THE BOOK OF MORMON SLEUTH

BOOKS BY C.B. ANDERSEN

The Book of Mormon Sleuth
The Book of Mormon Sleuth 2: The Lost Tribe
The Book of Mormon Sleuth 3: The Hidden Path
The Book of Mormon Sleuth 4: The Forgotten Treasure
The Book of Mormon Sleuth 5: The Secret Mission

THE BOOK OF MORMON SLEUTH

The Secret Mission

C. B. ANDERSEN

DESERET
BOOK

SALT LAKE CITY, UTAH

For Gwendolyn
(1963–2005)

Library of Congress Cataloging-in-Publication Data

Andersen, C. B. (Carl Blaine), 1961–
    The secret mission / C. B. Andersen.
        p. cm. — (Book of Mormon sleuth ; 5)
    Summary: When Mr. Omni invites the Andrews family to his southern
California cottage to help solve a mystery connecting the original
Mission Viejo to the Mormon Battalion, they find answers using the Book
of Mormon.
    ISBN 978-1-59038-906-5 (paperbound)
    [1. Mormons—Fiction.   2. Book of Mormon—Fiction.   3. United States.
Army. Mormon Battalion—Fiction.   4. Family life—Fiction.   5. Mission
Viejo (Calif.)—Fiction.   6. Mystery and detective stories.]   I. Title.
    PZ7.A51887Sec 2008
    [Fic]—dc22   2007053017

Printed in the United States of America
Publishers Printing, Salt Lake City, UT

10   9   8   7   6   5   4   3   2   1

Contents

Acknowledgments

I gratefully acknowledge the continued efforts of the publishing and marketing departments at Deseret Book. The people sometimes change, but the commitment and dedication remains universal. With so many simultaneous projects, I'm amazed at the personal attention given by so many to each individual book.

I especially appreciate Chris Schoebinger and Lisa Mangum for refusing to allow those frequent, unrelated difficulties to get in the way of accomplishing the tasks at hand. I was shocked to learn that my long-time editor, Richard Peterson, would choose golf over editing, but I wish him all the best in his retirement and thank him for the countless hours he spent with this series of books.

I also acknowledge the patience and tolerance of my dear wife and children as they have come to learn that anything they say or do may well find itself in a published novel.

CHAPTER 1

Dodge Omni

"No!" I yelled as loud as I could. "Get away!"

Everything around me was dark and out of focus. I wasn't sure where I was, how I got there, or how to get out. He was coming. He was getting closer and closer. I stumbled into the darkness, trying to get away. But no matter how hard I ran, every time I turned around he was closer. I could hear his breathing. Why wasn't he gasping for air like I was?

Suddenly I heard someone calling my name from far away. "Brandon!" The sound was there and then gone quickly on the wind. I looked around frantically as I stumbled forward again, hoping to see who had called to me. It was a friendly voice—I wasn't sure whose it was, but I knew its owner would be able to help. Then I heard it again. "Brandon!" This time it was closer, but I still couldn't tell where it was coming from.

I jumped violently as someone grabbed my shoulders. I couldn't pull away from him!

Then he started shaking me—and I realized it was the person with the friendly voice. "Brandon!" he said again. His voice was clear now. It was my older brother, Jeff. "Brandon, wake up!" I struggled to open my eyes. It was the middle of the night, and the only light in our bedroom was coming from the streetlight outside. There was a dim glow around the blinds at the window.

"Were you having that same dream again?" Jeff asked quietly. He had climbed down from the top bunk and was leaning over me.

I swallowed hard. My throat was really dry. "Yeah," I breathed. My head was pounding. I reached up to rub my forehead and found it covered in sweat. I rubbed my hand across my chest to wipe off the sweat, but my undershirt was completely soaked as well.

"Omni?" Jeff asked.

"Yeah," I said. "Mr. Omni was chasing me again."

When I said the word *again*, I was reminded of the day these nightmares had begun.

A couple of weeks earlier I was in a grocery store with Jeff when we heard a huge crash at the end of the candy aisle. We looked up and saw an old man who had accidently knocked over a big display of cans. (At least at the time I *assumed* it was an accident—but the more I've thought about it since, the more I wonder.) Jeff and I walked over to the man, who was slowly leaning down to pick up the mess he had made, and I said, "Looks like you could use some help."

I'm sixteen and Jeff is a year older, but we still try to follow the old Scout motto to "do a good turn daily" whenever one of us thinks of it. This seemed like a pretty good opportunity—but I imagine it was probably our first "daily" good turn all week.

The old man tilted his head toward me just enough to catch a glimpse of my shoes out of the corner of his eye and then snapped in a gruff voice, "What's yer name?"

"Brandon," I answered slowly, reaching down to pick up a dented can near my feet. Jeff isn't real big on confrontation, so he slowly backed away from the mess and stood there with wide eyes and a tight mouth.

"Well, don't touch that," the old man growled as I continued to reach for the dented can.

I immediately froze, waiting for some further explanation.

The old man continued speaking without looking up, "So, Brandon, you think I look like I need help, huh? Well yer wrong!

Be on yer way—both of ya." With that he gestured with his hand down the aisle and returned his focus to the mess he had made.

"I didn't say you *needed* help," I tried to explain. "I only said it looked like you could *use* some." I laughed a little to try to lighten the situation. He didn't respond, so I stood there smiling at the back of his bald head. Yeah, this guy was bald—as bald as a billiard ball—front to back and side to side. Then I added, "I know *I* always like having help even when I don't necessarily *need* it."

(This was absolutely true! I had accidently knocked over displays in this very same grocery store at least a half dozen times in my life. Luckily, I always had a bunch of friends there with me when it happened, and they usually helped me clean up the mess; it never occurred to me at the time that having all of those friends around is probably *why* the cans kept getting knocked over. Maybe throwing a Frisbee inside a store isn't such a great idea?)

Anyway, without looking up, the old man snarled, "Never judge a man until you've walked a mile in his moccasins."

Moccasins? *Moccasins?* I stared at him in disbelief for a moment—this guy was clearly crazy—and then spun around and walked back up the aisle.

My granny, a full-blooded American Indian, whom I'd never heard use the word *moccasin*, by the way, used to say, "Don't judge a book by its cover." And, I suppose the old bald man was simply trying to say the same thing as Granny: People don't always turn out to be what you first think them to be.

In this case, though, I wasn't convinced. The guy at the grocery store *was* weird. And now he was showing up in my dreams—make that nightmares—and morphing into Mr. Omni.

Mr. Omni. Just the thought of him brought on a feeling of dread, even when fully awake. I first met Mr. Omni (pronounced *Omnee*, not *Omni* like the book in the Book of Mormon) a couple of years ago, and my immediate impression of him—like my impression of the bald guy at the store—was not a very good one. In fact, neither were my second, third, or fourth impressions of this weirdo. Jeff, Shauna, Meg, and I were stranded with the strange Mr. Omni for about two weeks. And the entire time we were with him I was totally convinced that we would all be lucky to survive.

At the time I tried to take Granny's advice, and I *promise* that I made an effort to not judge Mr. Omni by his appearance; but let me describe this guy. He had not a single hair on his head—not one eyelash, and no eyebrows whatsoever. It looked like he soaked his head in some sort of hair remover every morning. His skin was pasty, his lips were pink and always wet, and he had big gaps between his teeth that showed whenever he smiled—and he smiled *way* too much. (Smiling is OK, generally, but he seemed to smile at other people's discomfort. Or maybe he was just clueless. Either way, it got old pretty fast.)

The guy was a total pain for two straight weeks. Shauna, who is twenty now and more optimistic than the rest of us Andrews siblings, claims he turned out to be "not-so-bad" in the end. But I don't remember anything "in the end" that would have changed my opinion of Mr. Omni, so I really don't have a clue what she's talking about. In fact, I never really try very hard to remember anything about the experience; I was happy to leave Mr. Omni buried in some distant memory in my brain.

But that was not to be.

After all, why leave a terrible memory buried somewhere inside of you when you can live it all over again?

The night after Jeff and I met the old man with no moccasins in the grocery store, I had a dream about it, a dream that keeps coming back. It always starts out exactly the way it happened in real life, but then suddenly the man with the bald head looks up at me and he is Mr. Omni! He has the same sick, wet lips that I remember and not a hair anywhere to be seen. But then he starts chasing me and I start running for all I'm worth. I've never figured out where I'm running to, but everything gets dark all around me, and Mr.

Omni gets closer and closer as I frantically try to get away. I've had the same nightmare two or three times a week since then. Jeff knows about it because we share a bedroom, but I haven't told anyone else and I told Jeff not to tell anyone either.

The dream I'd just woken from was no different. And Jeff's worries started out to be pretty much the same.

But then, he expressed something new: "Remember when the angel Moroni visited Joseph Smith during the night?" Jeff asked.

"Yeah," I answered, wondering what he was getting at.

"Well," Jeff continued, "do you also remember that the angel told him to tell his dad about it?"

"Are you serious?" I asked Jeff with total disbelief on my face. "This is nothing like that. I'm having nightmares—not visions with angels!"

"I still think you should tell Dad," Jeff said.

"If an angel tells me to," I answered, "then I will."

Jeff just stared at me.

"We both know," I defended myself, "that Dad will probably just tell me it's because I'm sleeping too much or not enough or—or I need to eat cheese before I go to bed or something equally and totally unhelpful, OK?"

With that, I pretended to go back to sleep. But as I lay there in silence I was doing anything but sleep. I kept replaying the dream in my head and thinking about Jeff's idea to tell Dad.

My dad is awesome. That said, I know of two areas where he is totally lacking. The first is his ability to show compassion when I am in distress (which is why I hadn't yet bothered to tell him about my nightmares). The second is that he has absolutely no idea how to do a normal family vacation. By normal, I mean something like what some of my friends get to do once in while, like taking the family to SeaWorld or renting a houseboat or something. Instead, my dad comes up with the most off-the-wall ideas!

Case in point: The bombshell he dropped during dinner the next night. "Hey, guys, do you remember Mr. Omni?" Dad asked.

The whole family was there. The four of us who knew Mr. Omni responded with petrified silence. Twelve-year-old Meg wore a look of complete panic. Our mom and our younger brother and sister, 10-year-old Chelsea and 8-year-old Danny, had never met Mr. Omni, so they had no idea that a pleasant dinner conversation had just turned ugly—very ugly. The only sound was Meg's fork slipping from her fingers, clanking on her dinner plate several times and then bouncing to the floor.

Dad looked at her without saying anything, waiting until the echo of the bouncing fork died away. Then he apparently realized that this was one of those rare moments that he had everyone's undivided attention, so he took advantage of the opportunity by saying, "I had a nice long chat with Mr. Omni this afternoon. He seems like such an agreeable man. I thought it might be fun to spend a week with him."

I was stunned. *Sure,* I thought, *he's agreeable to anybody else's suffering. He's also agreeable to anything that might make him more rich!* I racked my brain trying to remember *what* we had told Dad about Mr. Omni and those two long weeks I had tried so hard to shove to the back of my mind. Could Dad *really* have forgotten it all already? The answer was obvious: he could. Dad is really good at the "forgive and forget" thing. Sometimes I wonder if he forgives simply *because* he forgot. Dad continued before any of us could answer. I'm not sure why Chelsea and Danny didn't say anything; maybe they could feel the fear in the air.

"Let me back up," Dad continued. "Mr. Omni called me today and invited us to spend a week with him at his cottage in Southern California. Apparently there are some very old ruins on his property that he has been excavating and he has found some interesting information about some early LDS Church members down there. He said he even found an old copy of the Book of Mormon."

6

"Maybe it's an original, like yours," Mom smiled at me. I stared back with an unchanging expression.

"It could be," Dad said, "because the site he is excavating is from the mid-1800s. Anyway, Mr. Omni thought we might find it interesting and was also hoping that we might be able to help him figure out a couple of things. Apparently he has a bit of a mystery on his hands." Dad bounced his eyebrows a couple of times and got a silly look on his face. I guess he was trying to get us excited. It didn't seem to be working, so he ignored us and said, "I told him it sounded *fascinating*. I know it's short notice, but I talked to Mom about it and we're going next Monday."

We all stared at Dad in disbelief. No one made a sound.

Mom finally interrupted the painful things we were imagining by saying in a comical, nasally voice, "Your stunned silence is very reassuring." It was one of our favorite movie lines, and generally it evoked laughter, but not this time.

Shauna was the first to make a blatant attempt to get out of it. She was breathing shallowly when she said, "Paul and I were planning to work on wedding plans that whole week."

Shauna and Paul had known each other for about a year and had been engaged for a couple of months. They were planning to get married in October.

"I know," beamed Dad. "It's perfect! Mission Viejo is not far from Mr. Omni's cottage and so Mom and I thought that you could do some wedding planning with Paul's parents."

"I already spoke with Paul's mother," Mom said. "She is so excited."

"Oh," Shauna said, surprised. Then a smile began to creep across her face. "So I will be with Paul and his parents and not with Mr. Omni all week?"

"Well," Dad stammered, "yeah, I guess. We still need to work out the details."

"Sounds great," Shauna smiled.

Betrayal! I couldn't believe she would run out on the rest of us like that. Actually I could believe it, though. Lately she hadn't been able to have a single conversation with *anyone* about *anything* without somehow getting Paul or the wedding into the conversation—and it never took longer than about the second sentence. (Grocery clerk to Shauna: "How are you today, Ma'am?" Shauna to grocery clerk: "I'm fine, thank you. And I'll be much better in about twenty minutes when I see my fiancé for the first time today. We're getting married in October.")

Trying not to sound as horrified as I felt, I asked, "Are the rest of us going to be stuck at his 'cottage' all week?"

"What do you mean 'stuck'?" Dad asked. "Don't you think it sounds interesting? You like a little mystery, don't you?"

The stunned silence returned.

"But, no," Dad continued slowly, "I thought we would go to some local attractions." He spoke as though he was just then thinking about it for the first time.

"Like SeaWorld?" I asked, thinking I had better start giving him some good ideas.

"Sure," Dad answered, acting like he never would have come up with such an idea on his own. "We could do an amusement park."

"Or two," Jeff finally joined in, eyes still wide with panic. "Or three."

"OK," Dad nodded. "Does anybody have any other suggestions besides SeaWorld?"

"Wait," Danny said. "Is this like the video game where you can't go into 'C World' until you've already passed 'A World' and 'B World'?"

"No," I said intently. "It's not a game." I realized that I was also speaking really loudly. Apparently a result of deeply ingrained fear. Everyone was staring at me. I whispered intently, "It's a matter of life or death!"

Meg nodded slowly in agreement and I heard Jeff gulp. Shauna looked like she felt bad for our misfortune, but she obviously felt that saving herself was the only thing she could do. She probably justified her actions by thinking that by saving herself, she was also saving Paul from a lifetime of grief and loneliness.

The next few minutes were spent talking about the various attractions and amusement parks where we might be able to spend some time. I was hoping Dad would end up with a list of one amusement park for each of the days we'd be down there. And hopefully these would be places that opened early in the morning and closed at midnight or later. Mom agreed to do some checking to give us more options. I looked down at my plate, which was still half full of food, but my appetite was gone. My advisor in the Teachers Quorum used to tell us that certain comments could "quench the spirit" in a quorum meeting. I think my appetite was quenched by the words "Mr. Omni."

I sat quietly stabbing at my food until it was time to do the dishes. Unless we have something really important to do, we're usually not allowed to leave the kitchen until the dishes are done; we all clean up together. So I didn't bother to ask to be excused. I was too wrapped up in my own depression to notice if anyone else was feeling the same way; I imagine they probably were. The discussion about what we might be doing in California continued as we cleaned the kitchen. Mom and Dad worked hard to make it all sound fun and exciting; but Chelsea and Danny were the only ones who appeared to be falling for the idea. They had heard of some of the places Mom and Dad were talking about, but had never had the pleasure of personal experience. We were just finishing up the final touches when Mom told Danny and Chelsea that they could go play. Quiet returned to the kitchen when they left. I was happy for them that they were looking forward to the trip, but it was nice to not have to endure so much excitement when I was feeling the exact opposite.

"Dad," Jeff said after a minute or so as he was putting the broom and dustpan away. "Has Brandon told you about his nightmares?"

Dad looked a little surprised. "No," he said. Then, turning to me he asked, "Have you been having nightmares, Brandon?"

"Uh," I hesitated. Then I said, "No, I haven't."

Jeff looked stunned. "*What?*" he asked me, looking incredulous. "What do you call them, then?"

I smirked slightly before responding. Then I finally said, "One."

"Excuse me?" Dad asked.

"One," I repeated. "I haven't been having nightmares, plural." I paused and glanced over at Jeff before continuing, "I have only been having one nightmare—multiple times."

"How often?" asked Mom.

"Since when?" asked Dad.

"Ever since we saw this wacked old man in the grocery store two weeks ago," answered Jeff. "He sort of looked like Mr. Omni, and Brandon has been having nightmares about him ever since."

I'm sure Jeff thought he was doing me a favor by answering the question for me.

"Personally," Jeff continued, "I think it's a warning."

"A warning?" Mom asked.

"A sign," Jeff said. "I think it's a sign that we are supposed to watch out for him. He's crazy!"

"Ohhh," Dad scoffed. "Don't be dramatic."

"I'm not the dramatic one," Jeff said. "That's Brandon. Mom says that all the time."

No one responded to that. What could they say?

Finally Dad broke the silence. "I think," Dad said, "that it is indeed a sign."

"See!" Jeff said to me, raising his eyebrows with a knowing look on his face.

"I think it's a sign," Dad continued, "that it's time to convince each of you that there is nothing to be afraid of with regard to Mr. Omni."

Jeff's mouth fell open and he grunted slightly in Dad's direction.

"I know that you had a traumatic experience a couple of years ago," Dad said, "and you are probably just associating Mr. Omni with the fear of that experience. I have a feeling that this trip will actually end up curing Brandon's nightmares—or rather his *one* nightmare that he has had multiple times."

As we walked down the hall a minute later I said, "See, Jeff. I told you it wasn't worth telling Dad about it. Now he's just more convinced than ever that staying with Omni for a week is the best vacation idea he has ever had."

Jeff didn't respond for a minute. But really, what could he say? He stared at me for a couple of moments. Every few seconds he acted like he was going to say something hopeful, but then he would suddenly look discouraged again and let out a small sigh. He did this at least two or three times before finally just shaking his head and mumbling, "Sorry, dude."

"Don't worry about it," I said. After another moment I asked, "Do you want to play some B-ball?" We had an old basketball hoop at the side of our driveway. It was well-used on warm summer evenings like this one.

"OK," Jeff agreed after a moment.

We went outside and shot around for a few minutes before starting a game of Speed. I had almost forgotten about Mr. Omni when one of the quick shots I took hit the front of the rim and bounced hard toward the end of the driveway. I ran fast, but wasn't able to stop the ball before it rolled over the curb, across the street, and under a parked car.

"You're out!" Jeff called, announcing the end of the game as I stuck my head under the back bumper of the car to get the ball. Since the game was over, I made no attempt to hurry. After retrieving the ball I just sat on the curb for a moment catching my breath.

11

"Whose car is that?" Jeff asked, walking slowly over to where I was.

"I don't know," I admitted, realizing that I had never seen it before. It was a small, old gray thing.

"What kind of car is it?" Jeff asked. I guess he had never seen one of these either.

I read the words mounted to the trunk on the back and caught my breath with surprise.

"You won't believe this," I breathed.

"What?" asked Jeff, approaching the car.

"You want a sign?" I asked, louder now, pointing to the car. "Here's your sign."

When Jeff saw the words on the back of the car, he looked just as stunned as I felt. Mounted on the back of this car were the words "Dodge Omni."

CHAPTER 2

Articles of Faith Unplugged

"I thought I knew every model of car that was made by Dodge," Jeff said, "but I've never heard of a Dodge Omni!"

"This thing looks like it was probably old and rusty before we were ever born," I said. "That's probably why you've never heard of it." Then I asked, "Do you think it's pronounced like Mr. Omni or like Omni in the Book of Mormon?"

"If it's really a sign," Jeff said, "then I'm sure it's pronounced *exactly* like Mr. Omni."

The warning on the back of the old car pretty much eliminated any enjoyment we were getting from basketball, so we put away the ball and trudged back into the house.

"Hey, Dad," Jeff said as we came into the kitchen. Dad looked up from the list he was making on the back of a long envelope. He was sitting at the kitchen table.

"Yes?" Dad smiled.

"Have you ever heard of a car called a Dodge Omni?" Jeff asked.

"Not for a long time," Dad said. He immediately sat back in his chair and sort of stared off into space like he was having a really pleasant memory. I had never before seen such a dreamy look on his face. While they were talking, I grabbed Dad's favorite huge, black dictionary from the bookshelf and opened it on the kitchen table.

"Did I pronounce it right?" Jeff asked. "Or is it like Omni in the Book of Mormon?"

"No, you said it right," Dad answered lazily. "Our next door neighbor had a brand new Dodge Omni when they first came out. I was in high school. I remember thinking it was a pretty weird car."

"Well there's one parked in front of our house right now," Jeff said. "And Brandon and I think it's a sign."

"A sign of what?" Mom asked. "How?" She had been standing at the kitchen counter looking through a cookbook.

"Think about it!" Jeff said. "*Dodge Omni!* As in Dodge Mr. Omni."

Neither Mom nor Dad responded. I didn't see the looks on their faces as they thought about Jeff's comment, though, because I was too busy looking up the word *dodge* in the dictionary. I found it while they were still thinking.

"According to your favorite dictionary, Dad," I said, "*dodge* means 'to avoid or elude or evade by a sudden shift of position or by strategy.'" After I finished reading the definition I looked up to see Mom and Dad both staring at me with totally blank faces.

"In other words," I added, "that old car is telling us what we should do with your vacation plans, Dad."

At first Dad looked stunned. Jeff's eyes got real big, real fast, as if to say that he would not have had the guts to be as blunt as I was, but I know that he agreed 100 percent with what I was saying. After a moment Dad looked like he was about to say something, but the words seemed to be stuck in his throat. The silence continued as we all kept staring at each other. I didn't care what Jeff thought; I knew I was right and I was just waiting for Dad to finally admit it. The expression on Dad's face gradually changed from looking stunned to seeming slightly amused.

"Is it still there?" asked Dad.

"Is what still where?" I asked.

"This car," Dad answered. "I think I would like to see this 'sign' of yours."

"Gladly," I said, standing up and heading for the door. Jeff was right behind me.

"How does it look?" asked Dad as he followed us. Mom followed, too.

"Old," Jeff said. "Old and rusty and ready to fall apart."

We all went outside to look at the Dodge Omni. As soon as he saw it, Dad started yakking about his neighbor's car that had looked just like it thirty years ago or something. I was going to ask him if it looked old and rusty when it was brand new, but we were there to look at "the sign." Dad kept walking around the thing and talking about this feature or that feature. I finally had to look away for a minute because he was starting to make me feel dizzy. And besides that, he was missing the whole point! Then he started talking about all these other strange cars that came out when he was in high school. When Dad starts reminiscing it can take *months* to get him back on track. We didn't have the time to wait, so I blurted out, "So are we going to follow the advice of this old car or what?"

Dad stopped talking about old cars and turned to look at me. With half a smile he said, "You're not serious." He paused a moment before asking, "Did you really just say 'advice'?"

"OK," I grunted, "How about 'counsel'—or how about 'instructions'?"

"You can't be serious," Dad repeated.

"Don't I act like I'm serious?" I asked desperately. "Of course I'm serious."

"You think this car—because of its name—is giving you *advice*?" Dad stammered.

"Not just me!" I said with exasperation. "All of us!"

Dad stared at me for a moment before simply laughing, shaking his head back and forth, and heading into the house.

"If you don't want to go stay with Mr. Omni," Mom said, "then I think you're going to have to come up with a much better argument than the name of an old car." She smiled and started back into the house as well. Over her shoulder she called, "It was a nice try, though. Maybe you two should keep working on it. You just might come up with something that Dad *is* willing to buy."

Jeff and I just sat glumly on the curb and stared at the words some more. I think we both realized that if Dad wasn't going to go for a message as *blatant* as "Dodge Omni" right in front of him, then nothing was going to work.

"I think it's hopeless," Jeff mumbled, shaking his head from side to side.

I agreed, but I didn't bother to make the effort to say it aloud.

The next few nights I didn't have the nightmare anymore. Instead, I could hardly sleep at all for fear of seeing Mr. Omni again in person. I kept thinking about his constantly wet lips and the gaps between his teeth. He had now taken over my conscious thoughts instead of just the unconscious ones. The Dodge Omni was gone the next morning and we never did see it again, but its absence seemed as telling as its presence had been: the message had been delivered and we could either choose to follow or choose to ignore the warning. I caught myself looking at the spot where it had been parked every time I went outside.

Saturday mornings are generally my favorite because Dad actually lets us sleep in. Of course, "sleeping in" isn't as great as it sounds; he still wakes us up for family devotional at 8:15!

For devotionals on Saturdays and Sundays we usually read a talk from the latest general conference edition of the *Ensign*. Mom always goes to the Distribution Center and buys everyone in the family their own copy of the conference *Ensign*. After reading a talk together, we go around the room and each say something we like about the talk. We can pick a favorite line or paragraph or just a general idea. I didn't used to like it very much, but lately I had noticed that whatever talk we read seemed to have something that fit perfectly with whatever my latest biggest problem was. I was pretty disappointed this time, though, 'cause I couldn't find anything that I thought would make it obvious to Dad that a vacation at Mr. Omni's cottage was the wrong thing to do. I think I was hoping for something about following signs or staying away from rich men with no hair or something like that. But nothing came even close.

When we finished, Dad announced that we had to have our suitcases packed before we could go anywhere or do anything else that day. That stank. We tried to argue for a minute, but that just started him into this big, long explanation about how we were leaving first thing Monday morning, and we weren't going to pack on Sunday, and he didn't want us to have to stay up late Saturday night to get it done, and—well, I don't know what was coming next, but it didn't matter. I quickly realized that it would probably take longer to listen to Dad's explanation of his crazy reasoning than to just go and get packed. I started to wonder if I should feel bad for walking out in the middle of his sentence, but then I realized that he probably did it all on purpose!

Early Monday morning a limousine driver showed up at our front door. I answered the doorbell and said, "Hello," but my eyes were immediately drawn past the driver to the huge limo parked along the front sidewalk. It seemed to extend almost from one end of the house to the other. Seeing that thing almost made me forget about my fears for a while. I think it was the first time I had been outside for days that I hadn't thought about the Dodge Omni—maybe because the limo hid the empty parking spot from view. It was the kind of limousine that looked like it was part SUV. It was high off the ground and had huge tires with deep, rugged tread.

"Is Mr. Andrews home, please?" asked the driver in a very formal voice.

"Yes," I answered absently, my eyes still being sucked in by the limousine.

"I am David, your driver," he said. "Will you kindly inform Mr. Andrews that I am here?" He bowed low as he spoke.

"Sure," I said, finally taking the opportunity to check him out for the first time while he stared at the ground in front of me. He wore a matted, black suit with shiny, black shoes. His black and gray cap was tucked under one arm as he continued to bow. "I'll be right back," I added.

After I was halfway down the hall looking for Dad I realized that I probably should have invited him inside, but since I had left the door wide open, I figured that was good enough.

"Is the limo here?" Danny asked no one in particular as he pushed past me. "Whoa!" he breathed loudly as he approached the open front door and obviously found his answer. Then he laughed with excitement. By the time I found Dad and returned to the front door, just about everyone else was already outside staring at and talking about the limo. Shauna's fiancé, Paul, had shown up in the meantime. He had put his suitcase on the sidewalk and poked his head inside the limo.

"Good morning, Mr. Andrews. I am David, your driver." The man in the black suit bowed again.

"Good morning," said Dad.

"May I present your accommodations for the journey to the airport?" asked David, turning toward the limo and gesturing toward it with one hand as if to guide Dad in the direction he was to go.

"Of course," Dad nodded.

David led Dad to the limo, and the rest of us followed. He opened a set of double doors near the front of the limo and another set near the rear.

With a wave of his hand, David asked, "May I assume the accommodations are satisfactory?"

"Uh, yeah," Dad stammered a little, looking tentatively inside. "Yes. Absolutely."

"Very well, sir," said David. "Please make yourselves comfortable." He picked up Paul's suitcase, put it in the back of the limo, and asked, "Do you have any more traveling cases or other items for the journey?"

"Uh, yeah," answered Dad. "Just inside the front door."

"Very well, sir," David said. And then, without moving his feet, he acted like he was reaching toward the front door and asked, "May I?"

"Of course," Dad said.

"Very well, sir."

As David began to walk back to the house, Dad said, "Let me help you."

"Thank you, sir," said David.

The rest of us immediately took David at his word and climbed inside to see if the "accommodations" were indeed "satisfactory." The thing was amazing. The inside looked like a big, long lounge with couches all the way down the side opposite the doors. The other wall of the limo (with the double doors) had a TV with a DVD player and wireless headphones near the front, and it had a video game system hooked up to a different TV with tons of games near the back—also with wireless headphones. In between the TVs, along the same wall, there was a refrigerator full of drinks and cabinets full of snacks. I had never seen anything like it in my life.

We had just barely begun to figure out what everything was when Mom came and said that all the bags were loaded in the back of the limo and so we needed to have a family prayer in the house before we left.

"Would you like to join us for a prayer before we leave?" Dad asked David as we made our way back inside.

"Thank you kindly, sir. I would be honored."

We knelt in a circle in the family room, leaving an obvious open place for David. He looked around hesitantly before kneeling. He was next to Paul and Shauna. He seemed to notice they were holding hands and quickly glanced around at everyone else to see if hand-holding was part of the ritual and if he might be expected to do the same—he seemed pleased to note that they were the only ones.

Dad said the prayer. I used to be nervous when Dad would invite people that he had just met to join us in our family prayers, but he had done it so often while I was growing up that I hardly thought twice about it anymore. I knew that Dad would not change his prayer at all when we had guests either. He always prayed that we would be accepting of others as well as kind and generous towards them.

"Thank you for joining us," Mom smiled at David as she stood up.

"I am honored to be asked," said David. He smiled and we all quietly stared at each other for a moment. Then David extended his hand toward the front door and asked, "Shall we be on our way?" He still held his cap under one arm as he spoke.

"Let's do it!" Dad said with gusto.

"Wahoo!" yelled Danny, and he took off running toward the front door. Chelsea ran after him and we all heard the door slam. By the time I got to the door they were already out of sight, apparently lost somewhere inside the limo.

Jeff and I ran after them, scrambled inside, and found seats in front of the TV that was hooked up to the video game machine. We started fishing around in the cupboard where Jeff quickly found a game, held it up above his head, and said in his very best announcer voice, "Welcome to the game called 'Monsteeerr Trruuckk Rall-lly!'" We had never played this game before, but I wasn't surprised that Jeff chose it. For as long as I can remember Jeff has always been in love with trucks. I wouldn't be surprised if the first word he had ever learned to say was "truck."

Jeff put the game in the machine while I started rummaging through the other cupboards for something to munch on. I quickly found various individual packages of cookies and other junk food that had never *once* appeared in our cupboards at home. I tossed a couple in Jeff's direction while I chose two or three for myself. Now it was Jeff who called out, "Wahoo!" just like Danny had done a moment earlier. I think Danny recognized his own expression coming out of Jeff's mouth, so he came over to see what we were doing.

"Do you want to play with us?" Jeff asked Paul.

"Of course," answered Paul.

"Can I play, too?" Danny asked.

"Su-u-ure," Jeff answered. "Which paddle do you want?"

"Is there an orange one?" asked Danny. "Orange is my favorite color."

"Uh-h, nope," Jeff answered, "but there's an orange truck in the game! Do you want to use the black paddle and drive the orange truck?"

"Oh-h!" Danny breathed, nodding his head. "I want to do that, because that's like Halloween, huh, Jeff?"

"Yes, it is," Jeff said in a playful voice. I'm sure none of us had any clue what Halloween had to do with anything, but if it made Danny happy, then great.

Then the four of us settled in for a nice long trip to the airport with grins on our faces, game paddles in our hands, and a mixture of salt and sugar on our lips and fingers. I think I had totally forgotten about Mr. Omni by this time!

Unfortunately, the ride to the airport turned out to be not nearly as fun as I thought it would be. Usually when we went to the airport we spent an hour in the car and it could get pretty boring. I was definitely excited by the prospect of an hour in the limo playing video games and eating all the junk we had found. But we had just barely begun to figure out the Monster Truck Rally when the limo came to a complete stop and David got out. I don't think I would have noticed a thing if it hadn't been for Danny.

"Mom," Danny asked, climbing over my legs. "Where's that man going?"

"The driver?" Dad asked.

"Yeah," said Danny. "What is he doing?"

"He said he needs to make sure the plane is ready for us before we get out," Mom said.

"The *plane?!*" I asked, looking up from the video game just as my monster truck was about to try to jump over twelve cars lined up side by side. Looking through the windows I saw planes all around us. "How can we be at the airport already?" I asked.

There was a huge crashing sound that came from the game, and Jeff laughed and said, "Your truck just landed upside down right in the middle of the cars you were trying to jump!"

"Jeff!" I said with exasperation. "We're at the airport already! Who cares about the game?"

"What?" Jeff asked, finally realizing what was going on. "How can that possibly be?" he asked.

"We're at the *Provo* airport," Mom smiled, "not the Salt Lake airport."

"Provo has an airport?" I asked incredulously. "*W-why?*"

"For airplanes," Meg said. She is learning from Dad the fine art of the obvious—and completely unhelpful—comment.

Jeff grunted. "No kidding," he said flatly.

"Did it just open?" I asked. "Why haven't we ever come here before?"

"Because it's just for small, private planes," Mom explained. "It's been here for a long time."

Jeff and I just stared at each other with our mouths hanging open. Neither of us had any idea that because Mr. Omni had sent his private plane for us we were going to the *Provo* airport instead of the one in Salt Lake—total bummer!

"Is that the airplane we're going on?" asked Chelsea.

We all looked in the direction that Chelsea was staring and saw a sleek plane with a single jet engine on each wing. There were windows that wrapped around the front of the plane for the cockpit and there was a doorway right next to it with a short staircase that looked like it had been folded out from the doorway. There were about ten windows down the side between the door and rear of the plane.

"Do you think that whole thing is just for us?" asked Meg. "Or will there be other people in there, too?"

"There will probably be some people acting as the crew," Mom answered.

"But I think we will be the only passengers," Dad added.

I could feel the nervousness rising inside of me, maybe because we were just sitting in the limo by ourselves. To no one in particular I asked, "Has anyone seen any sign of David?"

"There's one up here," Chelsea answered unexpectedly. "Look!" she said, pointing at a chain hanging from the rearview mirror. At the end of the chain was a six-pointed star made from two overlapping triangles—one pointing upward and the other downward.

Dad laughed when he saw what Chelsea had found. I grunted and said, "That's not *exactly* what I meant."

"What are you talking about?" asked Danny. He always wants to know what is going on whenever he hears someone laughing.

"See that chain with a star hanging from it?" asked Mom. Danny nodded without speaking. Mom continued, "That's called a 'Sign of David.' Some people call it a 'Star of David' because it looks like a star. The name 'David' comes from King David in the Bible. That symbol is used to refer to descendants of King David."

"Isn't it used today for people who are Jewish?" asked Meg.

"Yes," answered Mom. "King David was Jewish."

"So was Jesus," said Chelsea.

"And Mary and Joseph," added Mom. "That's why Joseph and Mary had to go to the 'City of David' (also called Bethlehem) to be taxed at the time Jesus was born."

"Is David, the driver, Jewish?" asked Meg.

"I don't know," Mom smiled. "Maybe."

David returned a few moments later and climbed into the driver's seat. Looking into the rearview mirror, he said, "Mr. Andrews?"

"Yes," answered Dad.

David continued, "The crew of Mr. Omni's plane has informed me that they will be ready for your boarding in a few minutes."

"Sounds fine," Dad smiled.

"If you please, sir," continued David, "we should remain in this vehicle until they are ready for you."

"Sounds fine," Dad said again.

After a momentary silence, Danny asked David, "Are you Jewish?"

David looked up in the rearview mirror without answering. Then he reached for the chain and held it in his hand as he turned around in his seat so he could look straight at Danny instead of using the mirror. "No," he smiled. "But I have a good friend who is. He and I have been friends since we were about your age. He and his wife and children are some of the finest and kindest people I have ever known. I don't see them as often as I would like to, so I keep this to remind me of them." David paused for a moment before adding, "I am also reminded that Jesus was a Jew. He treated all people with respect."

Mom asked David some questions about where he grew up and where his friend lived now. She always talks to complete strangers about things like that. I'll bet she knows more details about the lives of the employees at the grocery store than their manager does. She's amazing.

Dad said we could keep playing until it was time to get out of the limo and board the plane, but the mention of Mr. Omni's name drove any thought of fun completely from my mind. Jeff and Danny kept playing, but I just left my truck crashed upside down on the cars it had been trying to jump. Instead, I stared absent-mindedly out of the windows. At first I caught sight of a nearby plane with

24

the words "OMNI Enterprises" printed on the side. It wasn't too big of a stretch to figure that this must be Mr. Omni's plane. My stomach flipped as I read his name again. If ever I was tempted to spray graffiti, now was the time. I found myself imagining the word *Dodge* spray painted in front of the word Omni. It made me smile in spite of my fear. I had to force myself to look somewhere else. Soon I found myself watching a man who was washing a small airplane. It looked like there was probably room inside the plane for only two people. I had never before seen such a small airplane—and I have never seen anyone be so intent on washing anything so perfectly.

The man had a long-handled brush that he used to carefully and completely scrub a small section of the plane. Climbing up on a ladder, he then used a hose to rinse that section for at least a minute before using a rag to carefully dry the section he had just rinsed. After drying the area, he would seem to find little specks of something or other that needed to be removed and then he would polish that area with his drying rag once more. I figured at the rate he was going it was going to take him about five hours to wash the entire two-seater plane.

Finally, I just burst out laughing and asked anyone who might be listening, "*What* is that man *doing?*" Everyone in the limo turned to see what I was looking at. They all stared for a moment before I added, "He is totally insane! Have you seen the way he is washing that plane?" I shook my head back and forth several times, still laughing and said again, "*What* is he doing?"

"I believe I can answer that, sir," said David.

"I would love to hear it," I said.

"It could be," said David with a sideways glance, "that he is washing his airplane." David stared at the man for a few seconds before continuing. "But I believe it would be more accurate to state that he is, in fact, *worshiping* it, sir."

"Worshiping?" I asked with a slight laugh.

"Yes, sir," David answered. "He is either a perfectionist and detail oriented . . . or he is worshiping that airplane."

I looked over at Dad who had a wry smile on his face. He bounced his eyebrows a couple of times as I continued to study him. I had the feeling Dad enjoyed David's comment.

"Danny!" Chelsea called unexpectedly. "Are you ready to learn another Article of Faith?"

"No," Danny called back flatly, apparently too involved with his monster truck. After another moment Danny asked, "but what is it?" He continued to play the game without looking up.

Chelsea, on the other hand, had a look come over her face that made me get the feeling she was about to announce something that was extremely serious.

"The Eleventh Article of Faith," Chelsea said. She spoke each word deliberately—as though she were speaking into a microphone on a stage in front of several hundred people. "We claim the privilege of worshiping Almighty God according to the dictates of our own conscience, and allow all men the same privilege, let them worship how, where, or what they may."

"What does that mean?" Danny asked absently.

"It means," Jeff said, "that we're not going to give that man a hard time about worshiping his airplane."

"Chelsea," Dad asked, "what did you mean when you asked Danny if he was ready to learn *another* Article of Faith? Have you already taught him one?"

"Uh-huh," Danny answered for her. "She's helping me get ready for my baptism day."

Chelsea nodded agreement and added, "Danny said he wanted to learn them before he got baptized."

"How many Articles of Faith do you know, Danny?" asked Mom.

"Three," said Danny. His turn ended, and so Jeff started putting the game away.

"Will you quote one for us?" asked Dad.

"Which one?" asked Danny.

"It doesn't matter," Dad answered. "Whichever one you would like to—just be sure to tell us which one it is before you start."

"OK," said Danny. "The First Article of Faith. We believe in God, the Eternal Father, and in His Son, Jesus Christ, and in the Holy Ghost."

"That's right!" said Mom. "What does that mean?"

Danny thought for a moment as he watched Jeff finish putting the video game machine away. "It means," Danny said, "that we worship God and not airplanes."

Everyone laughed. David clapped his hands together and threw his head backwards in delight. He laughed for a moment and then said to Danny, "Well spoken, sir!"

CHAPTER 3

Plane and (Other) Precious Things

If ever there was a plane that someone would want to worship, I think the one that Mr. Omni owned might be it. We had no idea what was waiting for us. As we were making our way from the limo to the plane, Mom said, "Everyone who wants their backpack needs to get it from David before they get loaded up with the suitcases."

"Very well, madam," David said as he stood next to the trunk of the limo waiting to hand over backpacks to anyone who wanted them. Mom and Dad always have us bring backpacks on vacations that we can load up with anything we might want—as long as we include a copy of the scriptures as well. I wanted mine on the plane because I had a book in there that I was reading and I didn't know if Omni's plane would have a video game system like the limo had.

After getting our backpacks, David escorted us to the staircase that had been lowered from the side of the plane. I thought David might be going with us, but it turned out that he had been hired simply to pick us up at home and bring us to the plane; he had never even heard of Mr. Omni. *Lucky for him*, I thought.

After I had climbed the steps to the door in the side of the plane, I looked down and saw David and another man taking all of our suitcases from the limo and loading them into a place near the back of the plane.

When I turned back to the door of the airplane and stepped inside, I was amazed by what I saw! It was the most ritzy place I think I have ever been inside of in my life. It looked like a room inside of a mansion—except for the fact that it was long and skinny and had a rounded ceiling. Still, it looked really fancy. There were a man and a woman near the front of the plane and another woman further inside acting like she was just waiting to bring us whatever we needed.

"I am your captain and pilot for today's flight," said the woman near the front of the plane.

The man standing next to her said, "And I am the co-captain and co-pilot."

Mom and Dad both greeted them as they walked past. I was too busy trying to figure out the difference between a "captain" and a "pilot" to bother to say anything to them in response. I was wondering why they felt they needed to say both words. I also noticed that they acted like they had specific marks on the floor for their feet and they were standing precisely where they were told to by some choreographer. Weird.

"Please find a place to sit," smiled the young woman further inside the plane. She had long, blonde hair, large eyes, and a beautiful smile. "My name is Melinda," she continued. "I will be your hostess today. As soon as you have made yourselves comfortable in the cabin, I will be happy to provide snacks for you. If you need anything at all at any time while you are on the aircraft, please feel free to let me know. I do hope the accommodations are satisfactory."

"Thank you," Mom said. The rest of us mumbled something similar as we surveyed the "aircraft" and its "accommodations." (I realized that this was the second time in one morning I had heard someone say something about "satisfactory accommodations" and I had a feeling it wasn't going to be the last time during this trip.)

"Brandon?" whispered Jeff into my ear. "Have you ever wondered why they call this a 'cabin?'"

"Yes," I answered, glancing in his direction. "Obviously, it's not a *log* cabin."

"Ha!" Jeff laughed.

The "cabin" was arranged with multiple sitting areas such that pairs of seats were placed facing other pairs of seats. The large, cushy chairs were all covered in soft, white leather. There were drink holders in the arms of each of the chairs. In the middle of each of the sitting areas there were small, low tables that were made of rich, dark wood that had been polished until it was very smooth and really shiny. The carpet was white—which I have always thought is a pretty dumb color for carpet, because it needs to be cleaned so often. (Of course, *that* might be exactly why they do it: so other people know how rich they are because they can afford to have their carpets cleaned every single week! I guess another advantage to having carpets cleaned so often is the fact that you would never have to buy a vacuum—let alone use it.)

There was a flat panel TV mounted on the wall at the front of the cabin and another one near the back. I couldn't tell if there was a game system hooked up to either of them, or DVD players or anything else for that matter. There was a shelf—or a countertop—running the full length of the wall opposite the sitting areas, with cabinets underneath. The cabinet doors were made of the same shiny, dark wood as the tables, but everything was closed up so there was no telling what might be inside any of them.

"Books!" Meg called out with excitement. It was the first time I had noticed that the countertop was full from end to end with books. It seemed appropriate that Meg would notice the books and be excited by them, while I found myself wondering about hidden video game systems. I smirked at myself.

"Oh, yes!" said Melinda. She stooped over and smiled, asking "Are you Meg?"

"How did you know?" asked Meg with wonder.

"Because these are here for you!" Melinda said, standing up

straight again and moving toward the long line of books and gesturing toward them with her hand. It was the first time I noticed
her long, skinny fingers.

"They *are?*" asked Meg with wide eyes. Meg was currently
demonstrating two of her very favorite things in life: books and
questions. "How did you know I love books?" she asked.

"Mr. Omni called and asked me," Dad answered. "He wanted to
be sure everyone was comfortable during the trip." Turning to Jeff
and me, he added, "I think that's why there was a game system in
the limo."

"Is there one on the plane, too?" I asked, nodding toward the
nearest TV screen.

"Of course," smiled Melinda. "You will find game paddles and
headsets under the tables between the chairs. Several dozen of the
most popular games are pre-loaded and may be selected from the
menu using the keypad on each table." Then, looking at me more
closely, she asked, "Are you Brandon?"

"Ye-eah," I hesitated.

"Ah! Well, something else has been provided for *your* enter-
tainment," Melinda said, tilting her head to one side. Then she
moved to the back of the plane and picked out the very last book
from the long shelf. It was quite thick with a medium brown cover.
Almost immediately I thought I knew what it was, but as she
handed it to me I checked the spine of the book just to be sure. I
was right; it was the Book of Mormon. It was made to look like a
first edition that had been printed in 1830, but this one was practically brand new. Opening the front cover I quickly found that this
copy had been printed in 1995. It was what they called a "replica."
I had a real, live, original one given to me once that really had been
printed in 1830, so that's how I knew what the old ones look like.
But mine was well worn, the corners were rounded, and the leather
cover had changed over the years from the original light brown
color to a darker brown.

Turning the book over in my hands a couple of times, I wondered why Omni thought that I would find this new-old book more
entertaining than video games. But Meg got Melinda's attention
before I could ask. Meg was already looking over the rest of the
book titles on the shelf, seemingly more and more excited as she
glanced over the selections. "Are these really here for me?" she
asked with sparkling eyes.

"Mr. Omni asked me to extend his apologies to you," Melinda
said.

"What for?" Mom asked.

"Because the selection of books is so limited on the plane,"
Melinda answered. "Mr. Omni asked me to inform you that a much
more extensive library awaits you at the cottage."

Meg's excitement almost seemed to brim over. Then, quickly
nodding her head very slightly up and down several times as she
moved her eyes from one end of the long shelf to the other she said,
"This is fine! This is just fine for me!"

I started once more to ask about the Book of Mormon, but
before I could, Jeff said to Melinda, "If it's just a cottage, then how
'extensive' could this library possibly be?"

Melinda smiled as if to say she knew how difficult it must be for
someone so young to try to understand such a complicated concept.
Then she explained, "The word *cottage* does make one think of a
smaller home, and it is indeed quite a bit smaller than Mr. Omni's
primary residence. But I can assure you that it is large enough to
house an adequate library." She smiled and shifted her eyes to the
side for a moment before continuing. I think she was trying to
decide how or whether to say anything else. Then she added with a
wry smile, "I think Mr. Omni uses the word *cottage* as a term of
endearment as much as anything else."

"Oh," Jeff responded, and he looked over at me with sort of a
nauseated expression on his face. I agreed with his unspoken feeling that Omni sounded a little weird about the cottage—but what

was so new about this? Personally, I thought the guy was pretty much off his rocker in every way I could think of. I wasn't really interested in talking about Omni's oddities, however. The break in the conversation gave me the opportunity I had been waiting for to ask about the book in my hands.

"So why did Mr. Omni think that I would be entertained by this book?" I asked. "I already have more than one copy of the Book of Mormon."

Jeff mumbled under his breath in my ear, "Maybe he thought you would have a term of endearment for it."

Luckily Melinda didn't hear his comment, but Dad did. Dad quickly turned his head toward Jeff and gave him a look that clearly said he couldn't believe what he had just heard coming from Jeff's mouth.

"Sorry," Jeff mumbled, quickly glancing around to see if anyone else realized what was going on. I didn't think so. Turning to Danny, he said, "Hey, Danny, do you want to check out the video games?" I figured he did it to try to draw the attention away from himself.

Danny agreed, and Jeff quickly escorted him to the chairs near the back of the plane.

As they walked away, Melinda answered my question with excitement in her voice. "That's part of the mystery," she smiled. "Inside the front cover of the book you will find a note from Mr. Omni explaining the whole situation."

I opened the book and found a handwritten note.

Once she saw that I had found it, Melinda said, "If there is nothing else, I will attend to the preparations for departure." She looked around at each person and smiled.

"Thank you," Dad said. "I'm sure we have everything we need."

"Let's all find a place to sit," Mom suggested. "And be sure to put on your seat belts."

"Do I have time to pick out a few books?" Meg asked.

"A few?" Dad said. "No. One or two, perhaps. Remember that the flight should only be about an hour and a half."

"OK," Meg agreed.

I tried to read the short note, but because the handwriting was a little different I couldn't even figure out the first word before Jeff said, "Brandon, come sit over here."

I sat down and started to look at the note again, but then Mom said, "Brandon, put your seat belt on."

I was going to express my annoyance at the repeated interruptions, but I decided it would be easier to just do what she wanted and forget about it. After I snapped the seat belt together, I looked deliberately around the room at each person to give everyone a chance to tell me something else before I tried to read the note again. No one seemed to be paying attention, so I looked back at the note, noticing the uneven letters and sloppy printing. It read:

Escape as did Limhi.

"*Escape?*" Had I read that correctly? I looked at it again. I could feel the tension all through my body; it definitely read *Escape*. It was another sign! First the warning on the back of the old rusty car to "Dodge Omni" and now a note written by Omni himself that tells us to "escape!" The name "Limhi" I recognized from the Book of Mormon but I couldn't really remember anything about him— or how he escaped from anything.

I wanted to show the note to somebody, but who? Mom and Dad didn't believe the first warning, so I could only imagine how they would react to this one. I was sure Jeff would take it at face value, though. I looked over at him, but he was helping Danny get set up in his chair. Danny apparently was having trouble getting his backpack situated on the little table between them so that he could reach everything he wanted to while he had his seat belt on.

Seeing Danny's backpack reminded me that I had my own and that I had my scriptures in it. I quickly pulled out my triple combination (which includes the Book of Mormon) and looked in the index for *Limhi*. It turns out that he was king of the Nephites in 121 B.C. There were dozens of references listed after his name, probably a half column's worth. I read through most of them before I found anything that looked like it might be helpful. Finally I read:

21:36—22:2 studies how to deliver people from bondage

Is that what Omni could be talking about? I wondered. Looking back up at the top of the list of references I found that this one was in Mosiah in the Book of Mormon. I quickly turned to the last verse mentioned, Mosiah 22:2, and read:

And it came to pass that they could find no way to deliver themselves out of bondage, except it were to take their women and children, and their flocks, and their herds, and their tents, and depart into the wilderness; for the Lamanites being so numerous, it was impossible for the people of Limhi to contend with them, thinking to deliver themselves out of bondage by the sword.

This scripture scared me to death; we were trapped on this plane! Omni was trying to tell us that we were now in bondage just as the people of Limhi had been and it would be practically impossible for us to escape. But what was the part about departing into the wilderness? Was that a warning to get out now before the plane actually got into the air? Maybe we weren't really trapped yet, but were going to be trapped as soon as we got to Omni's cottage. Either way, this was not sounding good.

I looked in the index again to see if there was another reference that might give a better clue about how to escape. The next reference stated:

22:9–12 follows Gideon's plan to escape into the wilderness

There was the word *escape* again! And it was just a few verses later than what I had previously read—maybe I was in the right place after all. I read the verses and they talked more about gathering their flocks and then giving lots of wine to the Lamanites to get them drunk before heading into the wilderness. Was he serious? How were we supposed to do that? I was starting to feel more and more desperate. I looked around. Everyone still seemed busy with various things. So far, luckily, the plane didn't sound like it was getting ready to move yet. I turned back to the Book of Mormon and decided to try to figure out if there was anything more to Gideon's plan than just giving wine to his captors.

I started at Mosiah 22:2 again, and this time I kept reading. I was hoping to find something in between verses 2 and 9 that would give some more information. I finally found it in verse 6, which reads:

Behold the back pass, through the back wall, on the back side of the city. The Lamanites, or the guards of the Lamanites, by night are drunken; therefore let us send a proclamation among all this people that they gather together their flocks and their herds, that they may drive them into the wilderness by night.

I quickly counted that this verse used the word *back* three times in the very first sentence. Maybe that was the clue. Then I remembered that the flight attendant, Melinda, had gone to the very end of the bookshelf—at the *back* of the plane—to get this book with its note to give to me. I didn't know what to do! I looked around frantically, wondering how much time I had to figure this out before we were trapped. I quickly decided that the sooner we got out of there, the better.

Looking around I found that the pilots had disappeared. I assumed they were behind the door at the front of the plane that was probably the cockpit. Melinda was nowhere to be seen, but it sounded like she was at the back of the plane moving some things around. The *back* of the plane—that's where I needed to go. I had to find out if there was a way to escape at the back of the plane.

Making sure that Mom was not looking in my direction, I unsnapped my seat belt, stood, and scampered to the back of the plane and around a wall. Melinda was there. She seemed a little startled to see me.

"May I help you?" Melinda asked.

"Is there a door back here?" I asked, quickly glancing around trying to find the answer for myself.

"A door?" Melinda looked confused.

"To escape," I said. "A door for escaping!"

Now Melinda really looked confused. "In the case of emergency?" she asked.

"Uhm." I thought for a moment, then said, "Yes! For an emergency."

"Yes," she said, stepping to the side and pointing to the wall behind her. There was a door with a large twisting handle in the middle of it.

"Great!" I said. "How does it work?"

Now it was *Melinda* who was starting to look a little concerned. She hesitated before answering, "Just turn the bar in the direction of the arrow until it stops and then push the door out."

"Perfect," I said. Then looking straight into her eyes with the most serious expression I think I have ever had on my face, I said, "This is an emergency. The note from Mr. Omni in that book you gave me says that we are supposed to escape out the back."

"What?" Melinda asked, astonished. "No it doesn't!"

"I don't have time to discuss it now," I said. "We have to get out of here."

Running back into the main part of the cabin, I called, "Everybody out!"

There was stunned silence from the entire family. Melinda came running up behind me, but before she could say anything, I blurted out, "The note from Omni in the book says that we need to escape out the back! Let's go!" I grabbed my scriptures and quickly stuffed them into my backpack. "I don't know if the pilots are good guys or bad guys," I added, "so we better move fast before they figure out that we're getting out of here." Looking at Melinda, I asked, "Are you on our side or theirs?"

Melinda had such a shocked look on her face that I figured she was either a really good actress or she really had no idea what was going on. Maybe she thought she knew what was in the note in the book, but maybe someone had switched it without her knowing it! Either way, she was skinny, and I figured we would have no trouble forcing our way past her if we needed to.

"Let's go!" I called as loud as I dared, not wanting to alert the pilots.

"Not before you tell us what's going on!" Dad said.

Turning to Melinda, I asked, "Who wrote the note in that book that you said would explain everything?"

Melinda blinked a couple of times before answering in a breathy voice, "Mr. Omni."

"Well, there you have it then!" I said. "It says to escape!" I paused and looked around at everyone before I continued. "It says to 'escape as did Limhi.' Well, I looked it up in the Book of Mormon and found that Limhi escaped out the back. I'm not waiting around for any more explanations. I've been in Omni's clutches before, so if he is telling me to escape, then I am definitely out of here!"

With that I scooped up my backpack and the new-old Book of Mormon and ran toward the back of the plane. I hesitated as I realized that Melinda had burst out laughing. I stopped and looked back at her to see that she was practically hysterical with laughter. She almost couldn't even continue standing because she was laughing so hard. Finally she leaned over and sort of stumbled to the chair where I had been sitting. She sat in the chair rocking almost uncontrollably from side to side as she continued to laugh. I noticed there were tears streaming down her face as she reached up to wipe them away with her skinny fingers. She continued to laugh and cry and rock for at least a full minute.

I was not amused. I looked around at everyone else, though, and they seemed to think something was pretty funny, but it was obvious they didn't know what at the moment. They all seemed to be anxiously waiting for some sort of explanation from Melinda.

Finally, through small spurts of laughter, continuing to wipe her eyes and rock slightly back and forth, she said, "That—was not—a—message—for you!"

I was still not amused. I narrowed my eyes and asked, "What do you mean?"

Melinda continued to struggle to speak between giggles. "It is—a message—he found."

"Found?" I asked. "Found where?"

Turning her head in the general direction of Mom and Dad, but with eyes still so full of tears that she obviously couldn't focus on them, she asked in the same broken way, "Didn't—Mr. Omni—say something to you—about a mystery?" She took a deep breath and coughed a couple of times.

"Yes," Dad answered. "He said that he was having trouble figuring something out that related to some LDS church members living in the area around mid-1800s."

"Yeah," I answered in a disgusted voice. "Didn't he say he found an old Book of Mormon, too?" Holding up the new-old book in my hand, I said, "This isn't it. This was printed in 1995."

Melinda looked at the book and started to laugh again. Shaking her head back and forth, she finally blurted out, "Of course—of course not."

I just stared at her. She acted like she was going to say something else, but it was taking way too long for her to get control of her laughter, so I said, "Is this just a trick to keep us on the plane long enough to get into the air? I say we get off the plane and talk about this outside!" I wanted to get out of there.

"We're not getting off the plane, Brandon," Dad said. "As soon as Melinda can, she will finish her explanation."

Melinda took a deep breath and nodded. "Yes," she finally said. "Thank you."

We all watched for another few seconds as she wiped her eyes and cleared her throat. Then she said, "Mr. Omni did find an old Book of Mormon. I believe it's a first edition. This is just a replica."

"I know," I said. Mom threw me a sideways glance, letting me know that I should just be listening at this point. I scrunched my lips together.

"He also found some other notes," Melinda continued after a deep breath, "that appear to be referring to things in the Book of Mormon. He doesn't know exactly what they mean and thought you might be able to help him." She started to laugh again, but quickly swallowed it. "The note inside the book is simply one of the references that he was hoping you would help him with."

"We would be happy to help," Mom said.

"Apparently it was too easy for you, Brandon," Melinda smiled at me. "You found out what it was talking about before the plane even got off the ground." She looked like she was trying not to laugh. "I apologize that you misinterpreted the purpose of the note such that you thought you and your family needed to escape, however. That was my mistake. Mr. Omni did want me to talk with you more about it, but I think he had no idea you would be able to figure out the reference to Limhi so quickly."

I had the feeling that she was simply using flattery to keep me from doing what I was sure was right. We all just stared at each other for a moment.

Danny said, "So are we going somewhere on the plane? I want to play this game."

"I think we might be getting off now," Chelsea said.

"No," Mom corrected her. "We're not getting off now. We're all sitting down now and putting our seat belts back on and we're flying to California to spend a fun week at a cottage."

Dad said, "A fun, *safe* week."

I couldn't help but wonder when the last time was that a family vacation had turned out the way Dad thought it would.

CHAPTER 4

The Cottage

Reluctantly, I sat down and fastened my seat belt. I kept trying to decide if the explanation that Melinda had given us about the note was believable. I guessed it was believable by some at least: Mom and Dad. Jeff and Danny asked if I wanted to play a game with them, but I was still thinking. I told them to play without me.

The more I thought about it, the more I decided that Omni was the one to be worried about and it probably didn't make sense for him to be trying to give me a warning about himself. *Unless!* Unless it was his *subconscious* trying to warn us. Hadn't Melinda said that there was more than one reference to the Book of Mormon that he wanted help with? Why had he chosen this particular one to write down? When we were stuck with him for two weeks a couple of years earlier, we were never quite sure when or if he was on our side or not.

Finally I decided that I was making myself crazy thinking about it; I might as well try to get my mind off of Mr. Omni. I spent the rest of the flight playing various games with Jeff and Danny. The system was totally amazing. The headsets we wore had a speaker for one ear and a microphone. We could hear both the sounds of the game as well as each other's comments through the speaker. It was set up so that we could even tell it to record certain phrases we said and play them back whenever we wanted or whenever we made a particular move. It was really cool! Danny thought he would be really tricky when we were playing a football game, so his recording repeated, "I'm gonna run for it!" whenever he was throwing a really long pass. It only took a couple of times to figure out what he was up to, but we tried not to use it against him.

Melinda regularly came around and offered us snacks and drinks. We got pretty good at telling her what we were interested in without taking our eyes from the screen. She came by so often that I almost got the impression she was getting paid by how much she could give away. One time when Jeff was changing games, I took the opportunity to check for expiration dates, just in case that was the reason she was trying to give so much stuff away. They were all good, though.

I was just starting to have a good time when Melinda came and stood where we could see her, but didn't say anything. I figured she was waiting to get our undivided attention, so I waited until it looked like all three of us were in a pretty good spot in our car race and then I paused the game.

"Thank you," she smiled. "I need to let you know that we will be preparing to land in a few minutes so if you need to use the restroom please do so now. Everyone will need to keep seat belts fastened during the landing."

Jeff and I turned toward Danny with questioning looks. He looked back without saying anything for a moment and then simply stated, "I'm good."

Then Melinda added, "The temperature at the airport is 63 degrees, and it is raining."

"Raining?" I asked, turning to look out the window. I hadn't noticed it until now, but the windows were wet.

"It's been raining for over a week," Melinda added.

I continued to stare out the window wondering what this was going to do to our amusement park plans. Then, suddenly, I realized that the game was going again. Without warning, Danny had

42

unpaused the game and his car was now well out in front of both mine and Jeff's. All three cars had been pretty even until then.

"Hey!" Jeff and I yelled at the same time.

Danny burst out laughing and said, "Sorry!"

"No you're not!" said Jeff.

"Sorry you fell asleep!" laughed Danny.

"You're pretty sneaky for an eight-year-old," I said.

"I wonder where I *learned* it!" Danny laughed again.

"It's a good thing you're getting baptized at the beginning of next month," Jeff said, trying desperately to get his car to catch up. He was in last place now. "You'll think twice before doing stuff like that anymore, knowing that you'll have to repent for it!"

"Oh," said Danny, "so when are you getting baptized?"

"Hey!" said Jeff again.

I just laughed.

We finished the last round of the race game just as the plane was landing. It was kind of fun to keep trying to play with our seats leaning back as far as they were. We watched out the window as the plane taxied over to some large buildings with huge doors, big enough to allow the plane to get through. There were several planes about the size of ours inside the hangar. Our plane slowly pulled up next to a black limo and came to a complete stop.

"We are now ready to disembark," smiled Melinda. "I hope you have enjoyed the trip."

"The accommodations have been satisfactory," said Chelsea.

Melinda looked at her in surprise and stammered, "W-well, I'm glad to hear it!"

"You said that's what you hoped for," Chelsea explained.

"It is. You're right!" said Melinda. "And I hope you have a wonderful week. I will see you on Saturday for your return to Provo."

"I haven't finished any of these books," Meg said. "Can I take them with me?"

"Of course," said Melinda. "You are welcome to bring them

back with you on Saturday or you may even leave them at Mr. Omni's cottage if you would like."

Meg smiled and carefully put the three books into her backpack.

Danny looked out the window and called out, "Do we get to ride in another limo?"

"Yes, you do," answered Melinda.

We gathered all our stuff and made our way to the door of the plane. Of course the captain/pilot and the co-captain/co-pilot were standing on their marks again and telling us how much they enjoyed having us aboard. I thought, *Oh, c'mon! We only saw each other for ten seconds at the beginning and another ten right now.* But I must admit they did seem completely sincere when they said it.

When we got to the bottom of the stairs from the plane we were greeted by a huge man with straight, black hair and dark eyes. He was dressed sort of like David, the last limo driver, had been dressed, but he acted nothing like him. When I said "we were greeted" I didn't mean to imply that he actually said any words, because he didn't. He just stood there and pointed toward the open door in the side of the limo. Once it looked like we knew where we were supposed to be going, he went over to the side of the plane and started unloading our bags and placing them in the back of the limo.

This limo was not part-SUV like the last one had been, but the inside was laid out in very much the same way. We made ourselves comfortable and were checking out "the accommodations" when the doors began to slam shut. The first thump made us all jump. At least I think everyone else jumped, too, but maybe I just jumped so hard that it *looked* like everyone else was jumping. Anyway, the guy then got into the driver's seat, started the engine, and began to drive away. He still hadn't said a single word.

Mom, of course, being the way she is, simply had to start talking to this driver who obviously had absolutely no desire to talk to anybody. I think she took it as a personal challenge whenever she was near a complete stranger for more than a couple of seconds.

"Thank you for being willing to drive us around in this terrible weather, sir," Mom said. "But I hate to call you 'sir,' so may I ask your name?"

The driver spoke about five syllables that didn't sound like anything English or any other language I had ever heard. At the same time he spoke, a black window began to rise just behind him that completely separated us from each other within about three seconds. We all just stared at each other for a moment.

"What did he say?" asked Dad. "Was that his name?"

"Or was he saying something else?" Shauna asked.

We all just started to laugh. Obviously, there would be no more interaction with the driver. In less than an hour we found ourselves pulling up to a huge home with a long driveway. The driver got out of the limo and came around to open the doors for us. As each person stepped from the limo the driver opened an umbrella and held it out for them to take. Again he didn't say a word. Even when various people thanked him for the ride or the umbrella or for opening the doors he completely ignored us. After everyone was out of the limo, the driver stuck his head inside and seemed to be looking to make sure we hadn't left anything behind. Then he slammed the doors shut again, just as he had after we first got in. Without a word he gestured toward the walkway leading to the front doors of Omni's cottage.

"Thank you," Dad said to the blank stare on the driver's face as he stood in the rain without an umbrella. I guess he had given them all away. We all started toward the house, but I was not looking forward to going inside.

The long walkway from the drive to the front door was lined with precisely pruned trees every few feet. The landscaping around the house was also perfectly cared-for and filled with an amazing variety of different plants and small splotches of grass here and there.

Jeff leaned over close to me as we walked and said, "Think

there's any place around here that's big enough for *two* people to play soccer—or will we have to play only one at a time?"

I smirked in agreement, but I wasn't in the mood to laugh.

As we heard the driver start up the engine and begin to pull away, Mom asked, "What about our luggage?"

"I'm sure he'll take care of it," Dad answered.

"But if he's hired just for the day, then maybe he forgot," Mom said.

"Look at the license plate," Dad reassured her. "It says 'OMNI X,' so I don't think the limo was hired just for the day. I'm sure we'll catch up with our luggage soon enough."

Mom didn't look totally convinced, even after reading the license plate. As we got close to the door, it swung open unexpectedly and we were greeted by a small woman with a Spanish accent.

"Hello," the woman said. "My name is Irene. I am the housekeeper. Please come in."

"Come now," said Dad. "Is Irene your given name? And if it is, how do you pronounce it in your native language?"

The woman got a huge smile on her face. Her eyes sparkled as she said, "Yes, that is my true name from birth, but in Spanish we say it 'Ee-ray-nay.' I am called 'Ee-ray-nay.'"

"It's very nice to meet you," Dad said.

"Hello," Mom said—but that was all the time she was willing to spend on pleasantries at the moment. She immediately continued, "The driver left without unloading our luggage. Was that a mistake?"

"No mistake," said the housekeeper. "I have instructed him to take your luggage to your rooms. You will please find everything in its place when we show you where you are to be sleeping. But first you will be dining with Señor Omni."

Other than the word *Señor*, and her slight accent, I was sure that her English was better than mine, even though it wasn't her native language! A drastic difference from the driver.

"Oh, thank you," Mom breathed in obvious relief. "I was not planning to be doing any shopping our very first afternoon here."

"I'm sorry to hear that," boomed Omni's voice from down the hall, "because shopping is precisely what I had in mind for you."

It was him alright—just as I remembered him. No eyebrows, no eyelashes, no hair on his head whatsoever. His white, pasty skin was accented by his wet, bright pink lips. His smile was wide enough for all to notice the large gaps between his yellow teeth. My stomach tightened at the sight of him.

"Come in! Come in!" said Mr. Omni. "I am so pleased to have you all here. I am Omni and you," he said, continuing to speak to Mom, "must be Mrs. Andrews."

"Please call me Sarah," Mom smiled. "I'm delighted to meet you."

"Oh," said Omni, taking her hand, "I can assure you the pleasure is all mine." Turning to Dad he said, "Mr. Andrews, I presume?"

"Yes," said Dad, shaking Omni's hand. "But it's Craig."

Omni smiled and shook Dad's hand vigorously. "Of course," he said.

Turning to the kids, Omni's expression changed to something like a two-year-old having a pleasant dream. "Dear Shauna," he cooed, taking her hand. "How wonderful you look!" He paused and added, "And how wonderful your hand looks with that engagement ring! Congratulations!"

"Thank you," Shauna half-smiled with hesitation in her voice.

"And you must be Paul," Omni said next. "Congratulations to you, as well."

"Thank you," Paul answered.

Omni greeted each of us by name from oldest to youngest. He continued to act contented and dreamy as he greeted those of us he already knew but hadn't seen for two years. He stooped over as he introduced himself to Chelsea and Danny, telling them how happy he was that they would come to visit him and hoping they had "a wonderful time at the cottage."

Then, with a sweep of his arm, Omni said, "Please join me for an early lunch. Normally I would enjoy eating outside, but the rain is so noisy I asked to be served inside."

We were escorted down a long, wide hall. The floors were wood, but they were covered in the center by long carpets that looked very expensive. There were chandeliers hanging from the high ceiling. The hallway had small tables or single cabinets or narrow bookshelves or chairs every few feet along both sides. I half expected to see a suit of armor or something similar because this place almost felt like an old castle. There were even rugs hanging on the walls. It made me wonder if they were rotated once in a while with the rugs on the floor. I guess a wall is as good a place as any to keep a carpet when it's not in use. I wondered if they were hiding some cracks or peeling paint on the walls. I smiled at myself as I thought about that. Partway down the hall I noticed a grandfather clock on one side that read 11:45. Looking at my watch, I remembered that Utah was an hour ahead of California. Even after all the junk we had eaten during the trip, I was more than ready for lunch.

Soon we entered the dining room, where several platters of small sandwiches were waiting for us on a long, wide table that had probably twenty high-backed chairs around it. The table also had bowls of fresh cut fruit and we were each served a glass of some kind of fruit juice. Each place setting was china, and the utensils were gold.

"Please feel free to offer a prayer for the meal," Mr. Omni said to Dad. "I believe that is something that you would normally do."

"Thank you," Dad said, and then he offered a short blessing.

I had never seen a gold fork before, so after the prayer I picked mine up and looked it over pretty closely before I actually used it to stab a piece of cantaloupe and put it in my mouth. It was perfectly ripe—probably the best cantaloupe I can ever remember tasting. I think Danny liked it, too, because he kept the bowl close to him and kept digging around the salad with the large spoon, picking out only cantaloupe and putting it into his own bowl. If ever he accidently got a strawberry or grape or something, he would carefully spoon it into Dad's bowl. At least he knew better than to return it to the serving bowl. That's good.

For the first few minutes of the meal, Omni asked the typical questions about how our trip had been. Just like practically everyone else that day, he hoped that our "accommodations had been satisfactory." At one point, the driver of the limo entered the dining room and stood where Omni could see him, but he did not say a word.

"Yes, TB?" Omni said to him.

The driver said, "Luggage to be now in rooms."

Omni responded, "Thank you, TB."

He immediately spun on his heel and left the dining room.

"Is his name TB?" asked Mom.

"I have absolutely no idea what his name is," Omni laughed. "I asked him several times, but I could never understand his response!"

"We had the same experience," Dad nodded.

"So I just call him TB," Omni smiled, "because he is The Butler."

Several people laughed, but I didn't get it.

"T and B are the initials for the words *The Butler*," Dad explained.

"Oh," I said out loud. I didn't have anything else to say.

"Are butlers supposed to be drivers, too?" asked Meg.

"Well, no," said Omni. "Not normally. But my regular driver was with me at the time. TB drives when I need a second driver or when my regular driver has the day off. I'm really not sure how much he enjoys it, but that's the way it goes."

"So," Omni said, turning to Mom. "I know that you had intended to use your time this week to do some wedding shopping, so I have arranged for a car to take you wherever you would like to go."

"Oh, that's what you meant," Mom said.

Omni just smiled and nodded.

"We should call your mom at home," Shauna said to Paul. "She wanted to show us some places."

"Where does your mother live, Paul?" asked Mr. Omni.

"Mission Viejo," Paul said.

Omni burst out laughing. I jumped, almost dropping the gold fork on the china plate. I couldn't imagine what reason he could possibly have for laughing at that moment.

"How absolutely appropriate!" Omni finally explained. "Do any of you know what 'Mission Viejo' means?" Without waiting for an answer he said, "It means 'Old Mission'! It fits perfectly! When I tell you why you are here I'm sure you'll find it just as amusing as I do."

I had a hard time believing that would be the case, but I didn't bother saying so out loud.

"I'm anxious to hear all about it," Dad said with enthusiasm.

"Wonderful," Omni said, slapping his knee. "Then let me tell you what I have planned for you and the boys. Before I tell you any more about what is happening on this property, I would like you to go to old San Diego and see some of the historical sites there and learn about the Mormon Battalion."

"The Mormon Battalion?" asked Mom.

"That's where the whole story begins," said Omni with a weird tone in his voice. I think he was trying to sound mysterious or something. "I have arranged for another car for you for the afternoon. One car will go north and another will go south. Sounds fun, doesn't it?" No one really responded. "I wish I could go with you, but unfortunately I have other responsibilities here. Tomorrow morning, however, we'll meet for breakfast and I will tell you the whole story."

"What am I going to do?" asked Meg. "And Chelsea?"

"Why don't you come with us?" suggested Mom. "Does shopping sound fun?"

"Yes-s-s!" giggled Chelsea and Meg at the same time. I was surprised that Meg chose shopping over the big library that was supposedly somewhere in this cottage, but maybe she was growing into a more typical girl.

"What am *I* going to do?" asked Danny the same way Meg did.

"Would you rather go shopping," asked Mom, "or visit museums?"

"Those are my only choices?" Danny asked, sounding slightly depressed.

"Is there something else you would rather do?" asked Dad.

"I would rather eat more cantaloupe," said Danny, "but I can't find any more in the bowl."

"TB!" called out Mr. Omni suddenly.

The butler appeared almost immediately.

"Please bring more cantaloupe for Danny, the youngest boy," Omni said.

TB nodded, spun on his heel, and left.

"Come with us," Paul said to Danny. "I don't want to be the only boy and I know that my mom will want to meet you."

"Besides that," Mom added, "maybe we can do some shopping for you, too."

"OK," sighed Danny.

TB returned at that moment with a serving bowl that he placed in front of Jeff and immediately left again.

"Is that my cantaloupe?" asked Danny.

"I don't think so," Jeff said slowly. "These are cookies."

Omni laughed.

"Is that man going to bring more cantaloupe?" asked Danny.

"I doubt it," laughed Omni. "Either we're out of cantaloupe, or

TB just didn't understand in the first place. We never really know for sure with him."

"What is his native language?" asked Mom.

"We're not really sure about that either," said Omni. "He sort of came with the house. I would let him go, but I'm not sure how to tell him."

"You need a gift," said Chelsea.

"A gift?" asked Omni. "You're very kind, but I have everything I need. I don't need a gift."

"You need a gift of tongues," Chelsea said.

"Excuse me?" said Omni.

"That means speaking different languages," said Chelsea. "We believe in the gift of tongues, prophecy, visions, healing, interpretation of tongues, and so forth. That's the seventh Article of Faith of our church. I'm helping Danny learn all thirteen Articles of Faith before he gets baptized next month."

"That's wonderful!" exclaimed Omni. "Those sound like fabulous gifts. I like the sound of the interpretation of tongues." Turning to Danny, Omni asked, "Which gift sounds the best to you?"

"Right now?" asked Danny dejectedly. His elbow was on the table with his fist pushed up against his cheek. "I was just hoping for cantaloupe."

I'm pretty sure museums and shopping were not what Danny was hoping for in a vacation. I had to agree with him.

Omni laughed. "Shall I have TB wrap some up in a gift for you?"

Danny just stared at him. Omni quickly figured out that Danny was a little more serious about his current situation than that.

"Why don't you just go into the kitchen and show TB what you have in mind," suggested Omni. "That always seems to work for me—most of the time, at least."

Danny looked over at Mom like he wasn't sure he felt entirely secure with this idea.

"I'll go with you," Jeff blurted out.

"Me, too," I agreed, and stood up to show I was serious.

"Go with Jeff and Brandon," Mom nodded.

Danny, Jeff, and I went into the kitchen. None of us were sure what we might find. What we found was a large, quiet room with a huge, stainless steel table in the middle and various appliances around the edges of the room. It looked to me like there were enough stoves, ovens, griddles, refrigerators, freezers, and sinks to keep a small restaurant running.

The huge table in the center was loaded with various dishes and serving trays that had been brought in from the dining room during our meal. This was the most organized assortment of dirty dishes I had ever seen in my life. Along one long edge of the table were all the serving trays. The edge of each tray was lined up precisely with the edge of the table and it looked like there was the exact same amount of space in between each of the trays—about an inch. Along the other long edge of the table—on the side of the room next to the sinks—were all the dishes that we had been eating off of. Again, these were perfectly organized. The plates and bowls were all arranged in stacks of similar dishes; the large plates were in one stack, the small plates in another, the bowls in a third. Again, the edges of the dishes lined up with the edge of the table and had the same one-inch of space in between them. The glasses were lined up next to each other as well, two deep from the edge of the table, and the silverware was lined up with all the forks together, then the spoons, and then the knives.

"They're dirty!" I whispered. "Why would anyone *do* that?"

"Make them dirty?" asked Danny.

"No!" I hissed. "Stack them perfectly before they're even clean!"

Danny shrugged. Jeff smirked as he pointed to the far end of the kitchen and said, "Maybe it was him."

Slumped in a chair with his chin against his chest was TB. I hadn't noticed him before.

"Is he dead or just sleeping?" asked Danny.

"The Bible uses the same word for either one," I said.

We all cautiously walked closer to take a look. TB was in a wooden chair with a padded leather seat and a high back. His forearms were draped over the padded arms of the chair, each hand making a fist. Trying to get a glimpse of TB's face, Danny slowly bent his head down until it got lower and lower. Danny's head was almost on the ground when he finally stopped moving and quietly asked, "Is there any more cantaloupe?"

TB made no response. Just then the door near the chair opened and Irene came into the room. She looked at us, then at TB. Looking back at us, she smiled and put her index finger up to her lips, telling us to be quiet. At the same time, with the other hand she reached for a large card hanging from a string above TB's head and turned it over. The card was hanging below a clock on the wall. Printed on the card in large letters were the words "Back in 15 minutes." Leaving her finger against her lips, she motioned for us to follow her to the other end of the kitchen.

"He is always sleeping in that chair," Irene said quietly.

"Just for fifteen minutes?" I asked, chuckling at the sign.

"Does he know about the sign?" asked Jeff.

"He knows nothing of his sign," said Irene, smiling at Jeff. Turning to me, she said, "He holds his keys in his hand and awakens when they drop to the floor. It is never longer than fifteen minutes."

"No way," Jeff said. "This I gotta see."

Walking over a little closer again, we saw that she was right; TB had his keys in his right fist. The other hand appeared to be empty.

"It will be a few more minutes yet," said Irene. "Is there something I may help you with?"

"Cantaloupe," said Danny. "Is there any more? That man was supposed to get me some, but he brought out cookies instead."

"Let me check," said Irene. Moving toward the large table she said, "He would have put the fruit bowl along here."

"Is he the one who arranged all of these dishes?" I asked.

"Yes," said Irene. "He is always wanting everything to be precisely in order—whatever the order may be. Señor Omni will say that he has 'OCD.'"

"What's that?" Danny asked.

"Obsessive-compulsive disorder," laughed Irene.

"That's crazy," said Jeff.

"Yes," agreed Irene, "but very useful. When I want to keep him out of my way for a time, I simply rearrange the tassels on the rugs in the hallways. He cannot walk past without straightening them."

Jeff and I both laughed softly, glancing in TB's direction.

Danny was not amused. "Is there any more cantaloupe?" he asked.

"Perhaps in the ice box," Irene said. She quickly pulled a large cantaloupe from the fridge, smiled as she held it up for Danny to see, and then took it to the sink where she began cutting into it. As she worked she glanced at TB and said, "He may be close to waking up now."

We went over closer where we could get a better look. His fists looked like they were definitely starting to relax. We continued to watch as they gradually opened more and more until, about two minutes later, the keys fell from TB's hand and rattled loudly on the tile floor. TB immediately jumped and then took a long relaxing breath without opening his eyes. After a loud exhale, he leaned over and scooped up his keys. Standing up he looked around the kitchen and saw us for the first time.

"We are to be having now helpers in kitchen?" asked TB. "For why?"

"They wanted to see your OCD," said Irene frankly. TB didn't respond. Irene added, "From your dishes to your nap, you put on quite a show."

TB nodded slowly and said, "I have been telling you before, this is not disorder—this is *gift!* I am feeling sorry for all else in the world who are not possessing my gift."

"Maybe we should call it OCG, then," said Irene. "Instead of OCD."

"This is being acceptable," nodded TB and with that, he turned and left the kitchen.

Irene shook her head from side to side as he left, and then she handed a small bowl of fresh cut cantaloupe to Danny and pointed to a stool in the corner. Danny dug in with vigor. He looked like he was in bliss. I wondered how long it would last. I decided I was not going to be the one to remind him about spending the rest of the day shopping. Later, I realized just how lucky he was to be spending an afternoon wedding shopping!

CHAPTER 5

The Mormon Battalion

Old San Diego was actually quite a bit more interesting than I thought it would be. Dad, Jeff, and I had a pretty good time. The narrow streets were full of restaurants with outdoor tables, all kinds of various shops selling all sorts of souvenirs, and street vendors selling tortillas, ice cream, and other food. It was still cloudy and cool, but at least it had stopped raining for the time being. Many people that we saw were wearing jackets; Dad had insisted that we bring ours along. There were people all over the place walking every which way. The outdoor tables were mostly full, and some of the chairs were actually partway into the street, but the people sitting in them didn't seem to notice any danger from the cars passing by— of course, with all the people, the cars were moving pretty slowly. TB was our driver again. Omni's regular driver took everyone else to meet up with Paul's mother and go shopping. TB maneuvered the limo carefully in and around all the people who were walking lazily in front of us or sitting on chairs halfway in the street.

"Are we just going to drive around?" I asked. The dark window between the driver and the passengers was still up.

"I'm not sure what the plan is," Dad answered. "Mr. Omni said he wanted us to learn about the Mormon Battalion, but that's really all I know. Hopefully TB knows what he's doing."

"We could bang on the window and try to ask him," suggested

Jeff, "but even if he decides to open the window, I kinda doubt we'd be able to understand his answer."

Dad and I nodded in agreement. After a few minutes of driving slowly through the streets, the dark window between the driver and the rest of the passengers came down as the limo came to a stop. We looked outside and saw that we were in front of the Mormon Battalion Visitors' Center. TB reached through the window and held up a small gadget that he apparently intended for Dad to take from him. Dad took it and turned it over in his hands a couple of times. It looked sort of like a pager.

"What's this?" Dad asked. "Will it buzz when you want to pick us up?"

"No," said TB gruffly. "You are to be pushing green button when you be finish."

"Oh," said Dad. "So when we're ready to be picked up I just push this button and you will come get us?"

TB nodded, but didn't say anything.

"Will you pick us up here?" Dad asked.

"I find you where you be," said TB. He pointed at the device in Dad's hand and repeated, "I am seeing at all times where this be."

"Oh," said Dad with surprise. "It must have a GPS in it. That's great." Then he asked, "How much notice do you need? How long will it take you to get here?"

"Fifteen," said TB.

"Just fifteen minutes?" said Dad. "Sounds great. I think we will probably want to be here for at least a couple of hours, so you won't need to worry about us until then."

TB nodded again, then he got out and came around to open the doors for us. As we got out, TB handed each one of us an umbrella even though it wasn't raining. We decided it was easier just to take them than to try to explain why we didn't need them. TB got back into the limo and drove away.

"Do you think he has any clue what's going on?" asked Jeff.

"It'll be fine," Dad said. That was reassuring, in a head-in-the-sand sort of way.

Jeff and I followed Dad into the visitors' center. Dad pointed out some umbrella stands near the entrance and we all left our umbrellas there. I must admit that I knew practically nothing about the Mormon Battalion before we went through the visitors' center. I was amazed by what I learned. We were greeted by a senior missionary couple by the name of Elder Rasmussen and Sister Rasmussen. They took Dad, Jeff, and me on a tour and showed us all sorts of really cool things.

The Mormon Battalion was a group of nearly 500 men who joined the United States Army in 1846 during the Mexican War. The Church and its members were in great need of money, and Brigham Young encouraged them to join when a representative from the U.S. Army in the West came and found the Mormons in Iowa. At the time, they were traveling to Utah to get away from persecution in Nauvoo. In addition to the men, there were thirty-two women and at least fifty children in the company. They marched about 2,000 miles from Council Bluffs, Iowa, to Southern California near what is now the U. S. border with Mexico. It was the longest military march in American history!

Brigham Young made several promises and prophecies regarding those who joined the Mormon Battalion. I think probably the most important one was that if they would join the army and march to California, they would never have to fight. He also told them that their children would one day bless their names and that men and nations would rise up and bless them also. Most of the women that went were hired by the army to do laundry, but some went just to be with their husbands.

The Battalion had all sorts of problems along the way, including their food being sent by the army to the wrong place, various sicknesses, and their commander (who was not Mormon) getting sick and dying. Whenever they got paid along the way, most of the money was sent back to family and friends in Winter Quarters.

Along the way, many of the company became sick, and company leaders decided to have them spend the winter in Fort Pueblo, Colorado. Those who were well marched on to Santa Fe, in what is now New Mexico. Once there, even more who had become sick were sent back to Fort Pueblo, including most of the women and all of the children. The Saints in Fort Pueblo spent a mild winter under the leadership of Captain James Brown, where they had time to become healthy again and prepare for travel in the spring.

The men who remained left Santa Fe for the final push to California on October 19, 1846, hopeful that the trek would take another sixty days.

Unfortunately, they were still a ways off after sixty days of travel, and food was scarce. At one point, the soldiers came across a group of Indians and Spaniards who traded dried food with them. One member of the Battalion wrote in his diary about these same Indians and Spaniards, who told the soldiers that there was a Spanish settlement only about three days away where they could get some more provisions. The soldiers were so hungry that they decided they were going to head for this town, even though its settlers were on the other side of the war! After about three or four miles, the colonel in charge suddenly made a right-hand turn and started heading for California again instead of the town. The soldier who wrote about this in his diary said they learned later that the Spaniards had been watching their march and had gathered a cavalry near the town and were planning to attack the Mormon Battalion.

In the end, it took the Battalion 102 days, not sixty, to get to San Diego. The thing that amazed me was that by the time they got to California, the war was over! The Mormon Battalion was never asked to fight at all. Brigham Young had been right. The men were signed up for a year, though, so they settled in the San Diego area and did work around there until their year was up. They actually ended up doing a lot to help the people living in that area. They repaired fences and replaced the bricks down inside wells and things like that.

The visitors' center had a flag that was carried for the 2,000-mile march. It had the words "Mormon BattaLION" on it. Elder Rasmussen told us that the reason the letters "LION" were uppercase was that Brigham Young was known as "the Lion of the Lord" and they wanted to honor him.

When we were done with the tour, Elder Rasmussen and Sister Rasmussen told us that we could walk around and look at the displays for as long as we wanted to.

In the theater at the visitors' center, a short film was playing, so we decided to watch it and then we walked around and looked at some of the displays a little more closely for a while. Dad wanted to spend more time looking at various things than either Jeff or I did, so we wandered on ahead of him.

We were in a different room when I saw something that made my heart skip a beat. Actually, I saw some*one* that made my heart skip. If Omni was bad to be around, then the man I had just seen was absolutely horrible. His name was Dr. Anthony. He was a historian that had been haunting our family for years! He was wearing a baseball cap, and had his shoulders hunched over, but I think I would recognize those wire-rim glasses and that dark, stringy hair practically anywhere. He was wearing a jacket with the collar turned up, which partially hid his face.

"Jeff!" I hissed.

Jeff responded with a lazy, "Hmm?" He didn't even look up.

Hurrying to his side, but still watching the direction that the man had gone, I hissed again, "I just saw Dr. Anthony."

This time Jeff's response was much more what I had hoped for. "What?! Where?"

He was now looking intently in the same direction I was. I

didn't have to take my eyes off of Dr. Anthony to know this; I could tell just out of the corner of my eye.

"See the guy with the collar turned up on his jacket?" I asked. "That's him!"

"Are you sure?" asked Jeff, his voice tense.

"Yeah," I breathed. "Besides, who else do you know that would sneak around like that with his collar turned, trying not to be recognized?"

"I know a lot of people who would turn up their collars to try to keep warm and dry in a rainstorm," Jeff said.

"It's not raining anymore," I said. "Remember?"

"It wasn't when we came in," Jeff said, "but it could be now, couldn't it? Don't the shoulders of his jacket look wet?"

"Do you really not believe me?" I asked. "Or are you just *hoping* that I'm wrong?"

"I'm not sure," Jeff breathed. He was sounding nervous. "Probably some of both."

"Let's see what he's up to," I suggested. As I spoke, I immediately moved in Anthony's direction.

Jeff's cool, but he's not what I would describe as particularly brave or very adventurous. He apparently had absolutely no interest in following Anthony. Sensing that he was riveted to the spot where I had left him, I ran back, grabbed his arm, and pulled him with me. "C'mon," I hissed. "I don't want to lose him."

"Why not?" mumbled Jeff, stumbling along next to me.

I ignored the question and continued to move us both along as quickly as I dared.

"What's he doing here?" Jeff asked.

"How should I know?" I answered.

"Is he still working for Mr. Omni?" Jeff asked.

"How should I know?" I answered again. I tried to act like this question didn't matter, but in reality I could feel myself tense up at the thought of Anthony and Omni being on the same team again. That would *not* be cool.

Anthony seemed to know exactly where he was going and what he was doing. He was moving quickly and quietly through the visitors' center. We had to keep hanging back, though, because he repeatedly glanced over one shoulder or the other, as if checking to see who might be watching him. He hesitated for a moment at a door near the back of the visitors' center that had a sign on it stating "Employees Only." He then slipped quickly inside. From his behavior, it wasn't hard to guess that he was *not* an employee.

I opened the door slowly just a few seconds after it closed. The hallway inside was mostly dark. Sneaking quickly through the door and shutting it as quietly as we could, Jeff and I paused for a moment. I was listening for sounds that might give us a clue as to which way Anthony had gone. Jeff, apparently, was simply wishing he was somewhere else—anyplace else!

"Let's get out of here," Jeff whispered. "Dad will be wondering where we are."

"Shh!" I hissed. We both knew that Dad was far too interested in whatever display he was currently standing in front of to have any idea that we were gone. Besides, I was sure I had heard some sounds.

Creeping down the mostly dark hall we found a door that was just slightly open. A small amount of light was coming from inside and we could hear some rustling of papers or something. Slowly, I pulled the door open, searching for any sign of Dr. Anthony or whoever was making the noise. Whether it was Anthony or not, I knew we weren't supposed to be in here, so I was really hoping not to get caught. But I had known Dr. Anthony long enough to know that whatever he was doing, it couldn't be good. I knew that catching Anthony in the act of whatever rotten thing he was up to was worth any risk we might be taking right now.

As the door swung slowly open, Anthony came into view.

There was not a lot of light in the room; there was only a desk lamp in one corner near the door. The room was long, and the walls were lined with what looked like huge filing cabinets for papers that were larger than normal size. The open area in the middle of the room was maybe only three or four feet wide in between the rows of cabinets on opposite walls.

Anthony was near the back of the room with one of the file drawers open. I pulled the door open far enough out into the hallway so that Jeff could see the same thing I was seeing. We watched as Anthony pulled a long tube out from inside of his jacket. He removed the cap from the end of the tube and then carefully pulled a rolled up paper from the tube. I noticed that he was wearing those really thin latex gloves that doctors and nurses wear. The paper looked like it was a light brown color. Flattening the paper, he slid it into the very front of the drawer. As he started to close the drawer, I realized that he would probably be turning in our direction any second so that he could leave. I think Jeff figured the same thing and was in the process of trying to get out of sight when he accidently kicked the door, causing Anthony to look up in surprise. Now there was absolutely no doubt. Even in the dark, I could see that it was definitely him. I think Jeff also made a positive ID.

Jeff, of course, did what any rational person would do: he ran for his life. I, on the other hand, was far more interested in seeing what Anthony had just put into the cabinet. I was afraid that if we ran, then Anthony would do something so that we wouldn't be able to figure out what he had been looking at—and I wanted to know! So I ran, too. I didn't run down the hall like Jeff had, but instead, I ran straight for Anthony. He screamed. He screamed like a girl. That's when I knew once and for all that it was him. I had heard Anthony scream in situations like this before and this scream was an exact match.

As I ran straight at Dr. Anthony, I started to yell. I screamed at the top of my lungs, "What are you doing in here?!"

Anthony looked around frantically for something to protect himself with. Finally, he picked up a nearby chair and began running straight back at me with the chair legs pointed straight at my head. I was surprised, but I wasn't backing down. Luckily there was another chair between us, and so I scooped it up as I ran. Anthony quickly decided that he didn't want a collision, so instead, he threw his chair at me as we got closer to each other. At that point I was sure glad I had a chair of my own. I held it up as a shield, closed my eyes, and ducked my head. There was a huge crash as the chair legs became entangled. I stumbled and fell with the two chairs on top of me. Before I knew it, Anthony had run past me and was headed out the door. I heard another scream from Anthony, followed by a big thud.

I heard Jeff call out, "Are you OK, Brandon?!"

I looked up and saw him coming through the door.

I mumbled, "I'm fine!" as I began to push my way out from under the chairs.

The door slammed shut behind Jeff as he made his way over to me and helped move the chairs from on top of me.

"Did *you* slam the door or was it Anthony?" I asked as Jeff helped me stand up.

"It wasn't me," Jeff said. "It must have been him."

"Do you believe me now?" I asked. "Let's go get him."

Just as I spoke we heard a loud crash from the hallway. It sounded like a bunch of boards and pipes being dropped on the floor. We could hear them being shifted around as we ran for the door. We turned the handle and pushed, but the door wouldn't open. We pounded our shoulders into it a couple of times and kicked it, but it didn't even begin to budge. We started yelling and pounding with our fists.

"Hey!" I yelled as loud as I could. "Let us out of here!"

"I don't think he wants to let us out," Jeff said.

"Of course he doesn't," I said between pounds. "I'm trying to get someone else's attention."

Just then the fire alarm went off.

"Oh, great," I said. "Now no one will ever be able to hear us."

"And they'll probably evacuate the building," Jeff added.

Jeff found a switch that turned on the overhead light, making it easier to see what was in the room. We looked around for a window or another door, but this one seemed like the only way out, so we continued to push on the door and pound and yell for a couple of minutes. Then we decided that the building was probably empty by now and we would just have to wait until they figured out we were missing and came looking for us. With the fire alarm still blaring, we agreed that it would have been pretty hard for anyone to hear us unless they were pretty close to begin with. It was probably another ten minutes or so before we heard someone calling out our names. It was kind of hard to hear above the sound of the fire alarm, though. I didn't recognize the voice. We immediately began pounding on the door and yelling again. Within a few seconds we heard the voice just on the other side of the door.

"This is the fire department. Are you OK in there?" the voice called.

"We're fine," Jeff called back.

"How many are in there and what are your names?" the voice asked.

"Just two of us," I said. "We're Jeff and Brandon Andrews."

"Your dad will be glad to know you're safe," came the reply. "Just give me a minute to remove all this junk from in front of the door."

We listened for about a minute to the sounds of boards and pipes being pushed out of the way and then the door swung open.

"Wow," said the fireman. "If I didn't know better, I would think someone wedged that door shut on purpose. Did you come in through this door or is there another entrance?"

"This is the only one we could find," Jeff answered.

"And it was *in fact* wedged shut on purpose," I said. "The guy's name is Anthony. Dr. Lawrence Anthony. He's a historian or something and we caught him in here putting a document back."

"We can talk about that outside," said the fireman. "For now we need to evacuate you two outside and get you reunited with your father."

We followed the fireman as he made his way quickly through the visitors' center. The fire alarm was even louder out here than it had been in the back room. The fireman escorted us out of the front of the building where we found two fire trucks, several police cars, and a whole crowd of people. Dad came running up to us and asked if we were OK.

"We're fine," Jeff and I said in unison.

"But we saw Anthony in there, Dad," I said.

"Dr. Anthony?" asked Dad with a surprised look and raised eyebrows. "Are you sure?"

"Absolutely," I said.

"No question about it," Jeff agreed, shaking his head from side to side.

"We need to talk to the missionaries," I said. "Where is Elder Rasmussen?"

We looked around for a moment and saw Elder and Sister Rasmussen talking to a police officer. We walked over near them and waited until they were finished. They apparently had a list of all the employees who were in the visitors' center at the time the fire alarm went off and they had now verified that everyone was out of the building and accounted for.

"We're still searching for patrons," said the police officer, "but there doesn't appear to be any signs of a fire anywhere. Someone must have deliberately triggered the alarm."

"I know who it was," I said. "His name is Dr. Lawrence Anthony." Turning to the missionaries, I added, "We saw him putting a document of some kind into a huge file cabinet in a back room. Come with us and we can show you what it was."

I started to head back into the building, but the police officer said, "Hold on there, son. No one is going back into the building until the alarm is turned off."

"But you just said," I started to argue.

"I know what I just said, young man, but I also said that no one returns to the building until the alarm is off." The officer gave me a stern look like he thought I might be the type of person who would ignore his instructions. I was trying to decide if he was right. The officer continued, "Since you seem to know something about what is going on here, I'm going to need you to fill out a police report. Now stay right here until I return."

Now I was really annoyed with myself for not looking at the paper when I had had the chance. I guess I was a little distracted. The officer was back in just a minute with clipboards, blank reports, and pens for me, Jeff, and the missionaries. It took probably ten minutes to get them filled out. I wrote Dr. Anthony's name on it in three different places. Dad was standing next to us asking questions the whole time we were writing. I don't know how many times I said to him, "Yes, Dad, I'm absolutely sure it was Dr. Anthony."

CHAPTER 6

And Their Names Were Taken

About the time I finished filling out the police report, the fire alarm inside was switched off. Most of the crowd was already gone by then, and it was starting to rain again. The police officer stood by the door and made sure that all of the employees were allowed back in first and then he let them control who else got in. Because of the confusion at the time of the fire alarm, the director of the center decided it would be best to close for the day and take an inventory to make sure nothing was missing. I wondered how long the document Dr. Anthony had returned had been missing before today.

Even though the visitors' center was now closed, the director and the missionary couple wanted Jeff and me to go back inside with them so we could show them what we had seen. Dad came with us, of course, and so did a police investigator. When we got to the door in the back that we had first seen Anthony go in, Dad said, "You didn't go through here, did you? It says 'Employees Only' on the door."

"We were following Dr. Anthony, Dad," I said. "We didn't really worry about what it said on the door, because we knew that he was up to no good!"

"Speak for yourself," mumbled Jeff.

"OK," I said. "I was the one who didn't really worry about it. I admit that I was dragging Jeff along behind me—pretty much against his will."

"It's true," Jeff agreed.

"Are you *sure* it was Dr. Anthony?" Dad asked again for about the twenty-seventh time.

This time I didn't bother to say that I was absolutely sure. I just gave Dad the same look that he gives me when I ask him to tell me the same thing for the twenty-seventh time. We walked down the hallway, but this time Elder Rasmussen had switched on the light, so it was much easier to see.

"Where did this mess come from?" asked Sister Rasmussen.

"That's what Anthony used to jam the door shut and trap us in the room," I said.

"This room is supposed to be locked at all times," said the director. Turning to Jeff and me he asked, "Was it locked earlier?"

"We don't know," I said. "Anthony was already inside when we got here. He had left the door open a little bit, so we just pulled it open the rest of way to see what he was up to."

"So you didn't see him taking anything?" asked the investigator. "You only saw him returning something?"

"That's right," I said.

As we entered the room I pointed at the empty tube that was lying on top of the cabinet and the drawer was still partway open. "See!" I said. "That's the tube he was carrying it in. And he put the paper in the very front of that drawer that's open."

"It's curious that he would leave the tube behind," mused the director. "I wonder why."

"Probably because we distracted him as he was finishing up," I said. As Sister Rasmussen straightened the chairs that Anthony and I had used to protect ourselves with, I explained how everything had happened.

"Can we look at the paper and see what it is?" I asked. "That might give us an idea of what he was up to."

"We probably shouldn't move anything in case the police want to try to get some fingerprints first," said the director.

70

"That's right," said the investigator.

"He was wearing gloves," I said, "so you probably won't be able to get any."

"But if he left the tube behind accidently," suggested the investigator, "then maybe he left some fingerprints there by mistake as well."

"I don't know why you think fingerprints are important," I mumbled. "Jeff and I know who it was. Don't we, Jeff?"

Jeff nodded in agreement.

"The more evidence, the better," smiled Dad.

"A jury is more likely to believe fingerprints than eyewitnesses," said the investigator. "Especially in a dark room where the witnesses were frightened."

I was going to say something about not being afraid, but decided against it. Instead I asked, "Isn't it possible that knowing what's on the paper could be an important part of the investigation?"

"Anything's possible," said the investigator.

The director pointed his finger at the drawer and said, "Perhaps we could use the tweezers to at least pull the document out and see what it is." Turning to the investigator, he asked, "Would that harm anything?"

"Just be careful not to set it down anywhere or touch anything that might smudge fingerprints on the cabinet or drawer," said the investigator. "We don't know when he put the gloves on."

The director got some tweezers and carefully lifted the document from the cabinet by one corner. "I know what this is," he said. "Do you see?" he asked the missionary couple.

"Of course," said Sister Rasmussen.

"I remember looking that over a few weeks ago," nodded Elder Rasmussen.

"What is it?" I asked.

As the director carefully dropped the paper back into the drawer he said, "It's a copy of a resident list or something like a census of the town of San Diego."

"A census?" asked Dad.

"Well, something like that," said the director. "We're not sure if it's a listing of all the residents of San Diego at the time or not. It appears to have been prepared in 1845 by a local Catholic priest named Villalobos. So it may just be a listing of those who were Catholic or those that had some other connection to the priest. We're just not sure."

We talked for a few more minutes about various things and then Dad said that he thought it was time to leave. We said good-bye to Elder and Sister Rasmussen and left the visitors' center, picking up our umbrellas on the way out. It was a good thing we had them, too, because it was raining pretty hard again. It was after 6:00 by this time and we were starving.

"Shall we try to find something to eat in Old San Diego before we have TB pick us up?" asked Dad. We thought it sounded like a great idea.

We spent thirty or forty minutes walking up and down various streets in the rain before we decided on a place to stop and eat. They served Mexican food that was really good. The tortillas were cooked for us while we waited. I had a chicken burrito that was the best I have ever had in my life. When we were nearly finished, Dad pulled out the GPS paging device and pushed the green button.

"I sure hope that thing works," I said. In about 15 minutes we saw the limo driving slowly up the street. It stopped right in front of the restaurant.

"Thank you for picking us up, TB," Dad said as we climbed in. "We're ready to go back to the cottage, please."

TB took the umbrellas from us one by one and nodded, but didn't say anything. Spoken language was definitely not one of his priorities. It had taken about an hour to get from Omni's place to Old San Diego, so we knew about how long it would take to get

72

back. I noticed that the window between us and TB was closed as usual. As we drove we started talking about Dr. Anthony again.

"Do you think Dr. Anthony is still working for Mr. Omni?" I asked Dad.

"I don't know," said Dad. He hesitated before saying, "I know you are sure that it was Dr. Anthony you saw, but I still find myself wondering if he hasn't just been on your mind because of being at Mr. Omni's home. The mind can really play tricks on you."

"But I'm totally sure, Dad."

"I know you are," Dad said. "But you can't tell me that you haven't been uptight and worried about visiting Mr. Omni, can you?"

"No," I admitted. "It's true. But I don't think I had thought anything about Anthony recently until I saw him today."

"That's fair," Dad nodded. "Maybe these things are all related."

We sat in silence for a few minutes until I noticed a police siren outside. TB pulled the car to the right-hand lane to let the car pass, but it stayed close behind us as TB eventually pulled onto the shoulder of the freeway and came to a complete stop. The siren stopped blaring, but the lights kept flashing. We could see the officer talking to TB at his window, but we couldn't hear anything that was said. Then TB got out and came around to open the doors for us.

"Highway Patrol," said the officer. "Please step out of the vehicle."

"Is there a problem, Officer?" asked Dad as he grabbed an umbrella and stepped out into the rain. Jeff and I did the same.

"We got a tip about a black limo with the license plate 'OMNI X,'" said the officer. "Something about stolen historical documents."

"You can't be serious," Dad said with complete astonishment on his face.

"Your driver has given me permission to search the vehicle," said the officer.

"It's fine with me," said Dad, "but I'm curious as to where the tip came from."

"I believe it was an anonymous phone call," said the officer.

"It was Anthony," I said.

"You're right," agreed Jeff.

"Who is Anthony?" asked the officer.

We explained to the officer what had happened to us earlier in the afternoon and all about Dr. Anthony. The officer listened carefully, but didn't say much. He spent at least ten minutes searching the limo, but didn't find anything. What was Anthony up to now? What a pain.

The officer thanked us for our time and apologized for the inconvenience. A few minutes later we were pulling up in front of Omni's cottage again. It was still raining. There was another limo in the driveway in front of us. It looked like the one that had taken everyone else shopping for the day. I noticed its license plate read "OMNI V." I pointed it out to Jeff and Dad.

"He must have a limo for every letter in the alphabet," I said. "I wonder where the 'OMNI W' limo is. The 'W' should have come between the 'V' and 'X.'"

"Maybe he didn't like that one," suggested Jeff.

When we went inside we discovered that the rest of the family had just gotten home, too. Soon we were escorted to our bedrooms by the housekeeper, Irene. We followed her up a large, wide staircase. It was so formal and fancy it reminded me of some old movie. I noticed video cameras mounted in the hallways as we made our way to our rooms.

"Please remove any wet clothing and freshen up as you need," Irene said. "Señor Omni is requesting that you join him in the dining room."

"Oh, OK," we said. "We'll be there in a few minutes."

Irene left, closing the double doors behind her. Danny, Jeff, and I were given a room together with three large beds. Danny jumped on his and quickly discovered that it was both really soft and really bouncy. This was the fanciest bedroom I had ever seen. All the furniture looked really expensive and really new. There were a half dozen pillows on each of the beds. I had absolutely no clue what a person was supposed to do with that many pillows. We soon found that our suitcases had been emptied and our clothes had been carefully arranged inside the dressers in the room. There was a dresser for each bed. We also had our own bathroom off of the bedroom that we could get to without even going into the hallway.

We weren't exactly sure what wet clothing we were supposed to change out of, but Danny figured it was getting close to bedtime, so he changed into his pajamas. Jeff and I decided to just remove our shoes and go to the dining room in stocking feet.

When we got to the dining room, everyone else was already there. Everyone except for Paul and Shauna, that is. It turns out that they went home with Paul's mom and were planning to spend the rest of the week with his parents. Omni was disappointed that they wouldn't be around, but said that he wanted to hear all about the events of the day. TB served us hot chocolate and cookies. (Danny asked him for cantaloupe again, and this time he got grapes.) No one in the "OMNI V" limo had much to report, except for Mom, who couldn't believe their great fortune regarding all the wonderful wedding purchases they were able to make that day. Meg was too busy reading one of the books she had brought from Omni's plane earlier that morning. I think the rest of us were just tired from a long, crazy day.

Everyone was amazed to hear all about the Mormon Battalion Visitors' Center—both the expected stories from history as well as the unexpected encounter with Dr. Anthony—and about our little visit with the highway patrol on the way home. Mr. Omni had a slightly amused smile on his face during all of our explanations. I was trying hard to see what he thought about Anthony, but I couldn't tell if he was surprised by it or not.

When there was a break in the conversation, I looked at Mr. Omni and said, "May I ask you a question?"

"Of course," he grinned.

"Does Dr. Anthony still work for you?" I asked. "Or do you still work together?"

"That's an interesting question," answered Omni. "Do you have another question you would like to ask?"

I stared at him for a moment, not sure what to make of his avoiding my question about Anthony. Finally I asked, "What was that note all about that said 'Escape as did Limhi' that was in the front cover of the book I got on the plane?"

Suddenly, Omni leaned forward and looked very interested in what I was saying. "Did you figure it out?" he asked intently.

"I think so," I said slowly. "I mean, I know who Limhi was and how he escaped. Is that what you wanted to know?"

"Excellent!" said Omni with enthusiasm. "That's what I was hoping for."

"Did I understand correctly that this was a clue about something here on the property?" asked Dad.

"Exactly," nodded Omni.

"Didn't you say that there were several clues?" asked Dad.

"Oh, yes," agreed Omni. "We'll get to those."

"Clues about what?" I asked. I was getting tired of him talking in circles and not really giving us any idea of what was going on.

"The *mission*," said Omni with passion. "I have clues about the *mission!*"

"What mission?" I asked.

Omni leaned back again, suddenly not looking so passionate. "Oh," he sighed. "We'll talk about that first thing in the morning. I will explain it all to you in the morning."

"Why are we waiting until tomorrow?" asked Danny. "We're all here now."

"Oh, but we're *not* all here," smiled Omni. "There is another person that needs to join with us first. In the morning we will talk until he arrives and then it will be time for 'Show and Tell.' I have been searching for something for several years. So we'll talk about my search. And then, after my guest arrives, together we'll show you what we found. You will hardly be able to believe it!" He was starting to get excited again. He licked his lips, leaving them shiny and pink.

After a pause, he said, "Any other questions?"

I asked, "Do you have a limo for every letter in the alphabet? I noticed that you have 'OMNI V' and 'OMNI X.'"

Omni threw his head back and laughed in response to my question. Watching him laugh drew my attention to the gaps between his teeth again and I was starting to get annoyed.

"No!" Omni answered eventually. "But I do have license plates for every Roman numeral value from one to twelve! What you thought were the letters 'V' and 'X' are in actuality the Roman numerals for five and ten!"

He obviously thought this was very funny and laughed about it all over again.

"Roman numeral twelve is the limit, of course," Omni explained, "because California license plates only allow for up to seven characters: 'OMNI' takes four characters, leaving just three more for the Roman numerals."

"Roman numeral eight won't work either," said Jeff.

"Yeah," I agreed. "It takes four characters to make an eight: VIII."

"Have you ever seen it written the old way?" asked Meg, looking up from her book.

Omni looked at Meg with a huge smile and a look of admiration on his face. He said, "Well done! How did you know that?"

Meg just shrugged her shoulders in response.

"Take a look at what she's always doing," I said. Meg looked down at the book in her hands and smiled sheepishly.

Omni explained, "Roman numerals are standard now, but they weren't always so. It used to be perfectly acceptable to write an eight with the letters 'IIX.'" Looking at Meg, he asked, "Is that what you were talking about?"

She bounced her head up and down in response. It's amazing what she knows.

"So where are all the other license plates you have between one and twelve?" asked Jeff. I'm sure he was wondering if there was a cool truck hidden in a garage somewhere close by.

"Oh, they're mostly at my other home," said Omni with a wave of his hand. "The 'X' has always been my favorite, so I try to keep the 'OMNI X' license plate on whichever vehicle I spend the most time in."

"Why is 'X' your favorite?" asked Chelsea.

"Thank you for asking!" smiled Omni. "I think I like 'X' because it can have so many different meanings and it is used in so many different ways."

"What do you mean?" asked Chelsea again.

"Have you ever heard of 'X' marks the spot?'" asked Omni. Chelsea nodded.

"It's an indication of something valuable," Omni continued. "Something that most others are probably not aware of—something secret and exciting."

Chelsea and Danny both nodded in agreement this time. It was nice to see Danny forget about his missing cantaloupe for a minute.

"But," Omni said, "an 'X' can also mean the exact opposite. It can indicate that something is gone or no longer valid. We sometimes use an 'X' to cross things out, don't we?"

"You're right!" agreed Chelsea.

"However," Omni went on. His face was more serious now. "I

believe my favorite meaning for 'X' is when we use it as the Greek letter *Chi*, which is the symbol for Christ. Have you heard of that symbolism before?"

Chelsea and Danny had big eyes now and were both shaking their heads slowly from side to side. I looked over at Dad and he nodded his head in agreement.

"Have you ever seen someone write the word *Christmas* with an 'X' in place of the word *Christ* at the beginning of the word?"

"I have," said Meg. She had returned to her book, but was apparently still listening to the conversation.

"Well," said Omni, "some people don't like that because they think it's an attempt to remove Christ from Christmas. But when it was originally written, it was actually just the opposite: it was *emphasizing* Christ by using the symbol for his name: the Greek letter *Chi*, which looks just like an 'X' in our alphabet."

Omni paused for a moment, made a deep sigh and said, "I love the letter 'X.'"

"Does the letter 'X' have something to do with the mission you're going to tell us about?" asked Danny.

A smile slowly spread across Omni's face. "I think they may be very closely related," he said. He paused before adding, "That will give you something to think about and dream about tonight, won't it?"

"It sounds to me like it's time for bed," said Mom. "That's the only mission we're going to worry about right now. Imagine a huge 'X' on each of your beds, because, as Mr. Omni has pointed out, 'X' marks the spot!'"

CHAPTER 7

The Mission

"Thank you for your hospitality," Dad said to Omni as we all stood up from the table and headed off to bed. "It's been an eventful day."

"Yes," Omni nodded. "Hasn't it?" Smiling, his eyes darting back and forth between the three of us that had been trapped with him two years earlier, he added, "The days always seem to be eventful when we're together, don't they?"

None of us really knew what to say in response to that. I sort of mumbled something and noticed that Jeff did the same. Meg just stared at her book, but I thought I saw her grip tighten as she continued to read.

"Yes, thank you," Mom said, saving us from the previous line in the conversation.

As we were leaving the room, TB came in and began to clear things from the table.

"Excuse me," Danny said. "Can I have cantaloupe for breakfast tomorrow?"

TB stopped what he was doing, turned to Danny, and gave a single nod before returning his attention to the tray that he was loading dishes on. I noticed that he seemed to be arranging them precisely on the tray.

"I think that means yes, Danny," Chelsea said as we left the room.

"I think it means that he recognized someone might be talking to him," said Jeff, "but nothing else. Not only is English *not* his first language, I don't think English is *any* of his languages."

Mom and Dad invited us all into their bedroom for a family prayer before sending us back to our own rooms. Mom and Dad had a king-sized bed, two dressers, and almost enough floor space for a three-on-three game of basketball. I noticed that the ceiling was probably even high enough for a hoop. The girls had a bedroom that was practically identical to ours: three beds and three matching dressers. Since Shauna was staying with Paul's parents, Meg and Chelsea had fun talking about how they might switch beds on different nights. They told us that their clothes had been unpacked just like ours, and they even found some of their things hung up in the closet. Their bedroom also had its own adjoining bathroom.

After Jeff said the family prayer we had a discussion about the remainder of the week.

"When do we get to go to D-World?" asked Danny.

"SeaWorld," I corrected him.

"Oh, yeah," he said. "But when?"

"I don't think we really want to do anything like that until the rain stops," Mom suggested. "So let's just see how it goes."

"It sounds like Mr. Omni has some things planned for us tomorrow, anyway," Dad said. "Let's plan on going later in the week."

As he said that I suddenly realized that there was a distinct possibility we would never hit a single amusement park while we were here. I remembered that Dad's plans and the family's reality just never seemed to cross paths.

"Oh, just so you know," Dad smiled. "I asked the housekeeper if we could use the dining room table for our family devotional in the morning."

The groans and moans were some of the best I had ever heard from my brothers and sisters. It made me really proud of them.

Dad laughed. "Wow!" he said. "That was impressive. I almost felt like you meant it that time." He made a small sigh and said dramatically, "But I know, deep down in your hearts none of you really believe that a vacation means a vacation from doing what's right. In fact, vacation means that we don't have to worry about anything unimportant—like schoolwork or sports—getting in the way of our favorite time of the day: family devotional!"

"Do we have to do it at the table?" asked Meg. "Can't we find some soft chairs somewhere?"

"I'm sure we could find some soft chairs somewhere," Dad nodded, "but we're not going to. Soft chairs put people to sleep, especially when they aren't really awake to start with! And besides that, I really like having a surface to write on." He paused and said, "So—yes, we have to do it at the table. Thanks for asking."

In a voice that sounded like a host at a Chinese restaurant, Jeff said, "Thank you! Come again!" I looked over at him in time to see him put the palms of his hands together and bow ever so slightly.

I don't think Meg enjoyed Jeff's contribution to the conversation.

"What time are we doing devotional?" asked Chelsea.

"I'm not sure," said Dad. "But I'll try to let you sleep as long as I can stand it, OK?"

"What does that mean?" she asked.

"It means that waiting for family devotional is like waiting for Christmas morning!" Dad said. He made a silly face and added, "I can hardly stand it!"

"Oh," Chelsea said without emotion.

"Don't forget to brush your teeth and say your own prayers," Mom reminded us as we all headed off for our own bedrooms.

"Uh-oh," said Danny with wide eyes. "I think I forgot to bring mine."

"Your prayer?" Jeff asked, insisting on being a pain.

"My *toothbrush*," said Danny with exaggerated lips.

Mom gave him a silly look and said, "We'll get you a new one tomorrow. But then you'll have to brush for twice as long every time for the next day!"

"OK," said Danny, looking dejected and swinging his arms back and forth as he left the room.

When we went into the hallway I was surprised to see TB standing at attention a few feet from the door, holding a large, silver platter. I wondered what treat he was serving now. I remembered wondering on the plane if we would be getting free food at every turn all week—it was starting to look that way.

Jeff got to the tray first and then burst out laughing. "I'm good, thanks," he called over his shoulder as he continued past the butler and headed for his room.

Before I could see what was being served, I heard Danny say, "How did you know?" Of course TB had no response. Then Danny asked, "Do you have an orange one?"

I couldn't believe it when I saw what was on the serving tray. There were, in a perfect arrangement, about ten toothbrushes of various shapes, colors, and sizes, all still in their packaging.

"Ha!" I said and then I added, "Look here, Danny. An orange one!"

"Oh, yeah," Danny smiled. Looking up into the butler's face, he said, "Thanks, Mister. Now I won't have to brush my teeth for twice as long tomorrow!"

"Every time," I reminded him.

"Yeah," said Danny. He rolled his eyes like he felt very lucky to have escaped that torture.

The next morning Dad woke us at 7:03 and asked us to be in the dining room in fifteen minutes for family devotional. I knew what time it was because of the green light display on the clock radio on my nightstand. After brushing my teeth and washing my face, I stumbled past the grandfather clock in the hallway, noticing that it read 7:12—way too early for any rational parent to expect a child to be awake while on vacation.

"Don't you think 7:00 is a little excessive?" I asked Dad as I put my scriptures on the table and plopped down on a chair.

"Does 8:00 sound better?" Dad asked.

"Yes! Tons."

"Well, that's what I was thinking," Dad smiled. "It's 8:00 in Utah."

I was trying to muddle through my brain well enough to come up with a brilliant response, but none was there. Luckily, I was saved by the butler, who entered the room carrying a tray of what appeared to be fresh-squeezed orange juice and glasses.

"That looks and smells wonderful," Dad said as we watched TB carefully place glasses and napkins in front of each chair around the table. After the glasses were in place, he held up the pitcher of juice without a word, and in a questioning attitude looked at Dad. "Yes, of course I would like some," Dad said. "Thank you."

TB then held the pitcher for me and I nodded and said, "Yes, please."

TB waited for each person in the family to come into the dining room and then offered to pour juice for them in the same way he had offered it to Dad and me: without saying a word. Just as we were all about settled, Mr. Omni came into the room. He was carrying a large glass of juice.

"Ah!" Omni said. "I thought I heard someone in here. I always enjoy a fresh glass of juice in the morning, so I'm happy that TB has provided it to you as well." Looking around the table, he said, "Starting the day with a little Bible study, are we?"

"Either that or the Book of Mormon," Dad answered.

"I see," said Omni. "I guess the term *Bible study* isn't quite broad enough. I suppose I should have said *scripture study* then."

"We believe the Bible to be the word of God," said Chelsea without warning, "as far as it is translated correctly. We also believe the Book of Mormon to be the word of God."

"Which Article of Faith number is that one?" asked Omni.

"Eight," Chelsea smiled and took a sip of orange juice.

"Interesting that you would refer to translation," said Omni. "Because we have been doing a lot of that around here lately." We all looked at him, waiting for more explanation, but then he said, "But I guess I'm getting ahead of myself again. I promised we wouldn't talk about the mission until the last guest arrives." With a wave of his hand he said, "Enjoy your scripture study," and left the room.

"OK," said Dad, "shall we get started?"

Just then, Omni poked his head back in through the door and said, "I almost forgot to tell you that 'Shiblon' is another clue that I think is in the Book of Mormon. Maybe you will run across that during your study." Then he was gone again, just as quickly as he had appeared. TB followed him from the room.

"What are we going to study today, Dad?" asked Meg. "Don't we usually do something different than just read when we have devotional on vacation?"

"Yes, we do," Dad nodded. "Let's have an opening prayer and then we can talk about that. Chelsea, will you offer the prayer, please?"

Chelsea said the prayer.

"Does anyone have any ideas of how we should have family devotional while we're here?" asked Dad. "We don't have to do anything different, though. We can just keep reading where we are. We're getting near the end of Alma. At the rate we're going, we'll probably finish Alma before the summer is over."

For our family devotionals Monday through Friday we would usually read from the Book of Mormon. At that rate we could read it once a year. Dad used the weekends to try to get us through all the conference talks in one *Ensign* before the next conference, but we didn't always make it. It was funny to hear Dad say "we'll probably finish Alma before the summer is over" because I knew perfectly well that he had a little schedule worked out that he kept in his scripture cover. He knew *exactly* how far we had to read each month to make sure we finished the whole Book of Mormon by the end of the year. I was betting that his schedule put us *exactly* at the end of Alma by the end of August.

"Why don't we read about Shiblon?" suggested Mom. "That might help us get ready for whatever Mr. Omni wants to tell us about."

"Yeah," I said. "And I can show you what I found out about the other clue he gave us—the one inside the front cover of the book."

"That sounds fun," Dad said. "Any other suggestions?"

Nobody offered any other ideas. Probably because they weren't really totally awake yet. So Dad decided to work on the clues.

"Where do we read about Shiblon?" Dad asked. Then he caught himself and said, "Or rather, first of all, who was Shiblon?"

"He was one of Alma's sons, right?" said Mom. "I think we read about him just a few weeks ago."

"Right," Dad said.

"Who can find the chapter?" asked Mom.

We all knew well enough by now that that was our clue to look up the word in the index. Before we could even start to turn there, though, Mom said, "Isn't it Alma 38?"

"That's right," said Dad.

Those of us who were starting to check the index decided not to bother and just turned to Alma 38.

"Shall we read it?" Dad asked.

As we read the chapter together, we stopped now and then, wondering what this might have to do with the mission Mr. Omni was going to tell us about. After reading the first five verses, Jeff said, "I'm not sure I like the sound of this."

"What do you mean?" asked Mom.

"Alma is telling Shiblon to have patience and that eventually he'll be delivered out of his troubles and trials," said Jeff.

"Why don't you like the sound of that?" asked Dad.

"Well, I've been thinking," said Jeff. I thought, *Oh, no. That's always dangerous*. I was smart enough not to say it out loud, though. I don't think that would have gone over too well during family devotional. Jeff continued, "Do you think this vacation might be the trials and troubles that Alma is talking about? Do you think we can endure to the end of the week?"

"Jeff!" said Mom.

"Just kidding, Mom!" Jeff laughed.

Neither Mom nor Dad looked like they believed him. I know I didn't!

When we got to verse 8, Danny said, "Hey, there's the word *mission* inside a different word, *remission*. What does that mean? Is that what the man is talking about?"

We talked for a few minutes about everything that Alma said Christ did for him when he was in pain and anguish. Then we continued to read until we got to the part about Jesus Christ being the only way that we can be saved. We talked about this for a long time, especially about what that means for people who don't believe that Jesus is the Christ or people who have never even heard of him. Chelsea was starting to feel bad just thinking about all the people who didn't know or believe in Jesus Christ.

"Don't worry," Mom said. "Heavenly Father loves all of his children so much. He will make sure that everyone knows what Jesus did for them. Everyone will get the chance."

We read to the end of the chapter and then Dad said a closing prayer. I thought about reminding him that we hadn't talked about the other clue, but I didn't feel like it now. I was starting to wonder what was for breakfast and how soon it would happen.

Immediately after we said "Amen" at the end of the prayer, the butler came into the dining room and began clearing the juice glasses and preparing for breakfast.

"Thank you for the juice during our devotional," Dad said. "How long do we have until breakfast is ready?"

"One half more past eight o'clock," said TB, in one of his rare speaking moments.

"Eight-thirty?" asked Dad. TB nodded.

Mom looked at her watch and said, "That gives everyone forty-five minutes to shower and dress before breakfast. You better hurry!"

The girls took off down the hall like the winner got free manicures for life. Since they were sharing a bathroom, there was no doubt about why they were in such a hurry. I figured that forty-five minutes would be pretty nearly impossible for either one of them by herself, let alone sharing with each other.

"Hey!" called Dad after them.

He didn't need to say anything else. They slowed down considerably but continued to giggle and pull at each other on their way down the hall. I knew Jeff and Danny and I didn't need to worry about hurrying because Jeff and I needed only about ten minutes each to get ready. And Danny was so fast I had the feeling he was in and out of the shower before he even had a chance to get wet. I suppose that saved him the trouble of drying off—as well as the time. In any case, I'm absolutely sure he didn't even reach for the soap—shampoo maybe, but definitely not the soap.

Breakfast was French toast served with an amazing selection of syrups, jams, and jellies. There was also plenty of various fresh fruits and juices. After the blessing, Mr. Omni explained that TB's four pitchers of milk were whole, 2 percent, 1 percent, and skim. After watching TB pour milk for several people, I decided I didn't dare have anything but juice. I watched carefully and noticed that there didn't seem to be any connection between what type of milk someone asked for and which pitcher TB poured from. I was really starting to wonder why Omni kept him around. Then I realized that maybe he had in fact let him go more than once, but because he didn't understand anything, he would have had no clue that he had been fired.

"Please don't read at the table," Dad said. I knew he had to be talking to Meg. Without a word, she immediately closed the book she was reading and slipped it under her thigh. She had been trying to spread jelly on a piece of toast with only one hand. I figured that was probably what caught Dad's attention. Even after she put the book down, though, she apparently had no intention of letting it go; I laughed to myself as I watched her still working on her toast with one hand.

As breakfast was winding down, Omni picked up his napkin from his lap and placed it very deliberately on the table next to his plate. "It's time for me to tell you why you are here," Omni said.

The room became immediately quiet. This is what we had all been waiting for!

"But, before I say anything more," Omni said, "I must ask a favor from each of you. What I am about to tell you and show you is currently known only to me and a few people that I have hired to help me. Please give me your word that you will not reveal any of this to anyone else before they are made public—which, by the way, I hope is only a few months away." Omni smiled. "Agreed?" he asked.

"Of course," said Dad. "Absolutely." Then Dad looked around the room at each of us and asked, "What do you think, guys? Can you help Mr. Omni keep his secret?"

Danny looked very serious as he nodded his head up and down.

Chelsea and Meg both said, "Uh-huh."

"No problem," I agreed.

"Sure," said Jeff.

"Certainly," said Mom.

Omni smiled and nodded. Then he spoke with great enthusiasm in his voice. "The Spaniards," Omni said, "began establishing Catholic missions along the coast of California in the late 1700s. They began in San Diego in 1769 and continued moving north until, by 1823, they had about two dozen missions from San Diego to San Francisco."

This is what we had all been waiting for? This is what he meant by "the mission"?

"Does everyone know what a mission is?" Omni asked. I think he assumed the worst from the blank stares he was getting from most of us.

Danny answered, "A mission is where Jeff and Brandon are going when they turn nineteen. And where I'm going, too, when I turn nineteen."

Omni laughed. "Same idea," he said.

Jeff looked at Danny and asked, "Do you know what we're going to do when we go on a mission?"

Danny's answer was immediate. "Teach people about Jesus."

"That's right," said Jeff. "And we will also help and serve people who need it."

"I know," said Danny.

"The type of mission that I am talking about is a place where priests lived," explained Omni. "They would share the gospel of Jesus Christ with the local inhabitants and would help people in need, often providing food, water, medical attention, or temporary shelter."

"So it's the same," said Danny.

"You're right," said Omni. Then he continued, "Because the missions were often far from established towns, they were usually built almost like a fort, with high walls all around and large doors that could be opened during the day, but closed at night to keep criminals out."

"Like robbers?" asked Danny with wide eyes.

"Like robbers," nodded Omni. He continued by saying, "Now many of these old missions still exist today." He suddenly burst out laughing. "Remember what I said yesterday about Mission Viejo?" he asked.

"It means 'Old Mission' in Spanish," Chelsea answered.

"Exactly!" laughed Omni. "And that's what we're talking about: old missions."

He looked around the room like he was expecting us all to laugh just as heartily at this wonderful joke, but I don't think any of us understood what he thought was so funny. He apparently figured that out after a moment and continued with his story.

"Several years ago I learned that the San Diego mission that was established in 1769 was actually on a different site than it is today. The church used the mission in its first location for a short time before deciding that there just wasn't enough water nearby. So they decided to move the mission further west, closer to the ocean. The mission has been at its current location for more than 200 years now."

Omni paused. He was leaning over his plate with his fingers laced together. He took a moment to look around the room at each of us seated at the table.

"So," he continued, "I asked myself probably the exact same question you are asking yourselves now: Whatever happened to the first mission that was built over 200 years ago? The only difference between you and me is that I decided to find out! And, luckily for me, I have the time and money to accomplish that goal." He shrugged his shoulders like he just couldn't help being the lucky guy that he was.

"So I started looking," Omni said. "I started researching and investigating everything I could find out about the area between where the new mission was built (and currently stands) and the mountains to the west of it. I did everything you can imagine. I hired geologists, I hired historians, I hired helicopters, and I finally figured it out! I kept asking myself and everyone else the same questions: Where is it? Where could it have gone? A mission is no small structure that could be beaten down by rain and blown away by the wind. And then one day I had an epiphany!"

"What's that?" asked Danny.

"A stroke of genius," said Omni quietly. "I suddenly realized where it went. Actually, the break came after I had been living in this area for a couple of years and learned more about it. Several years ago it rained and rained and rained one August, just like it is now. In the mountains east of L.A. the previous year there had been a huge forest fire that had burned off all the vegetation. Do you know what the vegetation does for the side of a mountain and what it can't do anymore when it's gone?"

"It holds it in place," answered Mom.

"Precisely," said Omni with excitement. "And when the vegetation isn't there to hold the side of a mountain in place and then it rains and rains, do you know what happens?"

"Mud slides?" asked Meg.

"Precisely," said Omni again. "And that's what I decided must have happened to the mission. I wasn't sure how close to the mountains the first mission had been built, but mountains are usually a good source of water because water runs down from them when it rains. It made sense to me that the mission might have been built quite close to the mountains and that therefore, it might have been buried by a mud slide. And since it had been abandoned, it also made sense that it could have happened without anyone taking much note of it or making any record of it."

Omni looked around at us again, his fingers still laced together above his plate. "I sent my geologist and my helicopter pilot out to try to find evidence of previous mud slides somewhere east of the current mission and guess what they found and guess what I now own!"

"What?" asked Chelsea.

"This house?" asked Meg.

"Close!" said Omni. "Come with me." He stood so quickly and unexpectedly and with so much excitement that several people jumped. He walked briskly out of the dining room, down the hall, and out onto a huge, covered patio that had an assortment of lounge chairs and tables. Beyond the covered portion of the patio was a large swimming pool with a diving board and a slide.

"Can we go swimming?" asked Danny.

"You'll need to ask Mr. Omni," Mom said, "but certainly not when it's raining." I noted that it was currently raining. Danny saw it, too, so he didn't bother to say anything else.

Pointing to the side of a large hill that was several hundred yards away from the back of the cottage, Omni said, "That's what they found."

"What?" asked Chelsea.

Omni answered, "That mountain. In Utah you would call that a hill, but here it's a mountain. And they found that over a hundred years ago part of that mountain slid down and buried the area that this cottage is built on. And can you guess where the San Diego mission is located today, relative to this property?"

"Is it directly west?" asked Mom.

Turning to Dad, Omni said, "Well done, Mr. Andrews! You have found yourself a woman who is sharp as a tack!" Dad smiled at Mom. Mom shrugged her shoulders as if she was trying not to look embarrassed.

"That's right; it is directly west from here," said Omni. "And as luck would have it, guess what property just happened to be for sale at the time I made this discovery?"

"This one?" asked Danny.

"That's right!" said Omni.

"Am I as sharp as a tack, too?" asked Danny.

"Yes, you are," smiled Omni with all the sincerity I have ever seen. "So I bought it! I bought it and immediately applied to the city for a permit to excavate the property between the house and the mountain. Anyone want to venture a guess as to what I found when I started digging?" Omni looked around at each of us again; the excitement in his eyes looked to be almost too much for him to contain.

I don't think anyone dared steal his moment of excitement by answering the question before he was ready. We stood in silence, staring at each other for about ten seconds before he said in almost a whisper, "The old mission!" Then he practically shouted, pointing his index finger into the air, "Mission Viejo!"

OK, this was the weird Omni showing up again.

"That's amazing," said Mom.

"Isn't it, though?" said Omni. "We have been excavating the site for over a year now and have the entire back wall exposed and you won't believe what we have found. You should know that at this point, very few people know about this. I want to get much further along before I make it public. But we have found some things that we're still trying to make sense of and because I hold your family in the highest regard—and I believe you could be of some help to me—I want to share it with you."

"When do we get to see it?" asked Meg.

"As soon as my other guest arrives," smiled Omni. "I just wanted you to know the history first."

"Who is it?" asked Meg.

"I call him my Doctor of Documents," said Omni.

"But most people just call me Dr. Anthony," came a voice from the doorway leading into the cottage. We turned our heads in unison to look at who had spoken.

CHAPTER 8

Doctor of Documents

Dr. Anthony looked sternly at each of us for a moment. Then he turned to Omni and said, "I'm late. I apologize."

"Did you have some errands to run this morning before dropping by?" asked Omni. He seemed to be looking at Anthony's face from side to side, as if investigating something.

Anthony stammered for a moment before saying, "Y-yes, well, no, I mean."

I looked Anthony over from head to foot. He looked different than I had ever seen him before, and different from how he had looked even the day before. His hair was shorter—it was also clean—and his glasses were different. Instead of the old, out-of-date wire frames, he had rectangular frames of black plastic. As I watched him I got the impression that the glasses were not very comfortable for him.

Then Dr. Anthony's expression suddenly changed from confused and uncomfortable to something much more sinister. "Actually," he said in a much more controlled voice, "I was delayed by a phone call from the San Diego police department." He glanced quickly, but menacingly, at Jeff and me. "It seems that someone—or two—made a claim that I was at or near a location yesterday afternoon where there was some type of disturbance. Such person—or persons—also attempted to allege some sort of crime, when in fact no crime was actually committed or reported."

"Isn't it a crime to pull a fire alarm when there is no fire?" I asked. "I believe that was reported. I wonder who is going to have to pay for all those emergency vehicles that showed up for no apparent reason."

Everyone on the patio looked back and forth at each other in silence for a moment before Omni took a deep breath and said, "Yes. Well, I don't believe any introductions are necessary, are they?"

Still no one said anything, but the adults all just sort of nodded at each other.

"But where was I?" asked Omni. "Oh, yes, my Dr. of Documents. First of all, what is a Dr. of Documents? He is a man who holds a Ph.D. in history and specializes in historical documents." Omni gestured toward Anthony as he said this. He continued, "And why do I need a Dr. of Documents, you ask?" The excitement returned to his voice as he said, "Because I found a document!"

"What is it?" Mom asked.

"A journal," breathed Omni. His lips were wet and his smile was wide. "A 150-year-old journal," he said.

"Whose is it?" asked Dad.

"A priest by the name of Villalobos," said Omni.

I was sure that I saw Anthony cringe as this name was mentioned.

"Come, let's take a walk," said Omni, and he headed away from the house toward the hill that was several hundred yards away. I noticed that as soon as Meg stood up from the table, she opened her book again and read as we walked away from the house.

"These coverings are nice," said Mom.

There was a wide sidewalk that led from the house to the mountain. Every few feet there were poles and thin ropes holding up a framework for a green covering or awning over the sidewalk. I hadn't started to follow yet. I was still trying to decide if I wanted Anthony behind me or up where I could keep my eye on him.

"I'm glad you like them," said Omni. "The path is actually wide enough for a golf cart, but I really prefer to walk." Anthony rolled his eyes. "I do have enough carts for all of us to ride," Omni continued, "but then we couldn't talk on the way. Walking is much better, don't you think?" He didn't wait for a response. "The coverings keep the sun off on warm days and the water off when it's raining."

Anthony still wasn't moving and, even though it wasn't my nature to want to let him get his way, I decided to go in front of him so that I could hear what Omni was saying.

"Luckily for us it's not raining much right now," Omni said, "because it gets a bit noisy when the rain is falling. Now, I told you that we had exposed the entire back wall, but I didn't tell you that we found rooms all along the back wall that opened into the center courtyard of the mission. We have excavated much of the courtyard near the back wall down to what we believe was the original ground level. Luckily, the mud slide was small enough that the weight did not destroy the roof, and the rooms were completely intact."

"No way," said Jeff.

"What kind of rooms were they?" Mom asked.

"Bedrooms," said Omni. "Four of them. Mostly there were small cots for sleeping and a chair or two. But one of the rooms seemed to be quite a bit nicer than the others. It had a rug on the floor, coat pegs on the wall, and it also had a small writing table. On the table was a lamp, two or three writing implements, and the journal."

"What are writing implements?" asked Danny.

"Pens," said Jeff.

"Close enough," smiled Omni.

"Have you read the journal?" asked Mom.

"Unfortunately for me," said Omni, "it is written in Spanish. I am many things, but I am not a Spanish speaker. That's another reason that Larry is here." Omni turned and gestured toward

Dr. Anthony. Omni continued, "He is translating the journal for me. By the way, how is that coming along, Larry?"

"Fine," said Anthony. He almost acted like he thought the answer was none of Omni's business. That seemed strange, since it was Omni who found it on the land he owned. It was getting hard to decide who was stranger, Anthony or Omni.

"Oh!" said Omni suddenly, turning back to the rest of us. "I almost forgot what we found hidden between a couple of boards in the cot in that room. Any guesses?"

No one had a guess.

"A copy of the Book of Mormon," said Omni. Nodding in my direction, he added, "An original printing just like the one I sent on the plane for you, Brandon."

"Wait a minute," I said, "I thought this was a priest in a Catholic mission. Why would he have a Book of Mormon?"

"Exactly!" said Omni. "That's the right question! And, luckily for us, the answer is in the journal. But Brandon, you're right. Thinking about what you just said, then, it's not too surprising that we found the Book of Mormon hidden in the cot, is it, rather than lying on the table in plain sight?"

"But if he wrote about the Book of Mormon in his journal," I said, "wouldn't that be just as dangerous as leaving out the book itself?"

"A journal would not only be common," said Omni, "it would likely even be expected of a priest and wouldn't look out of place. Also, most people living at that time in this area would not even have had the ability to read, so they wouldn't have been able to discover anything from the journal, anyway."

"That makes sense," said Jeff.

"So *why* did a Catholic priest have a copy of the Book of Mormon?" I asked again.

"I'm so glad you asked," laughed Omni. He didn't seem to realize that this was the second time I had done it. "I mentioned earlier that priests would often help people in need, including those needing medical attention. And that's what he did. According to the journal, in 1848 a man who called himself a Mormon was injured while traveling near the mission. He had been in the U. S. Army, stationed in San Diego."

"That sounds like the Mormon Battalion," said Jeff.

"Exactly!" Omni smiled. "His friends had left San Diego as soon as their enlistment was up, but he had stayed behind a while and was traveling alone. He was now on his way to Utah, where he had never been before, to meet up with friends who had moved there during the time that he was stationed in San Diego." Looking at Jeff, Omni said, "Now you see why I wanted you to know about the Mormon Battalion."

"How did he get hurt?" asked Meg.

"He fell," said Omni. "He was apparently looking for some shelter for the night on the mountain when a cougar decided he looked like a nice meal and attacked him. Because it was dark, he fell from a ledge, sustaining a severely broken leg. Luckily he landed in a place that made it difficult for the cougar to reach him. He had a gun and used it to scare the cougar away."

"Wow, he was lucky," said Mom.

"Are there cougars that live by here?" asked Danny with wide eyes.

"Yes," nodded Omni seriously. "They live in the mountains. Some people refer to them as mountain lions."

"Do they still hurt people?" Danny asked. He was looking a little concerned.

"Every year," said Omni, "we hear news reports of someone who is attacked by a cougar. It usually happens when someone is alone. They recently did a study with tracking devices and found that the cougars keep themselves well hidden, but they are often quite close to some of the walking and hiking trails around here."

That was a little scary. We all waited for him to continue.

"So, you're right, Mrs. Andrews," nodded Omni. "He was a lucky man. He was found a short while later by some Indians who likely heard the sound of his gun. They carried him to the mission in the middle of the night. The priest took him in, cared for his wounds, and gave him a place to sleep since he had nowhere else to go. He apparently stayed at the mission for several months until he was well enough to travel."

"So is that where the priest got the Book of Mormon?" Meg asked.

"That's what it says," answered Omni.

"Wow, that's amazing," said Dad. "I'm excited to see this place."

"Good," said Omni, "because we're there!"

"Whoa!" said Danny. My reaction was about the same.

We were looking down into a gigantic hole that had a long line of huge tents set up in the bottom of it. I was guessing that was where the back wall of the mission was. We could see glimpses of the side walls coming out from under the tents and heading toward Omni's cottage, but they were quickly buried under the ground that had not yet been dug away. The tents were set up on the flat area at the bottom of the hole. The ground all around the tents sloped upward out of the hole until it came up to the ground level for the rest of the property the cottage was on, including the walkway where we were standing.

"The tents are in place to protect the structure from the elements," said Omni. "Follow me and I'll show you what we found."

I was a little worried about getting muddy until I saw that stepping stones had been put in place from the walkway down the slope, almost like a staircase, and then across the courtyard to a slit in the side of one of the tents where people were probably supposed to go in and out. Omni made his way quickly down the slope and slipped through the slit in the side of the tent. All of us, including Anthony, followed not far behind him. Originally Anthony was

100

sort of hanging back, but now he was right with us. I was stunned by what I saw after entering the tent.

Mr. Omni had described it well, but I still wasn't ready for what was there. It was astonishing to see part of such a huge, old structure. There was a long, low building with a flat roof that looked very old and ready to collapse. I was amazed that it hadn't fallen down already.

"The walls are made of adobe bricks," explained Omni, "and the roof is some kind of ceramic material over a wooden lattice."

Along the length of the building were four doors that obviously led to the four bedrooms that Omni had talked about. From the looks of it, they were much smaller than I had imagined. And the doors were very short. It was obvious that we would need to bend over to get through the doorways. I noticed that the roof was only a few inches higher than the top of the door.

The side walls connected to the back wall at the ends of the long, low building. Again, we couldn't see much of these walls because they were quickly buried by the sloping ground just past the edge of the tents. It looked to me like there was still a whole lot of digging to do to find the side and the front walls of the mission. The back and side walls were the same height, which was much higher than the low roof over the four rooms and the wall with the doors. I figured the high walls around the outside were supposed to keep intruders out.

"Why is there a plastic bag on the handle?" asked Danny, pointing to the old door that Omni was about to open.

"To keep us from ruining it," said Omni. Then, speaking to all of us, he said, "As we go inside, please don't touch anything unless it is covered in plastic and only step where there is plastic on the floor."

As soon as Omni opened the door, Anthony pushed his way into the room ahead of everyone else. Surely he had been in there plenty of times before, so I immediately wondered what he might be up to. I was right about the doorway; it was so low that I think Chelsea and Danny were the only ones who could go through it without stooping over. And the ceiling inside was only slightly higher. I stood bending over slightly with my hands on my knees. Omni flipped a switch on a power cord that immediately lit up a couple of floor lamps. I wondered why Anthony hadn't done that, since he had made sure that he was the first one in the room. When the lights came on, we all looked around in complete amazement.

This was obviously the priest's room that Omni had described. There was a table with a chair, a small wooden cot, and a rug on the floor. The rug was covered in plastic and Anthony was standing on it. Even so, it was easy to see that the rug was very worn and I noticed it looked like it had a few holes in it. There was a large flashlight on the floor next to the table. I thought it seemed strange that the flashlight was under the plastic.

"Is that where the Book of Mormon was hidden?" asked Danny, pointing to the cot.

"Yes, it is," said Omni. He was beaming. He was obviously very pleased to be able to show off this place to some new people.

We went back outside and climbed the stepping stone stairway back up to the sidewalk. Then we walked around the back side of the tents. It looked like it was dug down to just about the same ground level behind the back wall as it was in front of the doors, in the courtyard. There was a backhoe parked between the back wall and the side of the mountain.

It had started to rain again. Omni was right about the rain being very noisy on the covered walkways. He suggested we walk back to the house where we could talk about things a little more. We didn't have to walk very far before I looked back and realized that the tents were already completely out of view. It was amazing to think about how big of a mud slide it would take to fill in that hole again and bury the mission. It made me wonder if it had happened all at once or over time.

When we got back to the house, Omni suggested that we make ourselves comfortable on the covered patio. Because it was a solid roof, it was much less noisy than the covered walkways. Anthony sat down, too, but well away from the rest of us. He was sort of acting like he wanted to eavesdrop more than actually participate.

Omni asked, "Does anyone have any questions before we talk about the other things we've learned from the journal?"

"How long is it going to take you to dig out the rest of the walls?" Danny asked.

"I'm not really sure," said Omni.

"How far will you have to dig to get to the front wall?" Chelsea asked.

"I don't know that either," answered Omni, "but I imagine the mission is probably pretty close to square in dimension. We'll have to see. But I'm excited to see what the doors in the front wall look like."

"Are there more rooms along the other walls?" Mom asked.

"I would think we'll find other rooms," Omni said, "because none of the rooms we found already look like they were used for any kind of storage. I'm sure there will be something like that, but we'll just have to see."

No one else had a question, but since Omni didn't have an answer for any of the questions anybody was asking anyway, there probably wasn't much point in asking anything else. I looked over at Anthony to see what he was up to. He just sat staring at the hill over in the direction of the excavation site.

"Well, then," said Omni, "I suppose it's time to tell you a little more about the priest, Villalobos. It turns out that the priest was being held captive by some other men who were living inside the mission walls."

"Really?" asked Mom.

"Well, remember," said Omni, "that in 1848, the year of the priest's journal, this was no longer an official Catholic mission. The real mission was now miles west of here. The other men living here apparently had some sort of enterprise going that they didn't want anyone else to know about. So they kidnapped this priest and threatened him with his life unless he agreed to help them make it look like this was a legitimate mission. That meant helping the needy and seeking converts to the church. Well, since this is what the priest wanted to do anyway, he agreed."

"He probably figured that was safer than trying to escape," Dad suggested.

"And then spending the rest of his life wondering when they might find him," Mom said.

"Right," Omni nodded. "So that's what he was doing here when the man from the Mormon Battalion was brought to him. The other men weren't too pleased with the idea of having someone else living inside the mission, but in order to continue to look legitimate, they allowed it."

"That makes sense," Dad said. "If they didn't let him stay, then others would probably find out about it and figure out that something was wrong with the mission."

"Anyway," said Omni, "they gave him his own room, and the priest would visit him regularly each day to take care of him. That's when he received the Book of Mormon."

"Did he read it?" Meg asked.

"They read it together," Omni explained. "The Mormon apparently used the book to help teach the priest English. The priest wrote that he knew a little English before, but by the time the man left the mission several months later, he was good enough with English to be able to read and understand the Book of Mormon without any assistance."

"That's great," said Mom.

"So now," said Omni, "we're to the part where I could use your help. Some time after the Mormon left for Utah, the priest wrote that he was making a plan to escape."

"Oh," I said, "is that where the words 'escape as did Limhi' came from?"

"Exactly," Omni said. "Do you have a clue what that means?"

"Actually, I do," I said.

"I already told you what it meant," said Anthony with a smirk. "I *am* a scholar of the Book of Mormon, you know."

"Well, I *assumed* that, Larry," said Omni. This was the first time since we had arrived that Mr. Omni was not smiling. "But I've been waiting for weeks now for some further explanation that fits with what we have found and you have yet to give it to me."

Omni continued to stare at Anthony for a moment as if waiting to see if he was going to tell him now or not. Anthony simply sniffed and turned to stare out at the hill again. Omni then looked back at me and smiled. "So what did you find out?" he asked.

"I found where it talks about Limhi planning his escape," I said. "It says that he got away by going through the back wall and a back pass on the back side of the city. It actually says the word *back* three times. I counted."

Omni suddenly became very thoughtful. I noticed that Anthony suddenly looked very fidgety and nervous. Omni rubbed his chin for a moment or two and then finally said very slowly, "That is what I found from my own research and what I discussed with Larry, but we have exposed the entire back side of the back wall of the mission already—and there are no openings anywhere along it." He thought for a moment longer before saying, "So how can that be?"

"I'm sorry I'm no help," I said quietly.

"Oh, no," smiled Omni. "Don't you worry! I'm not expecting you to solve all my problems. I invited you and your family here because I know how much you appreciate the Book of Mormon—I learned that the last time we were together. And that was such a disaster that I wanted to make up for it a little if I could."

I noticed that Dr. Anthony continued to glance nervously at Omni.

Finally Anthony said in a very unconvincing way, "Well, now you know why I never said anything more to you about it. It still just doesn't make any sense, does it?"

"Hmm," Omni said. "I'll need to think about that for a while longer."

"I don't see why," said Anthony. "It's obviously worthless information. The priest was obviously mistaken." Anthony acted like he was trying to figure out what to do next. Suddenly he stood and said, "I'm going to walk back over there."

No one said a word as Anthony left. Once he was gone, we spent the next couple of minutes talking about the way that Limhi escaped and what it might mean for the old mission. I can't remember everything, but various things were said by different people. Then came the best idea I heard about it.

"Maybe the wall you found is not the back wall," Mom suggested. "Maybe it's really one of the side walls."

Omni's eyes opened wide as he thought about this. If he had actually had any eyebrows, he probably would have been raising them right then. Omni nodded slowly and said, "I suppose that's a possibility."

We all sat in silence for a while.

"Oh, well," said Omni a few moments later. "Let's talk about the other clue. Did you find anything out about the word 'Shiblon'?"

"We read a whole chapter about him this morning," Dad said.

"Him?" asked Omni. "Shiblon is a person?"

"Well, yes," said Dad. "Shiblon was one of Alma's righteous sons. Alma 38 is a record of the instructions and teachings of Alma to Shiblon."

"That's curious," said Omni.

"What do you mean?" asked Dad.

"Well," Omni said, "the way the priest used the word didn't give me the impression that he was referring to a person."

"Really?" said Dad. "So how did he use it?"

"I can't remember the exact context at the moment," Omni replied, thinking slowly. "But it was definitely not like a person."

"I guess we haven't been very helpful with your clues after all," Dad said.

"Oh, don't worry about it," Omni said. "We'll get it figured out. I'm so glad to have you here this week."

Just then we all heard Dr. Anthony yelling something as he came running down the walkway in our direction.

"What's Larry's problem now?" Omni asked almost under his breath.

We all listened to see if we could figure out what Anthony was yelling about.

"What are they doing with the backhoe?!" yelled Anthony as he got closer.

"What are you talking about?" asked Omni.

"They're digging," panted Anthony. He had obviously just run very hard to get back to where we were sitting. "They're digging behind the back wall."

"It might not actually be the back wall after all," Omni said.

"What?" Anthony looked confused. "Yes it is. And they're digging back there. Why are they doing that?"

"They're digging a trench," explained Omni. "Because of all the rain we've been having we wanted to give the water some place to drain off, so they're digging a trench."

Anthony looked horrified. "But they're digging down below ground level! It could ruin everything!"

"What are you talking about?" asked Omni. "If we don't get all that water away from that old wall, *that's* what could ruin everything."

"Well, um," Anthony stammered, looking around frantically.

I got the feeling he was grasping at straws. "They shouldn't be working out there in the rain! Th-they could make a mistake and damage the wall! It would be a disaster!"

"They're professionals, Larry," Omni said. "I'm sure they have plenty of experience working in the rain. Everything will be fine."

"No! This is bad," said Anthony. "You *must* tell them to stop!"

CHAPTER 9

And Great Was the Fall of It

"I'm not telling anyone to stop working," said Omni to Anthony. "I'm *paying* them to work. So what is the real issue here, Larry? What is the real reason you're unhappy?"

Dr. Anthony's eyes opened wide like he had just been caught in a lie. "I-I don't know what you mean," he stammered. "I am just worried that those clumsy oafs will damage the site."

"Then *you* should go talk to them," Omni suggested. "I don't think they are clumsy oafs. I think they have done brilliant work so far. I'm also very pleased that they have not violated their non-disclosure agreements and told anyone about what we have found. But since *you* are worried about them, why don't you ask them if they are indeed oafs that are clumsy and what the likelihood is that they will be damaging the site by working in the rain?"

Anthony got a look on his face that clearly revealed how he was feeling about Mr. Omni right now. He was not a happy camper. The two of them just stared at each other. Omni had a semi-sincere smile on his face, while Anthony wore a look of loathing and hatred.

Finally Anthony spoke. "Speaking of non-disclosure agreements," he sneered, "did you get this bunch to sign them before you gave away all our secrets?" He waved his hand in our direction as he spoke.

"*Our* secrets?" asked Omni. "What makes you think they are *our* secrets?"

Anthony didn't respond.

"They are *my* secrets, Larry," said Omni. "That's why you, too, were required to sign the NDA. You are a business associate, whereas these people are my friends. I have asked them to keep what they see confidential for the time being, and, because they are friends, I have no doubt that they will honor my wishes."

"Yeah!" I said without thinking.

Anthony's head jerked in my direction. Now his look of loathing and hatred was aimed directly at me. I immediately regretted my outburst.

"I'll be going to the excavation site now," Anthony said, still staring at me. He turned slowly away, staring me down for as long as possible, but then he walked briskly down the walk toward the mission.

"I think it's time," said Omni after Anthony was well on his way, "to give you a tour of the cottage."

Meg looked up from her book and said, "The woman on the plane yesterday said you have a library here." Her eyes sparkled as she spoke. "Is that really true? Because I'm almost done with the books she let me bring from the plane."

"It's really true," smiled Omni, practically leaping to his feet. "Why don't we make the library our very first stop?"

"I love libraries!" Meg giggled.

"Before we go into any rooms, however," Omni said, "I'd like to show you the general layout of the cottage. It's quite unusual. As you know, there is a hallway running from the front all the way to the back. Then the architect put hallways with windows running the full length of the house both in the front and in the rear. It lets in a wonderful amount of light. This is true for both the main floor and the upper level. You'll notice that all of the rooms back onto each other in the center of the cottage."

"That is unusual," said Dad. "So does that mean that none of the rooms have windows?"

"Only the rooms at the ends," Omni said. "Because they have an outside wall on the side. So the only way for natural light to get into most of the rooms is through the doorways. That's probably why all of the rooms, except for the bedrooms, have double doors."

It was interesting to walk through the halls at the front and back of the "cottage" and be able to have a full view of everything outside. It was pretty different. After showing us how the halls were set up, Omni took us to the one at the back of the house. We followed to a room with double doors that Omni pulled open. The lights came on automatically when he walked inside. I was shocked when I saw what was in there. I don't think I had ever even imagined a room this large inside somebody's house before. It was two stories high with bookshelves from the floor to the ceiling on every wall. Right in the middle of the room was a huge, black, grand piano. There were large, soft armchairs placed randomly around the room, each with its own floor lamp.

"Whoa!" breathed Danny. "I think you have more books than the whole library at my school!"

"And a piano, too?" said Meg with excitement. "Did you know that pianos and books are my two very favorite things in the world?"

Danny then got a puzzled look on his face and asked, "But how do you reach the ones at the top?"

"With the rolling ladder," said Meg with excitement. "I have always wanted to be in a library with a rolling ladder."

"What are you talking about?" asked Danny.

"Look," said Meg. She practically pranced to the corner of the room where a ladder with wheels on the bottom was located. The ladder reached to the top of the highest shelf, where it was connected to a thick railing that went all the way around the room. She pushed the side of the ladder, showing Danny how it rolled along in front of the shelves. "Using this ladder," she explained, "someone can reach every single book in the room."

"Whoa-oh-oh!" Danny giggled. "Dad, we *need* one of these."

"That's too bad," said Dad, "because it's not going to happen."

Mom and Dad walked slowly along the bookshelves, reading some of the titles.

"You have an amazing collection," Mom said absently.

"Yeah," breathed Dad.

"Did you enjoy the selection of books on the plane?" Omni asked Meg.

"Uh-huh," she nodded.

"I'm so glad," Omni said. Then he pointed high up on the wall and added, "They came from that section right there, so you might be able to find something else that you like."

"OK," Meg said. Her excitement was still brimming over. She slowly and carefully pushed the ladder over to where Mr. Omni had pointed. Danny volunteered to help and quickly got on the other side of the ladder, pulling on it as he walked backwards.

"Thanks," Meg said to him, and then she climbed carefully up to where she could reach the shelves where Omni had pointed. Danny climbed up behind her and started looking at the books on a lower shelf.

"Wow!" Dad said after a moment. "This is quite a law collection you have here. Did you study law?"

Omni answered, "As a matter of fact, I did." Then he asked Dad, "Do you know something about law?"

"I do," said Chelsea, who had been standing quietly with her head all the way back, staring up at the highest shelves.

"Well, what do you know about law?" asked Omni.

Chelsea said, "The twelfth Article of Faith."

"Ah!" smiled Omni. "Will you tell me?"

Chelsea thought hard for a moment and then said, "We believe in being subject to kings, presidents, rulers, and magi-magistrates, in obeying, honoring, and sustaining the law."

"Wow!" said Omni. "So what does all that mean?"

"It means," said Danny, "that Mom doesn't think Dad should drive so fast."

Omni's mouth fell open in surprise. He nodded slowly a couple of times and said, "OK. That's why I have a driver, so I don't need to worry about such things."

Turning to Dad, Danny said, "Maybe you should get a driver, Dad."

"That's an idea," Dad said absently.

"I'll do it," I volunteered.

"Thanks, Brandon," Dad said.

A minute later Omni asked, "Well, shall we continue the tour?" No one spoke, so he said, "Anyone who would like to is welcome to stay here."

"I want to stay," said Meg, still poring over the books.

"I want to go," Danny said, climbing down the ladder to the second rung from the bottom and jumping the rest of the distance.

We left Meg behind and followed Omni to the next room he wanted to show us. As we walked down the hall, Dad asked, "When was this house built?"

"Around the turn of the century," said Omni.

"What does that mean?" Danny asked.

"Well," Mr. Omni said, "every hundred years, a new century begins. So technically, the beginning of a century is the turn of the century. But the expression itself generally refers to the early 1900s, though I'm not sure why. Maybe the expression was never used before the 1900s. In any case, historians believe the house was built around 1900."

"Are the video cameras that old, too?" asked Jeff. Dad gave Jeff a look like he couldn't believe he had said that.

"I always like to have a surveillance system," Omni smiled.

"You'll find cameras in the hallways and in the public rooms of the house."

No one said anything else for some time.

When we got close to the door of the room Omni wanted to show us next, he slowed down dramatically and turned to us with his finger to his lips, indicating that we were to be quiet. We all stopped dead in our tracks. Omni smiled and then turned back to the door and opened it very slowly. As he peered through the crack, I wondered what he might be looking at, because I could detect absolutely no light coming from inside the room. Suddenly Omni stepped back and swung the door wide open.

"Come in," he invited us.

Again, as we entered, the lights came on automatically.

"This is what I currently call the 'translation room,'" Omni said. "This is where Larry is taking care of the translation of the priest's journal."

The room looked like a huge, fancy office. There was a large wooden table in the center of the room with a single chair pushed up to one side of it. There were various books and papers scattered over the table. Directly in front of the chair was a laptop computer with a blank screen. At one corner of the table near the chair, the old journal that Omni told us about lay open. It was covered with a sheet of clear plastic. There was a box of latex gloves nearby.

"Luckily for us," said Omni, "it looks like Larry has not made it in here yet this morning. He hates to be disturbed when he is working. He practically throws a fit if he is interrupted. He always turns off the motion-detector lights and works using only the table lamp."

"So is he typing it out onto the computer?" Dad asked.

Omni nodded.

Mom looked closely at the old handwriting that was visible through the sheet of plastic on the open pages of the journal. "This is amazing," she said. "I don't speak Spanish, but even if I did, I

114

think I would have serious trouble just deciphering the letters. I'm impressed that Dr. Anthony is able to translate this."

"So am I," sighed Omni. "He's a bit difficult to work with at times—as you have surely noticed—but he certainly has the skills I need right now."

We looked around the room and talked about the journal for a couple more minutes before Omni took us down the hall to the next room on the little tour.

"I thought everyone else might like this room," Omni said as he pulled the doors open. Just like the library, the lights again came on automatically when we went inside.

This room was full of toys and games. Chelsea and Danny quickly found the biggest bin of snap-together building blocks that I have ever seen. They immediately decided they were going to build a mansion. Jeff and I were, of course, attracted to the video game system.

"Care for a little more Monster Truck Rally?" I asked Jeff.

Jeff closed his eyes, threw his head back and belted out in his announcer voice again, "Monsteeerr Trruuckk Rall-lly!"

"OK," I said, popping the game into the machine.

"Wonderful," said Mr. Omni. "Lunch will be served in about an hour. Enjoy yourselves!"

"We will," I called lazily after him and Mom and Dad as they left the room.

"OK," said Chelsea and Danny.

"Boo-yaw!" called Jeff.

"Do you think they have any idea what that means?" I asked Jeff after they were gone.

"How could they?" laughed Jeff. "I don't even know!"

An hour later we were having lunch around the dining room table. The meal of small sandwiches and fresh fruit looked very much like lunch the day before, but with such a huge variety of sandwiches, I figured we could have the same thing all week and not get tired of it. Mr. Omni had made sure to give Dad the opportunity to call on someone to give a blessing on the food before we dug in.

Near the end of the meal the housekeeper, Irene, came in and told Mr. Omni that two police officers were at the door.

"Let's please invite them in!" said Mr. Omni with a smile. "We are always anxious to cooperate with law enforcement." He seemed quite sincere.

"Yes, Señor," Irene said, and she scurried out of the room.

A moment later she returned with the officers, a man and a woman.

"Pardon the interruption," the woman said. "But we understand there may be a man by the name of Lawrence (or Larry) Anthony here."

"Of course," said Mr. Omni. "He is doing some work for me. Is there a problem?"

"Well, sir," the officer continued, "there may be. Can you tell us where we can find him?"

"I'll have him summoned at once," said Omni. Irene returned at that moment. Omni said, "Irene, will you please send TB in here?"

"Yes, Señor," Irene said, and she left the room again.

A moment later the butler came in and stood near Mr. Omni.

"TB," said Omni, "please locate Dr. Anthony at once and bring him here."

TB bowed slightly without speaking and walked briskly from the room. I realized that I was unconsciously shaking my head, wondering what the chances were that TB had any clue what he had just been asked to do. Leaning over so only Jeff could hear me, I said, "I think Danny has a better chance of finally getting his cantaloupe than for TB to get Anthony in here."

Jeff laughed.

"While we're waiting, sir," said the other officer, "we understand that a Mr. Brandon Andrews and a Mr. Jeff Andrews are staying at this residence. Are they available?"

Gesturing toward us, Omni said, "Right in front of you."

Jeff and I both sort of raised our hands a bit to let the officers know who we were.

"Did you two file police reports last night regarding the sighting of Mr. Anthony at the—," the officer paused while checking a paper in his shirt pocket and then said, "at the, uh, Mormon Battalion Visitors' Center at or near the time a false fire alarm was deployed?"

"Yes, sir," I said. Jeff just nodded.

"But you did not actually see Mr. Anthony deploy the alarm, is that correct?"

"That's correct," I said. Jeff nodded again.

"Thank you," said the officer.

Just then TB and Anthony entered the dining room. I admit that I was totally amazed by TB's success. Anthony looked very nervous.

"What's this all about?" asked Anthony, looking back and forth from the officers to Omni.

"They asked to see you," smiled Mr. Omni.

"Are you Mr. Lawrence Anthony?" asked the woman.

"Yes," Anthony answered warily.

"We need you to come with us to the police station at this time," she said.

"What?" said Anthony. "No! Why?"

"We just need to talk about a few things," said the other officer.

"Let's talk about them right here, right now!" said Anthony.

"Are you sure about that?" he asked.

"Since the guilty parties are in this room," Anthony gestured toward me and Jeff, "then, yes, this is where I want to talk about what you have to say."

"That's fine with me," the woman said. "What can you tell us about a 150-year-old document currently in the possession of the Mormon Battalion Visitors' Center that was written by a man named Villalobos?"

"I-I," Anthony stammered. "I have seen the document in question."

"Are you aware that the document currently at the visitors' center is a forgery?" asked the officer. Anthony's eyes darted about the room. "And that this document does not match photographs taken of the original document less than a year ago?"

Anthony looked suddenly indignant. "There's nothing wrong with that copy," he said. "I mean, with that document."

"Well, then," she asked. "Can you explain why there was an empty document tube found in a back room of the visitors' center with your fingerprints on it?"

Anthony looked nervous again. "N-no," he stammered. "But is that a crime?"

"Not in and of itself, sir," said the officer.

"Well, then," said Anthony, getting a little defiant. "And—and, by the way," Anthony said, "what makes you think they are my fingerprints?"

"You have an FBI file, sir," said the man, "and we have access to it."

Anthony looked really annoyed by that answer. He glanced at me and Jeff again, as if he thought it was our fault that he had an FBI file. Maybe it was.

"Well, then," said the woman, "can you explain why your fingerprints were found on the fire alarm not far from the room where the forged document was found and the document tube with your fingerprints was found?"

"I-I have no idea," said Anthony. "I-I'm a nervous man."

"I can see that, sir," smiled the officer.

"I often tap my fingers on various things without even realizing what I'm doing," said Anthony. I wanted to laugh right out loud. How lame can you get?

"Now, sir," said the officer, "we need to talk a little more about these items. Are you willing to come down to the police station with us?"

Anthony hesitated.

"Your cooperation—or lack of cooperation—in this matter will be quite prominent in our report today," the female officer said.

"Oh, all right," breathed Anthony. "I suppose I have no choice."

"Not really, sir," smiled the officer.

"Larry," said Mr. Omni. "Why don't you take the next couple of days off? It looks like the rain should be gone by then. We can start work again on Thursday." Turning to the officers, he asked, "Will Mr. Anthony be available by then?"

"It's possible," said the woman.

Anthony's eyes got big. Looking at the officers, he said, "Just let me get my jacket and umbrella. I'll be right back."

"We'll come with you, sir," said the man.

Anthony stopped short, like that was the last thing he had in mind. He glared at the officer coming toward him and then headed back out of the dining room. I noticed he was limping. I looked down at the leg he was favoring and saw a streak of mud down the side of his pants. As the officers both followed Anthony from the room, the woman asked, "Are you injured, sir?"

"No!" said Anthony. "Well, yes. I-I accidently ran into a chair a few minutes ago in the office where I was working."

"That's too bad, sir," said the officer. "I'm sorry to hear that."

They were getting far enough away by now that I couldn't tell if Anthony responded. Somehow I doubted it.

"TB," Omni said, "will you please go with the officers and Dr. Anthony and show them to the door? There is no need for them to come back through here."

TB nodded silently, as expected, and followed them down the hall.

"Wow, that was amazing," said Dad.

"Why didn't they arrest him?" I asked. "They found his fingerprints all over the place. They know he did it! Why didn't they arrest him?"

"Brandon," Mom said, "I'm sure they know what they're doing."

"They're going to let him go," I said with disbelief. "Just like always! The reason he has an FBI file is because he keeps doing things like this, but they keep letting him go! I don't think he's ever going to be punished for any of it."

"That's not what you're supposed to believe," said Chelsea. "We believe that men will be punished for their own sins and not for Adam's transgression."

"I like it!" said Omni. "Now which of your Articles of Faith is that one?"

"Number two," she answered.

I was about to complain some more when suddenly a man I didn't recognize came into the room. He was wearing a yellow hard hat, a rain poncho, and tall, rubber boots.

"Mr. Omni, sir, we have a problem," he said.

"Everyone," said Omni, "this is Kirk, my job foreman for the excavation." Turning back to the man he asked, "What's the problem?"

"We need to rent a crane," the foreman said.

"What for? And how soon?" asked Omni.

"As soon as possible," said the foreman. "We started digging the drainage trench along the back wall this morning, but we only got it about halfway done before lunch. When we returned from our lunch break, we found the backhoe on its side, down in the trench. I think a crane is going to be the only way we can get it out of there and set it up on its treads again."

"How did this happen?" asked Omni.

"At this point, I'm not sure, sir," said the foreman. "Kevin was at the controls, and he assures me that he left everything in the proper resting position. If he says so, then I believe him. I have never had a problem with him in the twelve years we've worked together."

"How soon can we get a crane back there?" asked Omni.

"I would imagine we could find one available this afternoon," the foreman said. "Most folks don't care to rent heavy equipment in the rain."

"Well, let's do it then," said Mr. Omni. This was one of the rare times he was not smiling.

Two and a half hours later, most of us were outside watching the crane hooking onto the backhoe and slowly lifting it out of the hole. The girls and Danny had come out for a few minutes but quickly lost interest and went back inside. None of us said much as we watched them set up the crane, not even Mr. Omni. He seemed a little discouraged. Even after the crane had arrived, it had taken quite a while for them to get all the legs securely set in the right places to make sure it was stable and wouldn't tip over when they started lifting the backhoe.

In a few minutes the backhoe was out of the hole and placed safely on level ground again next to the crane. We watched as the foreman and other workers had a lengthy conversation around the backhoe. They kept pointing to various places on the backhoe as they talked. Then the foreman made his way up to the walkway where we were standing with Mr. Omni.

"Is the machine damaged?" asked Omni.

"No, sir, I don't think so," the foreman said. "But we have another problem."

"Tell me," said Omni.

"That hoe is not in the position that Kevin left it," said the foreman. "He left the bucket lowered against the ground, but you can see now that it's been raised."

I looked and saw that the bucket at the end of the long arm of the backhoe was indeed a couple of feet off of the ground.

"But it's only a foot or two," said Omni. "Couldn't it have moved when it tipped over?"

"Kevin left it resting against the ground at the *bottom of the trench*," explained the foreman. "That's another six feet, at least. The only way it could have moved that far is if someone lifted the arm."

"I see," said Omni.

"And there's something else," said the foreman.

Omni just looked at him and waited for the bad news.

The foreman pointed and said, "Look at the front legs."

Omni responded with, "One of them was raised as well, wasn't it?"

"Yes, sir," said the foreman.

"There is no way that could have happened by mistake, is there?" said Omni. It wasn't really a question.

"No, sir," said the foreman.

Omni heaved a heavy sigh and said, "Thank you, Kirk. After that crane is gone, why don't you and your men take the rest of the week off. I'll still pay you, of course."

"Yes, sir," he said. "Thank you, sir. I'll tell the crew."

Omni looked out over the excavation site for a couple of minutes before sighing again and inviting us back to the patio. It was raining, so I was happy to be on the covered walkway.

As Dad found a lounge chair to claim, he said simply, "Sabotage?"

Omni didn't respond for a moment. Then he said. "It's not the first time."

"Really?" Mom asked. "What happened before?"

"Someone started a fire in the dry weeds at the base of the mountain," Omni said. "It was fewer than a hundred feet from the site." He really looked discouraged.

"When was that?" asked Dad.

"The twenty-first of July," replied Omni. "In the middle of the hottest and driest month of the year. I'll never forget that date."

"How bad was the fire?" asked Mom.

"Well, luckily," sighed Omni, "the wind took it up the hill instead of toward the site. It turned into something fairly significant, though. They had small planes flying all over above the hill, dropping flame retardant for a couple of hours before they got it under control. It still burned several hundred acres though. Perhaps you saw that the vegetation is all burned off the mountainside."

"No," Dad said, "I never really noticed. Is it only above your property?"

"No," said Omni, "it extends southward from here for about half a mile."

"Do the police have any leads?" asked Mom.

Omni shook his head. "It looks like it was started with some common fireworks. The main investigator wants to rule it an accident, but I don't believe it. The police file is still open for the time being, but if they don't solve it soon, I'm sure they'll move on to other things."

"Do you have any idea who or why someone would be doing these things?" Dad asked.

"Who?" said Omni. "I have an idea. But why? I'm still trying to figure that out."

No one said anything for a moment.

"Not to change the subject," I said, "but did anyone else notice that Dr. Anthony was limping and that he had a bunch of mud on his pants?"

Mr. Omni kept looking out toward the mountain as he said, "I'm not exactly sure that you *are* changing the subject."

CHAPTER 10

A Journal Day

Mr. Omni seemed somewhat depressed after talking about the two apparent sabotage attempts. Mom and Dad talked with him for a few more minutes about what he might do about the problem and why someone might be sabotaging the work. They didn't really seem to come up with any ideas.

"I'm afraid I need to apologize to you," Omni said to Mom and Dad.

"I can't imagine what for," said Dad.

"Well, I've just realized that I have been so intent on sharing my little project with you that I have not taken into consideration any other plans that you may have had. I do apologize."

"We didn't really have anything concrete in mind," smiled Dad, shaking his head back and forth. "We had thought that sometime during the week we might want to visit an amusement park."

"Or two," I added.

"Or three," whispered Jeff.

We were ignored. That was OK. We had actually gotten pretty good at being ignored. We had recently discovered that it was one of our best talents.

"I hope you understand," Omni said to Mom and Dad, "that you are free to use a car and a driver at any time. I have two available around the clock, so you are always welcome to at least one of them. If I am not using my car, you are welcome to use them both if you have the need."

"Thank you very much," said Mom. "You were certainly very gracious yesterday with the two drivers. But I honestly don't think we had really even thought about it today."

"Not at all," said Dad, shaking his head from side to side. "I've been fascinated by everything we have seen and heard since we got here. I think the boys have had a good time, too." Turning to us, he asked, "Haven't you?"

"Yeah," I nodded. "It's been great."

"It's been awesome," agreed Jeff.

I was serious and I'm sure Jeff was, too. The Mormon Battalion Visitors' Center was amazing, and Omni's excavation was totally incredible.

"I'm glad," smiled Omni. It was the first time he had shown the gaps between his teeth for quite a while.

"Hopefully the rain will let up later in the week," said Dad, "and then we can spend a day or two at an amusement park."

"It is supposed to clear by Thursday or Friday," Omni said. "I apologize for not inviting you here when the weather was better."

"Oh, don't be silly," laughed Mom. "You can't control the weather!"

"But I can try!" laughed Omni. After the chuckling died down, Omni said, "Thank you for indulging an old man."

"It's a pleasure to be here," Dad said.

I was surprised to realize that I felt the same way.

"Tonight," Omni said, "I have asked Irene to prepare a Mexican dinner for you using her own family recipes. The recipes are wonderful and I'm sure you will really enjoy the meal."

"It sounds fantastic," said Mom.

"Is there anyone in the family that does not care for Mexican food?" Omni asked.

"No," said Dad. "It sounds great."

Mr. Omni excused himself for the rest of the afternoon and told us to make ourselves at home. He would see us at dinner. Jeff and I decided to spend the rest of the rainy afternoon playing video games. Danny and Chelsea were in the game room with us, playing with an assortment of toys that was bigger than those in most stores I've been in.

Dinner was delicious. I have never had such good Mexican food. Irene admitted that when she cooks for her own family, she generally makes the dishes quite a bit spicier. "My family enjoys the red and green chilies," she said.

Near the end of dinner Omni told us that there was one more room he had intended to show us earlier, but we had been so excited about the game room that we had never made it there. It turned out to be yet another game room. But this one had air hockey, Ping-Pong, foosball, and pool tables. The five of us spent the entire evening there. Meg sat in the corner reading while the rest of us wore ourselves out playing games.

The next morning we had family devotional around the dining room table again. At least that was the plan. We all had our scriptures and were ready to study something, but we ended up just talking the whole time about Dr. Anthony and what had happened the previous day. We hadn't even cracked our books by the time Dad announced that we should be getting ready for breakfast. We said a prayer and went back to our rooms to shower and dress. Dad made sure that we all took our scriptures with us.

As we were eating breakfast, Omni started talking about the old journal again.

"How much longer do you think it will take Mr. Anthony to translate the journal?" Mom asked. "I'm sure you're anxious to learn what else is in there."

"I'm really not sure how much is left to translate," Omni said. "Hopefully, I'll get a chance to ask him soon. He's done such a good job so far. I'm sure glad he understands Spanish."

"Ha!" said Irene, who happened to be in the room at the time.

"Excuse me?" said Omni. "Irene, is there something you would like to tell me?"

Irene acted like she was trying to decide whether or not to say what she was thinking. Finally she blurted out, "I am the one who is translating. Señor Anthony has been giving me money to do this. I am sorry that I must be the one to tell you, but Señor Anthony does not know even enough Spanish to buy a taco!"

"*What?!*" laughed Omni. "Is this true? Why didn't you ever tell me this?"

"I was thinking it is not my place, Señor," Irene said. "But now I think I was mistaken. I should have told you the truth. I am sorry, Señor."

"No, no, don't be sorry," Omni said. "It's my own fault. I have known Larry for so long I made the mistake of just trusting him instead of verifying his claim. But from now on *I* will be the one who pays you for the translation, OK?"

"Yes, Señor," Irene said. "I have been doing the translation at night after my housekeeping duties have been completed. In the morning each day Señor Anthony is taking my translation and typing the words into his computer."

"Fascinating," Omni laughed again, shaking his head. "Larry hasn't given me much information during the last month or so. Have you been translating during that time?"

"Yes, Señor," said Irene. "The truth is that I have become faster and faster during this time. Each day it is becoming easier for me to read the old Spanish writing."

"Really," said Omni, his interest piqued. "I wonder if there is more information there than Larry wanted to share with me."

"I don't know," said Irene.

"I wonder," said Omni, raising his index finger and furrowing his brow, "if it might be possible to get a look at Larry's computer

127

and see what's there. I'll bet he's got a password on it, though. He is simple-minded enough that I might be able to guess it."

"You are not needing Señor Anthony's computer," said Irene. "I have the translation in a book—all the pages. I am writing very carefully, making the words easy for Señor Anthony to read. I think you also will have no trouble reading what I have written."

"That's wonderful!" exclaimed Omni. "This is the best news I have had in days. I'm sure I've never seen this book. Do you know where it is?"

"I always leave the book in the drawer of the table," said Irene.

"Ah!" said Omni. He looked around the room and said, "Let's have a look at it, shall we?"

Meg, Chelsea, and Danny were not really interested, so they headed to the toy room while the rest of us followed Irene to the office where Anthony had been translating—or rather, where he had been copying Irene's translation.

The table in the office looked just like it had the day before when Mr. Omni first showed it to us. The journal was still open underneath the clear sheet of plastic. Irene pulled the chair out from under the table, revealing a drawer handle. She opened the drawer and removed a bound, black book and handed it to Mr. Omni. It looked like a large modern journal. I thought that made it an appropriate book to use for writing the translation of the *old* journal.

"Thank you," said Mr. Omni, almost reverently. He opened the book and thumbed through the pages, revealing Irene's handwriting through about two-thirds of the book. He laid the book open on the table and leafed through several pages in the middle. It looked like she had only written on the right-hand pages, always leaving the left-hand pages blank.

"Why did you only write on one side?" asked Omni.

"Because sometimes Señor Anthony is wanting to make notes on the left side," explained Irene.

"Really?" said Omni. Then he started looking backward through the pages to see if he could find any place that Anthony had written anything.

"Here we go," Omni said. He pointed and said, "Look at this."

I looked and saw the words, "escape as did Limhi" written on the left side. Underneath were the words, "Need to find Limhi in the Book of Mormon," followed by the reference "Mosiah 22:6."

"That's the reference that I found, too," I said.

Omni read Irene's translation on the right side of the book and found a discussion about the priest's desire to escape; but the priest wasn't sure the best way to go about it. Then he mentioned Limhi as a possibility.

Omni started turning pages backwards again. A few pages earlier Anthony had written on the left side of the book the note, "Work must avoid the pattern of Lib to avoid discovery—No hills." Again, underneath this were the words, "Find Lib in the Book of Mormon," but this time there was no scripture reference written next to it.

"Perhaps we'll need your help finding this one," Omni smiled at me.

I was pleased at his confidence in me.

After thumbing through a few more pages, Mr. Omni stopped at a note that said, "Received a shiblon."

"Oh, that's right," Omni said. He looked at Dad and said, "Remember me asking you to find out what the word *shiblon* meant? Larry did tell me about this one. I couldn't remember what he said, but I remembered that it didn't sound like the name of a man. Hmm, it still doesn't sound like someone's name, does it?"

"Oh, that's right!" said Dad. "Shiblon is also used for a certain coin!"

Omni then said, "Well, it looks like I have some serious reading to catch up on today. Thank you so much for showing this to me, Irene, and for making sure we have a quality translation to work from."

As Omni was speaking, he let the rest of the pages fall until the book fell shut.

"Wait!" said Mom suddenly. "Was there a picture in there? A drawing?"

"Oh, yes," nodded Irene. "I copied this drawing from the journal."

"The drawing!" said Omni. "I almost forgot about that. I was captivated by it from the moment I first saw it, but it's been quite a few months now."

Omni opened the book again and started looking for the drawing.

"Please, sir," said Irene. "My copy is not nearly so beautiful as the original. Would you mind very much showing them the drawing in the priest's journal?"

"Of course," Omni smiled. He closed Irene's book and sat down in the chair. Carefully, he got a pair of latex gloves from the box on the table and pulled them over his hands. Then he gently lifted the sheet of clear plastic off of the journal and laid it aside. Even more carefully, he turned open the flimsy front cover of the old journal, revealing a drawing of a person that filled the entire page.

"We believe this is intended to be a depiction of Jesus," Omni said in a reverent voice.

"Notice the crucifixion marks on his hands and feet. Also notice the halo around his head."

The figure was dressed in a long robe that hung past the ankles, revealing only the wounded feet below. His hands were held out in front of his stomach in an unusual way, with the wrists touching each other and the palms facing forward. This made it easy to see the wounds. There were lines or streaks coming from the ends of the thumbs and fingers. The thumbs were pointed upward with streaks drawn to each of the upper corners of the page. The fingers were pointed downward with streaks going toward the lower corners.

"I've never seen anything like this," Mom whispered. "It's very unusual—but it's beautiful."

"It is," Dad agreed.

"What are those streaks?" I asked.

"They look like streams of light," said Mom.

"That's what I thought," agreed Omni. "It's as though the light emanates from his hands at the center, shining outward toward the four corners of the page."

We all looked at the drawing and discussed it for a couple more minutes before Mr. Omni carefully closed the old journal and replaced the plastic covering to protect it. He removed the gloves and said, "Shall we see what else we can learn from Larry's notes in Irene's book?"

"Sounds interesting," Dad said.

"I'll get my Book of Mormon," I said, and I quickly headed out of the office. I had left my scriptures in my backpack in the bedroom.

"Brandon!" called Jeff after me. "Will you bring mine down, too?"

"Sure," I said.

Dad was right behind me on his way to get scriptures for himself and Mom. We returned a minute later to find Omni thumbing through the pages of Irene's translation journal again. It looked like he had placed slips of paper in several locations as bookmarks.

"So who wants to take another look at the *shiblon* word?" asked Omni.

"I will," I offered. Turning to Jeff I said, "Let's see what we can find in the index."

As we started our search, Dad asked, "What was the other note that Larry made?"

Mom added, "The one that didn't have a scripture reference by it yet."

Mr. Omni checked his bookmarks until he found the one he was looking for and then quoted, "Work must avoid the pattern of Lib to avoid discovery—No hills."

The room was quiet for a moment, except for the turning of pages. Mom, Dad, Jeff, and I were all checking the Book of Mormon index while Omni kept reading Irene's translation.

"Look at this," Jeff said to me. "The first list here has references to Alma's son Shiblon." Pointing to his book, he added, "but there's another one below."

I looked where he was pointing and read the words "Nephite coin."

Looking at Jeff, I asked, "Coin, as in money, like Dad said?"

"I guess," Jeff shrugged.

"Excuse me, Mr. Omni," I said. "What did he write about the word *shiblon?*"

Immediately flipping to one of the bookmarks, Omni read, "Received a *shiblon.*"

"Thanks," I smiled. Omni flipped the pages back and returned to his reading.

"Sounds like money," Jeff smiled at me.

I looked over at Mom and Dad to see if they were listening to us, but they were engulfed in their own quiet discussion, pointing at each other's books and nodding as they spoke.

"Let's read the references," I suggested.

"It looks like they are all in Alma 11," Jeff said, "verses 15, 16, and 19."

"Cool," I said, quickly turning the pages in my Book of Mormon to find the chapter.

First I read verses 15 and 16 aloud:

A shiblon is half of a senum; therefore, a shiblon for half a measure of barley.

And a shiblum is a half of a shiblon.

"So he received a half measure of barley?" I asked Jeff.

"No," said Jeff, "it says he got some money that was *worth* that much barley."

"Oh, right," I said. "So how much is a measure of barley? Is it like a bushel?"

Jeff got an incredulous look on his face. "How should *I* know?" he asked.

I laughed. "Good point," I said. "What was the other verse? Was it 19?"

Jeff nodded. Verse 19 reads:

Now the antion of gold is equal to three shiblons.

We both jerked our heads immediately to look at one another. "Gold?" we said in unison.

"Does this mean he was paid in gold?" I asked.

I think we caught everyone else's attention, because Mr. Omni asked, "Did you find something?"

"I think a shiblon is a gold coin," I said.

"Really?" said Omni, looking pleased, but not nearly as intrigued as I was.

Mom asked, "Are you reading at the place where there's practically a whole page of verses about the money used in Book of Mormon times? Where were you just reading?"

"Alma 11," Jeff said, "verses 15, 16, and 19."

Mom and Dad turned the pages in their own books and read for a few seconds. Then Mom said, "Hmm. A shiblon is definitely a unit of measure for money." She paused for a moment and asked, "Did you notice at the top of the page that they describe different words for gold than for silver that has the same value?"

"Of course not," I admitted. "We just read the verses with the word *shiblon* in them."

"Look at verse 5," Mom said. "It lists all the words used for different amounts of gold. Verse 6 lists all the words used for silver.

Then in verse 7 it tells us which words for gold and for silver are equal to each other. That means that they used different words depending on whether the coin was gold or silver."

"So is a shiblon gold or silver?" Jeff asked.

"Let's figure it out," suggested Dad. "Look at verse 15 again—the first verse that you read."

"It says that a shiblon is half of a senum," Jeff said.

"And a senum is . . . ?" asked Mom.

No one spoke for a moment as we tried to find it. Then Jeff blurted out, "Silver! Verse 6 says 'A senum of silver.'"

"I think that's right," said Mom.

"But wait," I said. "Didn't we read something about gold in the last verse?"

"Which one?" asked Dad.

"Here it is," I said. "Verse 19. It says, 'an antion of gold is equal to . . . '" I stopped.

"It's just making a comparison again," said Jeff. "It looks like the antion is in gold—three shiblons is the same value in silver."

"What was the note again?" asked Dad. "The priest received a shiblon?"

"Correct," said Omni.

"It sounds like he was paid with a silver coin," said Mom. "That could have been anything. I'm sure that both Mexico and the United States were using coins made of silver at that time."

"One silver coin doesn't sound like very much," I said.

"It's half a measure of barley," Jeff said.

"Is barley worth very much?" I asked. "And what's a measure?"

"Throughout history," Omni said, "food and grain has generally been worth much more than it is today. Most people throughout history spent most of their labor each day obtaining and preparing food. It's only in modern times that we have forced the price of food down because of our increased ability to produce it. I suppose there's no way of knowing exactly how much 'a measure' might be, but I think a conservative guess might be enough grain for one person for a single day."

"Well," said Mom. "In verse 25 it talks about a man who offers another man six onties if he will deny God. It says that six onties 'are of great worth.'"

"Jeff and Brandon," Dad said. "Look at verses 11 through 13, and figure out how many measures of grain an onti is."

Working together, we quickly found that an onti was the same as seven measures of grain. "A week," Jeff said. "An onti is a week's worth of grain."

"Hmm," said Omni. "It does make sense that they would have a value for a week of grain."

"So how much would six onties be?" asked Mom.

"About a month and a half," I said.

"One and a half months' worth of food for a single person," Omni said. "In a time and place where they had to work so hard for food, I would have to agree that six onties sounds like they are of great worth."

"Cool," I said.

"But remember," Dad said. "The priest didn't receive six onties; he only received a single shiblon. That's only half of *one* measure, perhaps the amount needed to buy food for half a day."

"Oh," I said, realizing that he was right. "That's not so impressive."

"But that's weird that Alma used the same name for his son as one of their coins," Jeff noted. Changing his voice to sound deep and old, he added, "I would like you all to meet my son, Quarter. Over there are my daughters Nickel and Dime."

Omni asked, "Wouldn't it be better to name your daughter 'Sacagawea?'"

"Oh, no!" I said. "That means the son is only worth one fourth what the daughter is."

Mom heaved a heavy sigh and said, "Facts are hard to avoid."

Smiling, she added, "You may have noticed that Shiblon was apparently only worth half a day's grain. Ouch! Aren't you glad that we didn't name you after coins?"

"Despite the name," Dad said, "it looks like Shiblon turned out pretty good. I know of two pro basketball players that were each named 'Penny.' Now that's the lowest value you can get with U. S. coins. At least a shiblon wasn't the smallest they could have used."

"Good point," I said, quickly scanning the verses to see what the smallest coin was. "Whoa!" I said after a moment. "Bummer! Look at verse 17. The smallest silver coin was called a 'leah.'"

"Ha!" laughed Jeff. "I'll bet he thanked his parents every stinkin' day that they didn't give him that name. No wonder he was such a good kid. I can just hear it: You be good now, son, or we'll change your name to Leah. That's what your mother wanted all along, you know, and it's not too late."

I added in a high voice, "I'll be good, Dad! I promise!"

For some reason, Mom apparently felt the need to defend Shiblon's name. She said, "I imagine Alma's wife probably was just looking for something a little unique and found a name that she liked."

I got the impression she had had a similar experience. Suddenly I found myself going down the list of names of kids in our family, wondering which was the one that she thought was "a little unique."

"Mom and I found something interesting regarding the other reference," Dad said.

"So tell us about Lib," said Omni. "And the hills."

"Well," said Mom, "the index directed us to two different Jaredite kings who were named Lib. We read about one of them mostly in Ether chapter ten. The other one is in chapter fourteen."

"I read chapter fourteen," said Dad, "but the only thing in there about a hill is that they gathered for a battle near the hill Comnor."

Mom nodded and then said, "The word 'hill' wasn't in chapter ten at all. But it does talk about 'mighty heaps of earth.'"

"Sounds like a hill to me," said Jeff.

Mom directed us to Ether 10:23 that reads:

And they did work all manner of ore, and they did make gold, and silver, and iron, and brass, and all manner of metals; and they did dig it out of the earth; wherefore, they did cast up mighty heaps of earth to get ore, of gold, and of silver, and of iron, and of copper. And they did work all manner of fine work.

No one said anything for a moment. Then I asked, "Do you think the priest had a silver mine?" I paused as I thought more about it. Then I continued, "Maybe the priest wasn't talking about either Spanish coins or U. S. coins." I paused again as I looked around the room from person to person. "If he got a coin, then why didn't he just say what coin he got? But if he got a chunk of silver and didn't know exactly what it weighed, he might come up with some other name for it, don't you think?"

"There was a California gold rush in the 1800s," said Jeff, "but I don't remember ever hearing about a California silver rush."

"Actually," said Omni, "there were silver mines all over what is now Mexico and California. And there still are today."

"So do you think it's possible they had a silver mine?" I asked. I looked around again. "They could have had a silver mine! Right here!"

CHAPTER 11

Moving Mountains

"You could be right about there being a mine," Omni said. "In fact, that would explain a lot of things."

"Like what?" I asked.

"Well," said Omni, "it would explain why the men who had no business living in the mission wanted to be there. And it would explain what the work was that they were doing."

"You're right," Dad agreed. "Being surrounded by the high walls of the mission would make it much easier to hide what they were up to."

"But wait," said Mom. "Are you thinking that the entrance to the mine was inside the mission walls somewhere?"

"Perhaps," Omni said. "They would have had to tunnel down first and then head toward the mountain."

"How do you know the mine would be in the mountain?" I asked.

"That's where mines are usually located," Dad said. "It wouldn't have to be there, but it would make sense."

Mom added, "The journal said that their work had to 'avoid the pattern of Lib' in order to 'avoid discovery.'"

"What was the pattern of Lib?" I asked.

Mom answered, "Remember it said that they cast up mighty heaps of earth? People would quickly know what they had going on if they left mighty heaps of earth around."

"So what did they do with the dirt then?" asked Jeff.

"Well," said Omni. "They would need to get rid of it somehow. Most mining operations in the 1800s used a lot of water. If they had a river close by then I suppose they could have gotten rid of it by letting the water wash it away."

"Didn't you say that the mission was moved because there wasn't enough water at this location?" asked Dad.

"Exactly," Omni said, "so that method doesn't seem too likely."

Mom said, "Another way could be to just spread it out over a large area, so it wouldn't be noticed."

"That seems a lot more likely," said Omni. "There was nothing of consequence for miles around, so they could have just scattered it around outside the mission walls."

"It would still build up eventually," Dad said.

"That's true," said Omni.

"I saw an old World War II movie once," said Dad, "where the prisoners were digging escape tunnels and they had to get rid of the dirt."

"I remember that!" said Omni. "They put small amounts of dirt in bags that were hidden inside their pant legs. Then they walked around the prison yard and gradually opened the bottoms of the bags and let the dirt fall out from the bottoms of their pant legs."

"Right," said Dad, "and they had to kick it around a little bit to mix it in because the dirt from underground was so much darker than the dirt in the yard."

"They totally could have done something like that," I said. "They could have carried the dirt out in saddlebags tied to their horses. Then they would just ride a little way and open the bottom of the bags while riding and let the dirt fall wherever it would. That would totally work."

Mom, Dad, and Mr. Omni all looked skeptical about my idea.

"That's a whole lot of dirt to carry out in saddlebags," Dad said.

"I wonder if it says how they eventually solved the problem," said Omni. "I guess it's about time to stop relying on Larry to pass information along to me. I think I need to read this translation cover to cover."

"Sounds like a good idea," Dad said. "We'll leave you to it."

"Thank you for your help," Omni smiled.

I admit it was nice to see the gaps between Omni's teeth again. He hadn't smiled much since Anthony had left with the police the day before. He had been acting kind of depressed. But, apparently, the new discoveries had made him forget about that—at least for now anyway.

We had talked for over an hour since breakfast. Omni turned to the book and dove in head first before we even left the room.

As we walked down the hall, Mom asked, "So what would you like to do now?"

"Is it still raining?" Dad asked.

Because the back hall had an entire wall of windows that opened onto the covered patio, a quick glance told us that it was indeed still raining. Not fun.

"Why don't we grab a limo and go somewhere," Dad suggested. "I'm tired of being stuck inside. I'm sure the kids would enjoy a change."

"Grab a limo?" asked Mom. "Did you just say that?"

"Well," Dad laughed, "and a driver, too, of course."

Jeff and I immediately reminded them that we both had our driver's licenses now and we would be happy to take them wherever they would like to go.

"Hey, Brandon," Jeff laughed, "can you imagine taking a limo through the drive up window at Taco Bell or something?! That would be awesome!"

Mom and Dad ignored us. Mom asked him, "So where are you thinking about going?"

"I'm not sure," Dad said. "I was thinking maybe something like a bowling alley or a park—someplace the kids could get some exercise.

"OK," Mom said. "First let's find out if there's a driver available and then why don't we ask Irene or someone if they have any suggestions of where we could go."

"We could ask TB," I suggested. "I'm sure he'd give a great answer."

"Right," said Jeff. "And then he would bring us a platter of fried eggplant or something!"

It turned out Omni's driver was available. He checked with Mr. Omni to make sure he would not be needed for several hours. Irene assured us that she knew the perfect place for us to go on a rainy day. And she was absolutely right.

The driver took us to an indoor play place that was absolutely huge. I'm sure they could have fit an entire full-size soccer field in there—including bleachers. They had every sort of game you can imagine. They had video games and ball pits and batting cages and bowling and shuffleboard and pool tables and tube mazes fifteen feet off the ground that twisted in and around and above everything else that was going on. Jeff and I spent at least a couple of hours with a bunch of guys we didn't know running around with laser guns in a room that was made to look like a narrow canyon with caves running every which way. We all met and had pizza for lunch. Then we spent several more hours trying out all sorts of stuff. All in all, it was a pretty fun day, but we were totally beat by the time Dad finally pressed the little green button on the GPS gadget, and Omni's driver came to pick us up. We got back to Omni's cottage pretty late in the afternoon. Mom told Jeff and me that we stunk from running around so much all day, and so we had to shower before dinner.

After showering we decided to play pool until dinner was ready. Neither of us is very good at it, but we were having fun. At one point I had a particularly tough shot at a very sharp angle. I lined up the cue ball, trying to barely glance another ball, and shot it pretty much as hard as I could. Of course my aim was off just enough so that the cue ball missed, instead bouncing quickly from one side rail to another and back again. Because it was near the end of a game and the table was mostly already cleared, nothing got in the way of the bouncing cue ball. Jeff and I both laughed loudly.

As our laughter died down we were both startled to hear TB say, "Dinner to be served now." He was standing in the doorway as still as a statue.

"Whoa!" I said. "You scared me. How long have you been standing there?"

TB acted like he was slightly uncomfortable trying to formulate more than one sentence in a single conversation. Finally he said, "Long enough to be seeing the ball bounce forth and back three time."

Jeff laughed. "Your shot is famous, Brandon!"

I laughed, too. Then, feeling brave, I said to TB, "But I think you mean 'back and forth' and not 'forth and back.'"

TB's eye twitched slightly as if I had hit a mental nerve. Suddenly I was worried that I may have may him feel bad about not speaking English very well.

Then TB said, "No thing come 'back' until that thing has went 'forth.' To be saying 'back and forth' is to be speaking not in correct order."

With that he bowed slightly and left the room.

I looked at Jeff, who had a surprised expression on his face. "So, now you know," he said.

"Thankfully!" I said. "I've been trying to decide the right way to say that, but I keep going forth and back on it."

As we headed down the hallway, Jeff pointed at the grandfather clock and said, "Look, Brandon! The pendulum keeps going fro and to!"

We were both still laughing as we entered the dining room and sat down.

"Will Mr. Omni be joining us?" Mom asked TB, who was placing a platter on the table.

"Please to be eating when ready," TB said and he left the room.

We agreed that this must mean we were to eat without Mr. Omni, so we had a blessing and went ahead. We talked about the different things we had done during the day for a few minutes, but then the conversation soon turned to the priest and his journal. Meg, Chelsea, and Danny didn't know anything about what we had learned earlier that morning, so we did our best to fill them in. Just as we were finishing the meal, Omni came rushing in.

"I am absolutely famished!" he said as he sat down. He flipped open his linen napkin in the air and placed it across his lap, reaching quickly for the closest food. We instinctively began passing everything else we thought that he might want down in his direction.

"I haven't eaten since this morning," Omni explained as he began serving himself. "I have been wholly engrossed in that journal. I cannot wait to tell you what more I have learned."

He was such a whirlwind of activity that I just sort of stared at him. Mom responded almost immediately, however. "Sounds fascinating. Perhaps later this evening if you have time. . . ."

"I would be happy to tell you now," said Omni between bites and huge, gap-toothed smiles. "That is if you do not have other plans."

"Of course," said Dad. "We're all ears." I always thought that was a strange expression.

So, for the next few minutes Omni proceeded to tell us about what he had learned from Irene's translation of the priest's journal. He didn't let his explanations get in the way of his dinner, however, taking frequent, small bites and then swallowing quickly and wiping his mouth with his napkin before speaking or answering a question.

"It turns out," Omni began, "that the priest lived in the mission for quite some time. At first the priest didn't have much to do with making the mission look like it was the real thing. Not many people lived close by and so not many knew that it was a place where they could come for help. Also, the men didn't allow the priest to leave the mission walls. Of course, he wanted to, in order to spread the gospel and to visit the needy. When people would come to the mission for help—either for themselves or for others—they would sometimes tell him about others in need who were not able to travel to the mission for help."

Omni paused to take a bite.

"I'll bet that was frustrating for him," Mom said.

Omni nodded grandly several times until he swallowed. "Yes," he finally said. "The priest expressed that many times. After a while, the word began to spread that this mission was open again, so more and more people began to come to the doors seeking help. Of course the doors remained closed most of the time, even during the day."

Omni paused for another bite.

"So would they knock on the doors?" Meg asked.

"There was a bell with a rope," Omni said, after wiping his mouth. "People who found the doors closed would ring the bell and wait."

"That would be fun!" said Danny.

"We have a doorbell," I said.

"We do?" asked Danny with wide eyes.

"Yes!" I laughed. "But you push a button instead of pulling a rope."

"Oh, yeah!" said Danny.

Omni continued, "The man who gave the priest the copy of the Book of Mormon was actually one of the first to arrive at the mission in need of help. Because of this, the priest wasn't doing much else and had a lot of free time. That's when they read the Book of

Mormon together as he learned English. It wasn't too long after the Mormon left that the priest began writing about plans to escape."

Omni reached for his glass and so I added, "Like Limhi, right? Through the back wall, through the back pass, through the back something else."

Omni nodded. "That's right. But soon many more people began stopping by the mission seeking help from him."

"Do you think it was because the Mormon told others about the mission?" Mom asked.

"It's possible," said Omni. "I thought that, too, but I don't think there is any way to really know for sure."

"Did he change his mind about escaping?" asked Dad.

"I believe so," said Omni. "At least he didn't mention it again. Once he started spending so much of his time serving the local people he seemed to be pretty much consumed by that."

Omni took another small bite and chewed it quickly. He knew we were all anxiously waiting for more of the story.

"Things changed, though," Omni finally said. "The priest was getting desperate. He went to his captors and said he needed many more supplies if he was going to continue to help the people and at the same time help them keep their work secret."

"How did that go over?" asked Dad.

"Apparently much better than even the priest expected," said Omni. "He had obviously proven himself trustworthy over many months, and they agreed to help."

"Did they give him however much he asked for?" asked Mom.

"This is the part that I still don't completely understand," said Omni. "They agreed to give him one of their *ventures*."

"Ventures?" repeated Dad.

"That is the word that Irene used in the translation," nodded Omni.

"Did they have more than one mine? Did they just turn over the profits from a mine to him?" Mom asked.

"Or did they have other ways to make money?" asked Dad.

"I can't tell," said Omni. "I haven't read the entire journal yet, but it just isn't clear."

"Did you find out for sure if it was a silver mine?" asked Mom. "Or some other kind of mine?"

"I don't know," said Omni, "but they were definitely digging somewhere for something."

"Why do you say that?" asked Dad. "Did you learn more about these 'mighty heaps of earth' like Lib had?"

Omni smiled again. "Indeed. Apparently at night the men would load up the wagons at least a couple of times and sneak outside the mission to dump the soil in various places."

"It's got to be a mine," I said. "What else could it be?"

"I'm not sure," Omni said.

His thoughts seemed to trail away for a moment before he continued. "Anyway," said Omni, "there were several ventures already underway, and they told the priest that he could have one that was already in operation or he could have a future one."

"What did he choose?" asked Meg.

"He wrote that he wanted to choose the venture that best represented his Lord," said Omni, taking another quick bite.

"Wow," said Dad. "That makes it tough to narrow down. It could be anything."

Omni nodded. Then he said, "True. But quite a few months later the priest writes that the venture he had chosen was better than any of the previous ventures. He states that he was correct to use faith and choose a new venture based on its representation of the Lord, rather than judging for himself. He writes that some ventures had already received judgment and been given an appropriate name, but others were still awaiting judgment. His captors gave him the option to choose from those he already knew about."

"Judgment?" said Mom. "And then they received a name based on the judgment?"

Omni nodded.

"Another mystery," said Dad. Then he asked, "So how much more do you have to read?"

"Not much," said Omni. "I am almost finished with all that Irene has translated."

"Has she told you how much more still needs to be translated?" asked Dad.

"She is almost finished," said Omni. "So the journal may not be sufficient to place all the pieces of the puzzle together."

"Maybe the excavation will help," said Mom.

"I certainly hope so," smiled Omni. He had finished his dinner now and just sat comfortably in his chair as he spoke.

"Thank you for inviting us here," Dad smiled. "It has been such a pleasure to meet you and to share in this exciting discovery of yours."

"The pleasure is most assuredly all mine," said Omni. Then he said, "There is an interesting description of loading a wagon." He seemed to have almost forgotten about this. Remembering made his smile now even bigger than usual. "Whatever was being produced by these ventures was spread in the bottom of the wagon bed. Then it would be covered by other things, such as vegetables or sacks of food, to make it look like there was nothing of great value in the wagon. Once or twice a week a load would be taken and sold. The journal gives the impression that each load was sold for quite a lot of money."

The discussion between Mom and Dad and Omni continued for at least another hour as they kept guessing what different things might mean or what the different "ventures" might be. It seemed to me that they were almost talking in circles after a while, so I was getting bored. Chelsea and Danny had gotten bored quite a bit earlier, and so Mom had suggested they go find something fun to do. Meg was still in the dining room with the rest of us, but she was totally enthralled by whatever book she was currently reading.

Without a word, Jeff and I gave each other looks that made it clear we had sat in on the conversation long enough. So we stood and left the room as quietly as we could. Meg noticed and decided to follow. I'm not really sure why, though. Maybe she was just looking for a more comfortable place to sit and read.

Much later, after saying our prayers and going to bed, Jeff and I lay awake in the dark talking about everything we had heard that day.

"It's got to be a mine," I said for about the fourteenth time.

Before Jeff could respond, I continued. "Do you think the entrance is inside the mission somewhere?"

"It seems like it would be pretty hard to hide it," said Jeff, "if they constantly had people coming to the doors and asking for help."

"That's right," I agreed. "And remember that guy from the Mormon Battalion actually lived inside the mission for a while. How would they have kept it hidden from him?"

"I don't know," I said. "Maybe the entrance was inside one of the rooms."

We both lay in silence as we thought about this for a minute.

"You're right," I said suddenly. "There could be like a trapdoor in the floor that went down and then out the back."

"That's why!" said Jeff, sitting up in bed. At least I think he sat up. It was hard to tell in the dark.

"That's why what?" I asked.

"Anthony!" Jeff said. "That's why Anthony was so mad that they were digging that trench next to the back wall."

"No way!" I said. Now I was sitting up in bed. "Do you think he already found the entrance to the mine?"

"If he did," said Jeff, "then he would know that digging the trench might break into it."

"He's the one who sabotaged the backhoe!" I said. "He didn't

148

want them to find the entrance and so he made the backhoe fall into the trench before they found it."

We both just sat in the dark thinking about what all this might mean.

"Anthony's coming back tomorrow, isn't he?" asked Jeff. "We better tell Mr. Omni as soon as we see him in the morning."

"I'm not waiting," I said. With that, I was out of bed and putting on my clothes.

"What are you doing?" Jeff hissed in the dark. "You can't go wake him up now! It's the middle of the night."

"Who's waking anybody up?" I asked. "I'm going to find the mine."

"*What?*" Jeff said. "Are you crazy?"

"I can't sleep," I said. "And neither can you. We've been talking about this for hours. We might as well go check it out."

"I don't want to go," said Jeff.

"Then don't," I said. "I'll be back in a few minutes."

"I can't let you go by yourself," said Jeff.

"Fine," I said, pulling on my second shoe. "I'm ready to go. Are you coming with me or not?"

Jeff sighed and reluctantly got dressed. Then the two of us crept out into the hall. We picked up our jackets from the coat rack and put them on.

"What if there's no light out there?" Jeff said. "What are you going to do?"

"I don't know," I admitted. "Maybe we'll have to find a flashlight." Saying that reminded me that I had seen one in the priest's room in the mission when Omni had taken us in there. I asked Jeff about it, but he said he didn't remember seeing it. I actually don't think he was trying very hard to remember, though. He just wanted to go back to bed.

It turns out that there was no need to try to find a flashlight because the walkways all the way out to the tents had little lights along them every few feet. Even on a dark, cloudy night it was enough to see where we were going. I was happy to hear that the rain had quit for now. It had still been raining when we went to bed.

"Hold on," Jeff said suddenly. "I'll be right back."

Jeff took off on a dead run back toward the house and quickly went inside. He was only gone for about a minute. He was breathing hard when he returned.

"Where did you go?" I asked.

"It doesn't matter," Jeff gasped. Nodding in the direction of the excavation tents he said, "If we're really going, then let's go."

We crept down the stepping stones toward the tents. It was getting harder to see now because the little lights ended at the walkway. Inside the tent it was totally dark. I told Jeff to hold the tent flap open while I made my way over to the small door with the plastic on the handle. I opened the door and felt my way carefully over to where I had seen Mr. Omni turn on the lights the day before. It was so bright that I had to scrunch my eyes shut for several moments and then blink a few times before I could get used to the light. By the time I did, Jeff had joined me in the room. He pulled the small door closed behind him.

"Look," I said, pointing at the flashlight. "Do you remember it now?"

"I don't think so," said Jeff. "But why is it *under* the plastic?"

I looked around the room for a minute, checking out the floor for any signs of a trapdoor.

"Maybe," I said. "It's because the trapdoor is under that carpet and Anthony uses the flashlight inside the mine."

"Don't touch anything," Jeff warned.

"I just want to see," I said. Then I picked up the edge of the plastic and pulled it back, exposing the flashlight and the old carpet.

"Don't touch the carpet," Jeff said.

"How about if I put those gloves on first?" I asked. Next to the flashlight was a pair of gloves that I hadn't noticed before. I was picking them up and putting them on before Jeff could say anything.

"Bran!" he said. "I don't think this is a good idea."

"I just want to see if there's a trapdoor under the carpet," I said. "Then we can go back, OK?"

Again, I didn't want to wait for his response. Instead I just began to lift the edge of the carpet as carefully as I could.

"Look!" I almost yelled. "There it is!"

I had been right all along. Under the carpet, cut into the floorboards, was the outline of a square opening that I just knew couldn't be anything but a trapdoor. Jeff knew it, too. What else could it be?

Just then we heard a sound that made us both jump. The wall behind us was beginning to creak loudly. We both turned and stared at it intently. The longer I looked the more it seemed like it was starting to lean inward toward us. Then we heard a loud thump directly above us. We both jumped again.

"What was *that*?" asked Jeff. His voice sounded as shaky as I felt. I was scared.

"I don't know," I breathed, "but let's get out of here!"

Jeff ran for the door and pushed quickly on the door handle, which was covered in protective plastic. I was right behind him. But it appeared that he could push the door open only about two inches. I was stunned to see mud begin oozing in through the opening in the doorway more than halfway up the door. I looked over the top of the door and saw mud dropping in huge clumps from over the roof, where it was apparently building up behind the door.

"The building is being buried by mud!" I yelled.

"The mountain!" Jeff yelled back. "It must be a mudslide."

"All the rain!" I said with panic.

Jeff quickly pulled the door shut again to keep any more mud from coming inside. His eyes looked like they had suddenly sunken into his face.

"What do we do?" I asked.

"I have no idea," breathed Jeff.

We both looked around frantically for two seconds before I lunged for the trapdoor and yelled, "Follow me! It's our only chance!"

CHAPTER 12

Uplifted Hands

I quickly found the large gap along one edge of the trapdoor. Squeezing my fingers into the opening, I pulled the door up. It was hinged on one side, and so I laid it back against the chair that was already in the right place.

"Let's go!" I yelled.

"*What?*" Jeff yelled at me in disbelief. "Are you crazy? I'm not climbing down into some dark hole in the ground!"

I grabbed the flashlight on the floor by the table, switched it on, and shined it into the opening. We immediately saw a shaft that went straight down for about ten feet. There was an old, flimsy ladder mounted to the side of the shaft where the trapdoor was hinged. There were spider webs in the corners of the shaft. As we stood staring down inside there was a loud creak from the roof overhead.

"Let's go!" I yelled again. I wasn't sure Jeff would follow me if I went down first, so I wanted him to go ahead of me.

"I told you I'm not going down there!" said Jeff.

"You said you weren't going down into some dark hole in the ground!" I yelled. "It's not dark anymore!"

"No, it's not," said Jeff. "Now it's just a *creepy* hole in the ground that doesn't happen to be dark at the moment."

"If I go first will you follow?" I asked.

"What?" Jeff said. "No! I'm not doing it."

Just then something creaked again. It sounded like the back wall this time.

"Jeff!" I yelled. "I would much rather take my chances with a *potentially* creepy hole in the ground than get swallowed alive in a mudslide!"

"What?" Jeff said again. "What do you mean 'potentially' creepy? It's *definitely* creepy!"

This time everything around us seemed to creak at once—and it was the loudest time yet.

"I'm outta here!" I yelled and started quickly down the ladder. I was in such a hurry that I almost dropped the flashlight as I climbed, but luckily I held on.

When I got to the bottom I looked up just in time to see the bottom of one of the floor lamps coming straight down at me.

"Take it!" Jeff called. "That flashlight's not enough for me."

I reached up and took hold of the stand, setting it on the ground at the bottom of the hole as gently as I could. Jeff was not far behind.

"Luckily the power cord is long enough to reach down here," Jeff panted. I wondered how it was that power was even still reaching the lamp, with all the mud that was piling up all around the old mission.

Everything seemed really bright now with such a powerful light in such a small space.

"Did you close the door?" I asked, looking upward.

"The main door?" asked Jeff. "Yeah, I closed it as soon as we saw the mud."

"No," I said. "I mean the trapdoor."

"I'm not closing the trapdoor," said Jeff. "I don't want to get trapped down here! That's why they call it a trap!"

"Jeff," I said in frustration. "If that roof caves in, the thing that will trap us is mud pouring down the shaft."

Jeff just looked at me with wide eyes. I wasn't sure what he was thinking, but I didn't think we had any time to wait.

"I'm closing it!" I said firmly, and I quickly started climbing the ladder again.

There was more creaking and moaning from the walls and roof as I stuck my head up through the floor just long enough to grab the edge of the trapdoor and pull it down over the opening. Then I returned to the bottom of the ladder as quickly as possible. Jeff and I then just stood in silence for a couple of minutes, listening to the occasional moans coming from above. They were muffled a little by the closed trapdoor, but still very telling. I suddenly realized that standing at the bottom of this shaft in the direct line of anything that broke through the trapdoor probably wasn't a great idea.

"Let's look around," I suggested a little more calmly now.

There was a single tunnel that headed away from the wall where the ladder was mounted. The ceiling was low, only coming to about my shoulder. Jeff is a couple of inches taller than I am. The floor lamp was taller than the opening as well, and so its light shined only a short distance down the tunnel.

"Maybe we should move partway into the tunnel," I said.

"Why?" asked Jeff.

"In case something falls from above," I answered.

We moved into the tunnel, but just barely. Obviously, we had to crouch down to avoid hitting our heads. The ceiling and walls were completely covered in rough, wooden planks. And they were *really* rough. There were lots of wood slivers everywhere, and the boards themselves were not very flat.

"Now what?" asked Jeff.

"We wait, I guess," I said, not sure what else to say.

"For what?" Jeff asked.

"Until the mudslide stops and we can get out of here," I said.

"How are we going to know when it stops?" asked Jeff.

"When it stops making noise, I guess," I said.

We sat in silence for a few minutes. It was just a little cool down there, so I was glad we had grabbed our jackets. I tried to imagine what things must look like from the outside—how much of the mission might be buried and how deep the mud might be. I wondered how much of what had already been dug out by Omni's excavation would have to be dug out all over again.

"When we get out of here . . ." I said.

"How?" interrupted Jeff.

"What?" I asked.

"How?" repeated Jeff. "How are we going to get out of here?"

I stammered a moment before saying, "W-when the mudslide stops then they'll dig us out."

"How long do you think that will take?" asked Jeff.

"How should I know?" I asked.

"It took them months to dig it all before," said Jeff. "We'll be long gone by then."

I stammered again. "It-it's not the same this time. They'll be looking for us."

"Where?" said Jeff.

"Down here!" I said. "Where do you think?"

"Nobody knows we're down here," Jeff said softly.

"They'll figure it out," I said.

"Nobody even knows that there is any down here down here," said Jeff, a little louder this time.

"Anthony knows about the tunnel," I said. "He'll tell Omni."

"You don't know that," said Jeff.

"Which part?" I asked.

"Both," Jeff said. "You don't know that Anthony knows about the tunnel, and even if he does, you have no reason to think that he might tell someone about it. Nobody has any idea we're down here. *Nobody*."

Now I started to panic. "You're right," I breathed. I thought about all the mud that might be continuing to bury the door out of the priest's room. "Let's go try to push that door open again. Maybe with both of us . . ."

"Let's pray," Jeff said.

I looked desperately toward the ladder leading up the shaft. Then I suddenly realized that Jeff was right. How many examples are there in the scriptures about people who fail when they try to accomplish something by themselves; but when they finally remember God and seek his help, he provides it. It's not always in the way they want or think is best, but he always remembers those who remember him.

"OK," I said. "Let's take turns."

We both knelt on the hard dirt floor of the tunnel. Jeff prayed first and then I took a turn. The longer we prayed the calmer I began to feel. Why hadn't we thought of it sooner? Why did I always wait so long to ask for help, when Heavenly Father knows all and sees all and is just waiting for us to ask?

After we finished, I suggested that we try the door again. Jeff agreed, and so we headed up the ladder and through the trapdoor. One of the floor lamps was still in the room, and so it was easy to see everything. Mud was beginning to ooze through even tiny openings around the door, almost all the way to the top. We both pushed on the door with all our might, but it didn't budge in the least. We looked around for a couple of minutes and then decided it would probably be safer back down in the tunnel. We didn't like the occasional creaking sounds or moaning walls.

As we were climbing down the ladder, the floor lamp in the tunnel suddenly went black.

"Oh, great," I moaned.

"Where's the flashlight?" asked Jeff from above.

"I left it at the bottom," I said.

"Do you think you can find it?" asked Jeff.

"I think so," I answered. I made my way carefully down the ladder in the total darkness. I wasn't feeling very calm anymore. But it took only a few seconds to locate the flashlight and switch it on. I was shocked at how bright it was and at how quickly my eyes had adjusted to the blackness.

"Do you think both lamps lost power?" I asked.

"I don't know," said Jeff. "I don't see any light coming from up there, but I'll check it out." Jeff climbed back up the ladder and pushed the trapdoor open. "Nothing," Jeff called down. "The power cord must have gotten disconnected by the mudslide."

Jeff made his way back down the ladder. We sat on the ground in the tunnel and just stared into space. I thought about seeing what was in the tunnel, but I was in no mood to discover a silver mine that would make us rich just a few hours before we died.

"We shouldn't have come down," I mumbled.

"You're right," Jeff answered.

"You should have stopped me," I said.

Jeff didn't say anything. We both knew the truth.

"I know you tried to stop me, but you should have tried harder," I said.

"You're right," Jeff agreed.

"I'm going to be in so much trouble," I said. "If we ever get out of here alive, I mean."

"You're right," Jeff said again.

"Which part?" I asked.

"Both," said Jeff.

"You're going to be in trouble, too," I said.

"No, I won't," said Jeff.

"Why?" I asked. "Just because you tried to stop me? You failed!"

"I won't get in trouble because I was being a good Scout and followed the buddy system and didn't let you come out here by yourself," Jeff said. He sounded like he believed it. But he didn't sound like he really cared.

"You're probably right," I agreed. I was too discouraged to argue. Then I added, "I knew I shouldn't have come down here." No one spoke. "That's the worst thing about me," I said. "That's what I'm so bad at."

"What?" asked Jeff.

"Listening to the Spirit," I said. "I knew I shouldn't come down here. I knew you were right. But I figured if we just came and checked it out really fast then nothing could possibly happen. I think the Spirit tried to warn me, but I just never listen. But you do, don't you?"

"Hey!" Jeff said. "I almost forgot!" His voice was suddenly hopeful. I got excited just hearing him, without having a clue what he was talking about.

"What?" I asked, looking up. Then I remembered that he had gone back in the house. "Did you do something grand when you went back inside? What did you do? Is that what you just remembered?"

Reaching into the pocket of his pants, Jeff said, "I don't know if this will work or not, but the idea came to me to go grab this."

I looked in Jeff's hand and saw him holding up the little GPS gadget that we had used when we wanted the limo to come and pick us up!

"Jeff!" I yelled, hopping up on my knees. "You're a genius!"

Jeff shook his head slowly back and forth. "I just had a feeling," he said. "But I don't know if it will work down here."

"Push it!" I said with excitement. "Push the green button!"

"Everybody's asleep," Jeff said. "Shouldn't we wait until morning?"

"What are the chances that everyone is still asleep with a mudslide threatening to bury the house?" I asked. "Push the button!"

"I don't think the mudslide is making enough noise to wake anybody up," Jeff said. "I'm not sure . . ."

Without waiting to hear another word, I reached over and pushed the big green button while the device was still in Jeff's hand.

"Just because they're maybe still asleep now," I defended myself, "doesn't mean that this thing won't wake somebody up or leave a message or something." My mind continued to spin with excitement at this new prospect. "They'll be able to find us now!"

"Even under ground?" Jeff asked. "I don't think so."

"It works inside a building," I said. "Maybe we're close enough to the surface that it will still work."

"Maybe," said Jeff. "But if not, I guess it's a good thing that I pushed it when we were up in the priest's room." He gave me a huge smile.

As I continued to stare at Jeff, kneeling in the tunnel, I realized that he had probably just saved our lives. He was smart enough to listen to the Spirit and follow it, and I just knew that we were going to be rescued. When we did get out of this mess, I was going to make sure everyone knew how amazing Jeff was and how he saved our lives.

Feeling much better now, I said, "Hey, Jeff, should we do a little exploring?"

Jeff looked warily down the dark tunnel. "I don't know . . ." he started slowly.

"You never know what we might find," I said. "How would it be to show up with a huge bag of silver in each hand when we are rescued, huh?"

Jeff wasn't interested, so I thought of another approach.

"There just might be another way out of here," I suggested. "How crazy would that be if we just sat here waiting for someone to come dig us out when we could have walked out of here on our own through some other way?"

That got him. He was intrigued now. I knew he was still a little reluctant, but at least he was willing to give it a try.

With the flashlight pointed down the tunnel, I headed out first. Jeff stayed close behind. We had gone only a few feet when we discovered what looked like railway tracks. They weren't nearly as far apart as train tracks and they looked quite a bit thinner and lighter.

"This has *got* to be a mine," I said. Jeff didn't respond.

We walked quite a distance along the tracks. The tunnel seemed to be heading straight under the mountain. It wasn't long before the ceiling got higher and we were able to stand up straight. At the same time, the wood that had covered the entire ceiling and walls where we first entered the tunnel now became much more sporadic. Instead we found posts every few feet that created an archway overhead. There were signs that animals had been in the tunnel. We noticed what looked like little holes burrowed here and there in the walls with small piles of dirt that sometimes covered part of the railway tracks.

"It looks like no one has been down here for a long time," I said.

"Yeah," Jeff agreed. "I guess that means that Dr. Anthony hasn't discovered it yet, huh?"

A little bit further down, the tunnel suddenly opened up much wider. Instead of just looking like a tunnel for getting from one place to another, this area looked like someone had been actually digging against the walls. It extended as far as we could see. There was also a mining car on the tracks.

"Do you think it can still roll?" Jeff asked. He pushed on the car, and to the surprise of both of us, it rolled easily. "Wow!" said Jeff. "That's amazing."

We looked at the wheels more closely and found that they looked clean and that the axles had signs of oil on them.

"How long does oil stay wet?" I asked.

"No idea," said Jeff.

I shined the light further down the tracks into the tunnel. "Hey, Jeff," I said. "These tracks look clean."

Jeff followed the light and agreed, "You're right." He paused before adding, "Maybe Anthony has been down here after all."

I shined the light back in the direction we had come from and saw that these tracks looked much dirtier than the others.

"If Anthony is getting things rolling again," I said soberly, "then it looks like he hasn't made it all the way to the mission yet."

"So maybe there isn't anything in here worth taking out," Jeff suggested.

"Then why are the tracks clean part of the way?" I asked. "And why does it look like that car is cleaned up and working? Like I said, I think he just hasn't gotten all the way back to the mission yet. So whatever he's found that *is* worth hauling out just might still be down here."

Jeff nodded. As an experiment, I pushed the mine car about twenty feet down the clean part of the tracks. I was really surprised to find how easily it moved. Somebody had done some nice work.

"I hope you're planning to put that back," said Jeff. "What if Anthony notices that it's in a different place than where he left it?" Jeff continued before I could respond. "I mean if there really is another way in and out of here and Anthony knows about it, then I don't think I want him knowing someone has been here. I don't trust him to let us out!"

It was a good point, so I moved the car back to where we first found it. I was still holding the flashlight in my hand as I pushed the car back; the light was bouncing around on the ceiling as I moved.

Jeff said, "Hey, Bran, shine the light up there again. I thought I saw something."

I shined the light where he had pointed. This was one of the places where there was a wooden archway that I figured was there to support the tunnel. I was surprised to see what looked like a carving of a hand at the very top of the arch. The palm was facing forward with all the fingers curled up in a fist. The thumb was pointing to the side and slanted slightly upward. It made me think of how someone holds up their hand when they're hitchhiking.

"What in the *world* is that?" asked Jeff.

We looked at the carving for a moment and agreed that it

indeed looked like a hand. We talked for a minute about what it could possibly mean, but we really had no idea.

We decided to continue following the tracks for a while. We soon discovered another tunnel that branched off sideways from the main one. It had railway tracks going into it, but it didn't connect to the main track. It just sort of ended. Walking just a little further we found another tunnel with its own set of tracks and then we found a third one that branched off to the other side. The first two had each gone to the right, but the third was on the left.

Each of the tunnels had a wooden archway at its opening. We stood looking around the tunnel to the left and soon discovered a carving at the top of its archway, similar to the first one we had found. But this carving was of two hands: one was the same hitch-hiking thumb, but the hand to the right of it showed all the fingers—and the thumb—open, as if it was about to give someone a high-five.

"What is that all about?" asked Jeff.

"I have no idea," I admitted.

"Maybe we just didn't see the second hand at the other place," Jeff suggested.

We went back and looked at the first carving, but there was only one hand. Curious, we returned to the tunnels that had branched off to the right, wondering if we had missed carvings on the entrances. We had indeed. The first branch we came to had a single hand with both the thumb and index finger extended. Both were pointing upward. The next branch was almost the same, but had two fingers extended. We stared at the last carving for a few moments, trying to make any sense of it.

"Are these numbers?" I asked.

"Yeah!" said Jeff. "I was just thinking the same thing!"

"The first one had just the thumb up," I said, "like the number one."

Jeff nodded and said, "And the second had both a thumb and a finger extended, for two."

"Right," I agreed, "and this one has the thumb and two fingers for three."

"But what was the next one all about?" Jeff asked. "There were two hands, right?"

We went and looked at the tunnel on the left again. It did have two hands: the thumb extended on one hand and all the fingers extended on the other hand.

"That's six," I said. "That doesn't make any sense."

We decided to look for any more tunnels. We found another one on the right. We weren't looking for anything but carvings now. This one had a single hand with the thumb and all fingers extended.

"That would make sense for five," I said.

"So what happened to four?" Jeff asked.

"I have no clue," I admitted.

The next tunnel was also on the right. The carving on its archway had a hand with the thumb and all the fingers extended and a second hand with just the hitchhiker thumb again.

"Another six?" asked Jeff. "Weird."

We kept going deeper and deeper into what we were now convinced was a mine. We found three more tunnels that seemed to fit the counting pattern. The next one was on the left and had a hand with everything extended and a hand with a thumb and the index finger extended.

"There's the seven," I said.

The next tunnel was also on the left and had a carving that was the same as the previous one except for an additional finger, adding up to eight. The next branch was on the right side again and added one more finger to the carving, adding up to nine.

"They all make sense except for the four," Jeff said. "I'll bet if we keep going we'll find one with all fingers on both hands."

I don't think the thought ever crossed my mind to do anything else. The next tunnel did indeed have a carving on the archway with two hands and all of the fingers and both thumbs extended. This was obviously ten. But the hands were in a different position than the others. In this carving, the wrists were next to each other, the thumbs were pointing up and outward, but the fingers were all pointing down and outward. We stared at it for a couple of minutes, talking about how and why this one was different from the others. There seemed to be some extra lines coming from the ends of the thumbs and fingers.

"It's strange," Jeff said finally. "It's almost like the hands were carved over the top of something else—like an 'X.'"

That's when it hit me. "That's not an 'X,'" I said.

"I know," said Jeff. "It just looks like it started out as one. Or maybe someone was trying to cross it out.

"That's not an 'X,'" I said again. This time I could feel a smile starting to creep across my face. Then I added, "That's the number ten."

"I know," said Jeff. "It's both. It's ten fingers—but it sort of is in the shape of an 'X.'"

"No, no, no," I explained. "I mean that's a *Roman numeral* ten."

Even in the dim light I could see Jeff's mouth drop open as he finally saw what I was seeing.

"No way," said Jeff with a growing smile. "It is! You're right! The hands are shaped in an 'X' for the Roman numeral ten!"

"Exactly!" I said with confidence. We both just stood there smiling at our discovery for a couple of moments. Then I started thinking about the other carvings of hands. I hesitated. "But wait—think about the hands for number four. Are they Roman numerals?"

Jeff held his hands up, mimicking the carving that we had seen on the fourth tunnel archway. "It wasn't just a one and a five," he said. "It was a Roman numeral 'I' and a Roman numeral 'V.' Think about the hand with all the fingers showing: it looked like a 'V,' didn't it? And if the 'I' comes first, then that makes 'IV' for a Roman numeral four!"

I realized immediately what he was getting at. "I was thinking the hands for the fourth one and sixth one were the same," I said. "But I'll bet they were in a different order."

"Let's check it out!" Jeff said.

We went back and looked again. It was true: the single thumb was first on the fourth tunnel, but second on the sixth. We thought that was just about the coolest thing we had seen all week—and we had seen a whole lot of cool things. It was amazing to think that one hand could represent a 'V' or a 5, while two hands represented an 'X' or a 10. We just stood in the near darkness smiling for several minutes at how amazingly all these symbols seemed to fit together. It was pretty cool.

After a few minutes, we decided we should probably head back to the mission to see if anything had changed up there—hopefully for the better. As we were walking back I suggested to Jeff that he press the green button again just in case nobody got the signal the first time.

When we got back to the shaft leading up to the priest's room, I was happy to see that the trapdoor looked to be intact. We climbed the ladder and pushed the door open easily. I had been wondering whether the roof would have caved in and filled the room with mud, but it hadn't happened. For all we could tell, the creaking and moaning had stopped. We tried to move the door, but it seemed to be as solid as rock. It was not about to budge in the least.

"What now?" I asked.

"I don't know," Jeff said. "But I'm getting really tired."

"Yeah," I agreed. "It's got to be really late."

"Or really early," Jeff suggested. "I think we were wandering around down there for hours."

"You're probably right," I said. Then I asked, "Do you have your watch?"

"No," said Jeff, "but I wish I did."

"I think I'm going to start wearing my watch to bed from now on," I said.

Jeff yawned loudly. After smacking his lips a couple of times, he said, "I want to sleep somewhere."

"Not here," I said. "I'm still afraid the roof is going to collapse."

We agreed to climb down the ladder again and try to get some sleep just inside the tunnel. I told Jeff to press the green button one more time as we settled in, but then I quickly drifted off to sleep.

CHAPTER 13

The Breath of Life

Sometime later I woke with a start. It felt like hours had passed, but I couldn't know for sure. Everything was pitch-black, so I started to panic. I was sure that I had fallen asleep with the flashlight in my hand—and it had been on, of course. So, where was it now?

I began to feel around on the floor near where I had been sleeping, but I couldn't find the flashlight. I could feel the fear rising inside me as I began to feel around in the dark more and more frantically.

"What are you doing?" came Jeff's voice through the darkness.

"I can't find the flashlight," I said. I was surprised to hear the panic in my own voice.

"It's over here," said Jeff. "You fell asleep with it still on and I wanted to save the batteries." The tunnel suddenly filled with light, making me squint and blink. "I turned it off and put it out of the way, so I would know where to find it. Here." He held out the flashlight for me to take. He had been lying on the ground, but now he sat up with his back against the wall of the tunnel. I did the same.

"No, that's OK," I said. "Keep it." Rubbing my eyes, I asked, "How long was I asleep?"

"I don't know," Jeff yawned. "I was asleep pretty much the entire time that you were. I was almost gone at the same time as you, but then I woke up when I heard the flashlight roll out of your hand.

That's when I turned it off and fell asleep for good." Stretching, he added, "I didn't wake up again until I heard you fumbling around."

After he stopped talking I found myself getting a little bugged by how quiet it was. I hadn't really noticed it before.

"When was the last time you pushed the button?" I asked.

"The last time you told me to," said Jeff.

I just looked at him, wondering how long it would be before he got the hint and pushed the button. He just continued to look back at me. Since I had been so adamant before about him pushing it, I decided to give him a break and wait as long as I could stand it. I noticed myself getting more and more frustrated that he wasn't doing it. I was just about to say something when he spoke first.

"So aren't you going to tell me to push it?" he asked. His voice made it obvious that he knew exactly what was going on inside my head—and I was pretty sure he was enjoying it, too.

"Do I have to ask?" I sounded more intense than I wanted to.

"No," Jeff said casually. "I just figured I would wait and see how long it took."

Trying to appear to be much more patient than I really was, I decided to wait a little longer for him to push the button without being asked. I was starting to really get annoyed, though. Didn't he understand the seriousness of our situation?

Finally, Jeff leaned to one side while reaching into his pocket. "I think I'll try pushing the button again," he said. Even after he pulled out the GPS device he stared at it for a few moments, turning it over in his hands several times before he actually did push the button. Then he held it up to his ear and pretended like he was listening for something. "No response," he said flatly. Then he looked at it again and said, "I don't think this thing works."

I tried really hard not to let him know how annoyed I was. I forced myself to take several breaths in an effort to relax.

"Do you want to go up and try the door again?" Jeff asked after a few silent minutes.

I did. Jeff climbed the ladder, with me right behind him. I was a little worried about what we might find, but nothing seemed any different. We pushed hard on the door, but it still wouldn't move the least little bit. I noticed that the mud that had oozed around the door earlier seemed to have dried a little. I also noticed that it didn't look like any more had come in.

"That's good, at least," I said out loud.

"What?" asked Jeff.

"The building is still here, for one," I said. "And the mud looks like it has stopped trying to get in."

"Yeah," Jeff agreed.

We stood in silence for a moment before Jeff said, "Do you hear something?"

"Like what?" I asked quickly. I listened intently for whatever it was that he might be talking about. I was anxious to hear anything that sounded like good news.

Without answering, Jeff put his ear up against the door and said, "I think I hear something."

I quickly joined him at the door. There was a deep, rumbling sound that seemed to be slowly vibrating the door. "I hear it," I said. "I think I can even feel it a little bit."

I put my hands against the door jamb for a moment and then leaned my ear up against the wall. It was there, too.

"What do you think it is?" I asked.

"I think it might be a backhoe," Jeff said. "I think someone might be trying to dig us out."

That was an exciting thought. I listened for a few more moments and decided that I agreed with him. It did sound like some big equipment was doing something.

We began to get hopeful that we might be rescued soon, but we agreed that we would probably still be safer down in the tunnel than under a 150-year-old roof with a mountain on top of it. We made our way back to where we had been sleeping and sat down again.

"I'm hungry," Jeff said.

"I'm starving," I agreed. "I wonder how long it's been since we ate."

"I don't know," said Jeff. "I don't want to think about it, though. Let's talk about something else."

"Like what?" I asked.

"Something," said Jeff. "I don't know."

I watched as Jeff started shining the flashlight up and down along the walls and ceiling of the tunnel. I asked, "Do you think Anthony is the one who's been getting the mining car moving?"

"The way he was acting with the backhoe," Jeff nodded slowly, "I'm sure of it."

"Do you think anyone else knows about it?" I asked.

"I doubt it," said Jeff. "I don't think Dr. Anthony has learned to play well with others."

I had to agree with that one. I let just a small puff of air escape from my nose as I nodded. Then I asked, "Do you think he found any silver down here? And do you think he's stealing it?"

"I don't know," said Jeff. "Like you said earlier, it looks like that mining car hasn't made it out to this end of the tunnel yet, so unless he found another way out, then I doubt it."

We sat in silence for another minute or so as Jeff continued to shine the flashlight along the wooden ceiling and walls. Then he stopped short. I looked over at him and found him staring intently at a place on the ceiling right near where the tunnel opened up to the shaft that led to the trapdoor. We were sitting a few feet away from the shaft, still fearing what might happen if the roof above collapsed under the mudslide. I looked over to where Jeff was shining the light. He continued to hold it very still. I had no idea what he might be looking at.

"What?" I asked. "Do you see something?"

Jeff didn't answer, but began crawling toward where he had been looking, still staring intently at the ceiling. "I think there's something up there," he finally said.

Too tired to make the effort to follow him, I just watched. I figured that as tired and hungry as we both were, it was more likely that Jeff was having hallucinations than that he had actually found something worth taking the effort to go look at.

"No way," I heard Jeff say under his breath. Still holding the flashlight in one hand, he reached up with the other hand to where he had been staring and put his fingers into an opening between a couple of the rough boards used to make the covering for this part of the tunnel. He grabbed onto something and began to wriggle it back and forth. Within just a couple of seconds, his hand jerked out of the opening and he hit himself in the face with whatever he had been yanking on, dropping the flashlight in the process.

"Are you OK?" I asked, trying really hard not to laugh.

"You won't believe this!" called Jeff over his shoulder.

"You're *not* OK?" I asked. "I believe it."

Ignoring me, Jeff picked up the flashlight and shined it on whatever he had pulled from the crack in the ceiling. I couldn't tell what it was because he had his back to me. I figured he might be trying to hide a bloody nose.

"Guess what I found," Jeff said with amazement.

I couldn't imagine, so I didn't bother to try to guess. I simply asked, "What?" but without much interest.

"It's a Book of Mormon," said Jeff.

"What?" I asked again. This time I was a lot more interested. "Is it another old one?" Now I craned my neck to try to catch a glimpse of what he was holding.

"No," said Jeff, finally turning to show me and shining the flashlight on it. "It's a modern one. See?"

In his hand he held what looked like a black triple combination. It was inside a clear, plastic bag. I could see what looked like the typical gold writing on the spine of the three titles for the Book of Mormon, the Doctrine and Covenants, and the Pearl of Great Price.

"No way," I said. Then I asked, "How long have they been making triple combinations?"

"I have *no* idea," Jeff admitted.

"So check the print date," I suggested.

Jeff removed the book from the bag, opened the cover, turned a couple of pages and said, "Two thousand five."

"Wow. That's pretty new," I said. "It must have been put in there after Mr. Omni dug this place up."

Jeff asked, "Anthony, do you think?"

"It's *got* to be," I said. "Who else?"

Jeff stood, crouched over, and made his way back over to where I was sitting. "Hold this," he said, handing me the flashlight. Then he sat next to me and started thumbing through the pages. It looked practically brand new—completely unused. At least it wasn't used like any book I was used to seeing; some of the pages had bent corners (probably from being jammed up between the wooden slats), and the outside was kind of dirty, but there were no scriptures highlighted anywhere that I could see.

I was beginning to think the book had never been opened, but then, about two thirds of the way through I saw a scrap of paper in between two of the pages. I said, "Hey!"

Jeff said, "What was that?" He had obviously seen the paper, too, and immediately flipped the pages back until he found it. Jeff pulled the paper out and placed the open book face down in his lap.

"What is it?" I asked.

Jeff unfolded the paper twice. It was a full-size single sheet of notebook paper with handwriting on it. I had noticed that the writing did not look at all like Mr. Omni's from the note I had received on the plane several days earlier. This writing was cursive and much smoother. At the top were written the words:

173

Named as the children of Amulon

Then down the left side of the page was a list of names that I recognized from the Book of Mormon. All of this writing was smooth and neat, but then next to each name was written much more roughly something about "son of" someone or "son of" someone else. The complete list looked like this:

Nephi—son of Lehi or Helaman or Nephi or ?

Lehi—son of ? or Zoram or ? or Helaman

Laman—son of Lehi or son of ? or son of Laman or son of ?

Lemuel—son of Lehi

Alma—son of ? or Alma

Ammon—son of ? or Mosiah

Helaman—son of ? or Alma or Helaman

Korihor—son of ?

Samuel—son of ? or ?

Jesus Christ—son of God, son of Mary, son of Joseph

Timothy—son of ?

Moroni—son of ? or Mormon

Then, at the bottom of the page, were these words:

Cannot find any children of Amulon—Just search them all!

Jeff and I stared at the paper for at least 30 seconds before either of us spoke. Then I asked, "Is this supposed to be a genealogy?"

Jeff just shook his head slowly from side to side. "Weird," was all that escaped his mouth.

We continued to look over the list until I asked, "Who's Timothy? Is he in the Book of Mormon?"

"Let's check," Jeff said. He handed me the piece of paper, picked up the book from his lap, and looked at the open pages where the slip of paper had been. "Huh," he said. "This is the index and this page has *Amulon* on it."

I looked at the paper and saw *Amulon* both on the first line and the last line. "Who's Amulon?" I asked. "I don't remember him."

Jeff read from the index, "Leader of the priests of Noah."

"Oh, yeah," I said. "I forgot."

Jeff said, "Remember that the paper goes on the page with *Amulon*, OK?"

"OK," I agreed.

Then he started flipping pages, looking for "Timothy." He read, "Brother of Nephi."

"Nephi?" I asked. "I don't remember Nephi having a brother named Timothy. I thought they were just Laman and Lemuel and Sam and . . ."

"Not *that* Nephi," Jeff interrupted. "There was a different Nephi later. It says here 'Brother of Nephi 2.'"

"Nephi 2?" I asked.

"Yeah," Jeff said, like it was something that made perfect sense. Maybe to him, but not to me. Reading more, Jeff said, "Timothy lived later. He was raised from the dead by Nephi and later called by Jesus to be one of the twelve disciples." Flipping over a few pages he said, "Here it says that Nephi 1 is the son of Lehi 1 in the year 600 B.C. That's the one you're thinking about."

"Right," I agreed.

"They put numbers next to the name in the index when there is more than one person by that name," Jeff said. Turning the page, he pointed and said, "Nephi 2 is the son of Helaman 3 in the year 45 B.C." Moving his finger to the second column on the page, Jeff said, "It looks like Nephi 3 is the son of Nephi 2 and—let's see— Nephi 4 is possibly the same as Nephi 2 or his son. So I guess they're not sure if there are four Nephis or just three."

Looking at the paper in my hands, I asked, "So is that was this is talking about?" Pointing to the first name on the list, I said, "Look. It says that Nephi is the 'son of Lehi or Helaman or Nephi or ?' Are those the four Nephis?"

Jeff looked quickly through the four listings in the index again and found that they seemed to match up. The first three listings for Nephi each stated who his father was, but the last one was unsure.

"Is that what Anthony did?" I asked. "Did he just look up these names in the index, trying to find out who their fathers were?"

"I'll bet he did," said Jeff.

We looked up each of the names on the list and quickly found that Anthony's scribbling of 'son of' this person or that person matched exactly with the listings in the index.

"So what was he trying to figure out?" I asked.

"Look at the last line," Jeff answered. "He was trying to find out if any of these guys was a son of Amulon."

"We don't know anything about children of Amulon, do we?" I said, trying to remember.

"I don't think so," Jeff agreed. Then again he said, "Weird."

"Didn't you say the paper was by the index listing for 'Amulon'?" I asked.

"Oh, yeah," said Jeff, and he turned to the page where we had found the scrap of paper in the first place. He started reading aloud what it said by the name "Amulon."

AMULON—*leader of priests of Noah³, tributary monarch under Laman³ (see also Amulon, Children of; . . .)*

There was more, but he stopped short at "Amulon, Children of."

"Is that what he's talking about at the top of the page?" I asked. We both read again where Anthony had written, "Named as the children of Amulon."

"I think he was trying to find out how the children of Amulon were named," said Jeff. Looking back in the index, we found the listing for "AMULON, CHILDREN OF" right under the listing for "AMULON." Here there was a reference to Mosiah 25:12, so we looked it up. Here is what it says:

And it came to pass that those who were the children of Amulon and his brethren, who had taken to wife the daughters of the Lamanites, were displeased with the conduct of their fathers, and they would no longer be called by the names of their fathers, therefore they took upon themselves the name of Nephi, that they might be called the children of Nephi and be numbered among those who were called Nephites.

Jeff started laughing and said, "He missed the whole point!"

"What?" I asked, clearly slightly behind in this situation.

"This scripture is talking about people who wanted to be called by a name that represented something good," explained Jeff. "It doesn't matter what the actual names of Amulon's children were." Jeff laughed again and repeated, "He missed the whole point!"

"You're right!" I agreed, finally catching up.

We thought it was funny, but then the more we looked over the list and paper, the more we realized that there was still something missing. Where had the list of names come from? Where had Anthony gotten the phrase "named as the children of Amulon?" We didn't know.

We were tired and hungry, so we decided to go check the door again. We wanted to know if they were making any progress digging us out yet.

"Have you pushed the button lately?" I asked.

Jeff just looked at me without saying anything. Carefully, he put the scrap of paper back in the back at the "Amulon" listing in the index. Then he put the book back in the plastic bag and back where he had found it, in the space between a couple of boards in the ceiling.

"Why are you putting it back?" I asked.

"I just feel like we should leave everything the way we found it," said Jeff.

I nodded. I figured Mr. Omni would want to see everything down here and we could show it to him then. After that, Jeff pulled the GPS gadget from his pocket and pushed the button where I could clearly see it.

"Thanks," I said. He nodded and half smiled, but still didn't say anything. I'm sure I was making him crazy, but I thought it was important.

We climbed the ladder and pushed open the trapdoor. I went first with the flashlight. I was absolutely ecstatic after I laid the trapdoor back against the chair and looked at the door to the room. I could see light seeping in around the edges of the door along the top and most of the way down the sides.

"Jeff!" I called down to him. "There's light around the door!"

"No way!" Jeff called back.

"They're doing it," I said as I climbed up out of the hole. "They're close!"

It turned out they weren't quite as close as we might have hoped. It was still quite a while before we actually got out of there. After climbing out of the shaft, we rushed to the door and started pounding on it.

"We're in here!" we yelled. "Get us out!"

"Are you OK?" came the reply from a voice we didn't recognize.

"We're fine," we called back.

"How many of you are in there?" came the question.

"Two," we called.

"When was the last time you had anything to eat or drink?"

"Not since last night," I said.

"OK. What are your names?"

"Brandon Andrews and Jeff Andrews," we called back.

"Great," said the voice. "We'll tell your parents. We're going to have you out of there in a few minutes. There is still some more mud blocking the door."

"That's great," we called back. I think we were both really relieved to know that it would soon be over. I don't think we realized how uptight we were until we knew that the end was so near.

"We need you to move back away from the door until we get it open," came the voice.

"OK," we agreed.

We sat on the floor next to the wall as far from the door as we could get.

"Do you think we should close the trapdoor?" asked Jeff.

"Probably," I agreed. "And we should probably put all the plastic back down to try to keep the door and the rug protected as much as possible."

Jeff agreed, so we quickly closed the door and replaced everything that was on top of it. As near as we could tell, the room looked just as it had when we came into it hours earlier—except for the flashlight, which I continued to hold. We wondered how many hours it had actually been.

"Is that sunlight around the door?" Jeff asked. "Or do you think they set up floodlights?"

"I don't know," I admitted.

Sometime later the door was finally pulled open. Four men and women that we didn't know came rushing in with stretchers. They were dressed like emergency paramedics from ambulances or fire trucks or something. They made us lie on the stretchers and immediately put oxygen masks on each of us. After we assured them that we weren't hurt or in pain anywhere, they told us not to talk. While one of them was strapping me to the stretcher, another one was taking my temperature and my pulse and blood pressure. I imagine they were doing the same with Jeff, but I couldn't really see him.

Without warning, they quickly picked up the stretcher I was on and whisked me out of the room and into the bright sunlight outside. I had to shade my eyes. We had apparently been under the mudslide all night and into the next day.

I could barely open my eyes enough to see that there were people standing all around, watching me being carried out of the room, past a backhoe, up a steep hill, and toward a waiting helicopter. They informed me that I was to be taken to a hospital to be "examined following my ordeal." I could only guess that the same thing was happening to Jeff, as I saw another helicopter not far from the first one. As they were strapping me into the helicopter, Mom came up to me and squeezed my arm.

"I'm so glad you're safe," Mom said. "I love you!"

With that the helicopter door was pulled shut, I saw Mom wave, and I could hear the engine begin to speed up. Within a few seconds I felt the helicopter leave the ground as we took off for what I could only assume was the hospital. I was glad to be out of the underground mine, but couldn't help being pretty annoyed that we hadn't been given the chance to tell anyone where we had been or what we had found!

CHAPTER 14

They Shall Be Cut Off

The helicopter ride to the hospital was not fun. Since I wasn't injured or in pain and there was nothing wrong with me whatsoever, you might think it would be fun. But I never had a chance to think about it. As the helicopter took off I was still too busy being annoyed that I was there and not still on the ground telling Mr. Omni and my family what Jeff and I had discovered. Not long after we were in the air, though, my thoughts turned to how uncomfortable it was to be strapped into the stretcher, swaying back and forth as it moved through the air—or should I say forth and back?

I tried looking out the window, but because I was flat on my back way up in the air, all I could see was blue sky and really bright sunlight. I couldn't tell where we were going or where we had been. My face was starting to get hot under the oxygen mask.

"You're going to feel a little pinch," said the paramedic. At least that's what I think she said. I wasn't sure at first. But at the exact same time that I tried through the mask to ask her to repeat it, I felt the pinch. It wasn't small though, and I'm pretty sure I wouldn't have called it a pinch, either. It was actually much more like a "sharp jab" than a "small pinch." Right in my arm.

"We're going to give you some IV fluids," said the paramedic. "Since you haven't had anything to drink since last night, you may be dehydrated."

I nodded my understanding. I watched as she hooked up a bag

of clear liquid to a plastic tube and hung it upside down above me. Watching the bag swinging forth and back made me realize how much the helicopter was jumping around. The paramedic must have noticed because she said, "Just close your eyes and rest if you can, OK?"

I nodded again and closed my eyes. At first it seemed to just exaggerate the swaying, but soon I started thinking about other things. This was the first time that I realized that the sky had been blue. I didn't think I had seen a single cloud anywhere. I opened one eye momentarily just to make sure I was right. I was. This was the first time all week that I had seen anything but clouds.

After a few minutes we landed. I was pulled outside, placed on what felt like a really flimsy cart, and whisked into the emergency room of a hospital. They immediately moved me from the flimsy cart to a bed. After checking my blood pressure and pulse again, they said they would be back in a few minutes and then promptly forgot about me. At least that's how it felt.

There were people going this way and that way, but no one seemed to notice me or care about what I was doing there. I didn't see anyone that I knew. Soon I began to wonder if I had been brought to the wrong place; maybe no one even knew where I had been taken. I wanted to ask someone about it, but no one slowed down long enough for me to get their attention. I still had the IV bag and oxygen mask hooked up to me, so that made it a little difficult, too. The first chance I had to get someone's attention was when that flimsy cart was wheeled in again with another person that they moved onto the bed next to mine. At least I guessed that's what was going on—there was a curtain that separated us.

"Excuse me," I tried to say. My voice sounded funny because of the oxygen mask.

No one seemed to notice.

"Excuse me," I said again, this time a little louder.

"We'll be right with you," came a voice from behind the curtain.

Not wanting to wait, in case I was forgotten again, I asked through the curtain, "I'm just wondering where my family is. Do you know if anyone is coming to be with me?"

"Bran!" came Jeff's muffled voice. "Is that you?"

"Hey, Jeff," I called back. "It sounds like you have a mask on just like mine!"

"I guess so," said Jeff. "Did you get stabbed in the arm, too?"

"That's a good description of it," I said.

Someone helping Jeff get situated asked, "Do you two know each other?"

"We're brothers!" we both said at once.

"Would you like the curtain open?"

"Yeah!" I said.

The curtain was immediately pulled back. I was surprised at how Jeff looked, but I was really glad to see him. His face and clothes were really dirty. I looked down at my own clothes and realized for the first time that I was pretty dirty as well.

I couldn't wait to talk to Jeff.

When all the people had left to make themselves busy somewhere else, I said, "It's about time you showed up. I didn't like being here by myself."

"Have you seen anyone else?" asked Jeff.

"Nope," I said.

Jeff looked around and said, "I wonder if Mom or Dad or someone is going to be here soon to check on us. We should ask."

"Good luck with that," I said. "After they dumped me here, I was completely ignored until you showed up. And it was obvious they didn't even know we were together."

"We weren't," said Jeff. "We came in separate helicopters."

I couldn't see the expression on his face because of the mask, but I was sure he was wearing a smirk.

"Right," I said. I was too tired to say anything else. I had been kind of uptight during the helicopter ride, but now that Jeff was here I suddenly began to relax and feel really tired. I thought Jeff was tired, too, because he didn't say anything else for another minute or two. Maybe he was just thinking about everything that had happened.

"Have you had a prayer?" asked Jeff without warning.

"Huh?" I said, not sure what he meant. "We said a prayer together."

"I mean since we got out," Jeff explained. "I'm trying to be better about saying a prayer of gratitude after I get out of a mess."

"Right," I nodded. "Good idea."

Jeff offered to say it, so I told him to go ahead. He spoke really quietly. I'm sure it was to avoid attention, but with as much as we were being ignored, I didn't really worry about it too much. I remember saying "amen" at the end of his prayer, but not much else. I think I actually drifted off to sleep. The next thing I knew there was a woman standing between Jeff and me. She was taking down the IV bag.

"Hello," she smiled. "I'm a nurse. How are you feeling?"

I had to think about it for a moment before I could answer. "Fine," I sighed.

"I just need to ask you a few questions, OK?"

I just nodded. The nurse put a Band-Aid on my arm where the needle had been. She took off my oxygen mask and then proceeded to ask a bunch of questions about when I had last eaten or had anything to drink or whether anything hurt and a bunch of other stuff like that. She asked Jeff all the same questions after taking off his oxygen mask.

"There is someone here to take you two home," the nurse said. She was taking down Jeff's IV bag now.

"Great," said Jeff. "Does that mean you're done with us? Do we get to leave?"

"You should discuss the details about leaving with the person who is taking you," said the nurse, "I'll be done with you as soon as you prove to me that you're hydrated."

"How do we do that?" I asked.

"Use the restroom," smiled the nurse as she walked away. Then she pointed to a door and said, "Right there."

After we had done as we were told, Jeff and I were lying on our beds again talking.

"Who do you think is here to get us?" I asked.

"No idea," said Jeff. "Maybe we're supposed to call for someone." He pulled the GPS gadget from his pocket and pushed the green button. I noticed since it was his idea this time, he didn't feel the need to wait for me to say anything.

"You still have that thing?" I asked, questioning the obvious.

"I didn't see *you* having any lengthy conversations with anyone," Jeff said, "or giving anything to anybody. I was far too busy getting gang tackled and strapped to a board to even think about it. How about you?"

"Good point," I confessed.

Just then a police officer came up to us and said, "Hello, young men. I'm Officer Ivie."

"Hi," said Jeff.

"Officer IV?" I asked. "Like the IV that was just taken out of my arm. Why does the hospital need a police officer for IVs?"

The officer started to respond, but then instead, he just stepped closer and pointed to his name tag with the words, "Officer Ivie" printed on it.

"My last name is 'Ivie'," said the officer. "If I was here because of the IV in your arm, then this would have just the letters I-V instead of I-v-i-e."

"After this week," said Jeff, "I think we would read the letters I-V as a Roman numeral four before anything else."

Officer Ivie raised his eyebrows. "I see," he said. "I had heard that the two of you had quite an ordeal since last night, but I didn't realize it had been going on all week. You were stuck underground, right? How long were you down there?"

"Oh," said Jeff. "Right. Just since last night, and we did find some Roman numerals down there, but it seems like we've been colliding with Roman numerals all week."

"Colliding?" asked the officer. "That's an interesting choice of words."

"It's been an interesting week," said Jeff.

"I see," said the officer. "Well, I'm here to take you home."

"*You're* the person that's here to pick us up?" I asked. "Where's our mom and dad? Why aren't *they* here?"

"They would have been here if they could have," said Officer Ivie. "But the only road is currently buried by the mudslide."

"No way!" I said.

"I'm afraid so," said the officer.

"So did it bury the whole house?" I asked.

"Oh, no," said the officer. "The house is fine. The road is actually buried about a quarter mile from the house. The slide hasn't taken out any structures, but the road goes right next to the mountain at one point and the slide buried it."

"Is that why we were brought here by helicopters?" asked Jeff.

"That's right," said the officer. "And that's why you will be riding back home with me in a police helicopter."

"Is it safe?" I asked. "To go back near the mudslide, I mean."

"The home itself is so far from the base of the mountain that there is no danger of the slide reaching it."

"How many homes are blocked off?" asked Jeff.

"Just yours," said the officer.

"It's not ours," I mumbled. "We're just staying there for the week."

"Is it safe to be at a place with no road?" asked Jeff.

"Well," said the officer, "I discussed that with the chief. It turns out that it's just a short hike over to another road. Apparently, there's a good running trail there, so the chief said it would be fine. Besides, I guess you have a helicopter there, right? Or, at least, the owner of the house does, doesn't he?"

"Yeah, he does," nodded Jeff.

"So why didn't Mom and Dad use the helicopter to come pick us up?" I asked.

"I'm not really sure," said the officer. "I think they were planning to come, originally, but then we got a message that your parents just wanted us to bring you home."

"OK," we said. It sounded kind of weird to me, but whatever.

"I'm starving," said Jeff.

I had to agree. We hadn't had anything to eat since dinner the night before. I glanced at the clock on the wall which said it was now after 6:00 P.M. It's a good thing we're used to fasting for twenty-four hours once a month.

Jeff continued, "Can we get something to eat on the way?"

"On the way?" said the officer. "I don't know of any place with either a helipad or a 'fly-through' window—but you could get something here before we leave."

"At the hospital?" I asked.

"Sure," said the officer. "There are about twelve vending machines in the hallway full of a wide variety of flavored sugar, fat, and salt—in either liquid or solid form. Or we could head over to the cafeteria where they have a wide variety of food with absolutely no sugar, fat, or salt. I think they use a little pepper, though."

"Sounds great," I said flatly. Turning to Jeff, I asked, "Did that description cure your appetite or are you still hungry?"

"Let's check out the machines," he suggested.

We each got a few random things from the vending machines and then climbed into a waiting police helicopter with Officer Ivie.

"Wow," said Jeff as I started ripping open the various packages of junk food I had bought. "When you're done with that you're going to be full of more preservatives than an Egyptian mummy."

"What about you?" I asked, looking over at his food. I hadn't noticed until now that he had bought an apple and some grape juice.

"What's in that bottle?" I asked. "About 5 percent juice and 80 percent sugar?"

Jeff held the bottle up for me to read the large "100 percent juice" label on the front. He took a large bite of his apple and smiled at me through stretched out cheeks.

"I'm going for quick energy," I mumbled, wondering how Jeff had suddenly become a healthy eater and how long it would last. The sun was low in the sky as we made our way back to Mr. Omni's cottage. It probably could have been a pretty fun ride, but I was mainly concentrating on "dinner."

"I don't think we're in the right place," Jeff said a few minutes later.

I looked up from my food to see what he was talking about. I realized that the helicopter was slowing down as if it was about to land. We were approaching a small area that was well lit, but it was surrounded by a sea of shadows. It certainly looked like Omni's property, including the excavation site and the house and gardens, but only Omni's property had any lights.

"There should be other homes around," Jeff explained.

The police officer turned in his seat and said, "The mudslide knocked out power to most of the area here, but your home has its own generator. We wouldn't have brought you back here otherwise."

Jeff and I both nodded in understanding. I still didn't like him referring to the home as ours.

"The slide wasn't really that big," continued the officer, "but the edge of the mountain that came down had both power lines and

THE SECRET MISSION

utility lines on it—it even brought down a couple of cell phone towers."

Jeff and I nodded again; the helicopter was too loud to bother with talking very much. When we landed near the excavation site behind Omni's cottage a few minutes later, the only person we saw was TB. It was twilight now, but the lights along the walkways and patio were blazing. TB was standing as though he was expecting us. After the helicopter landed, he came up to the side and opened the door to the back seat where Jeff and I were riding.

"To be welcomed back," called TB above the sound of the helicopter. The rotor was still spinning overhead. TB gave a slight bow as he motioned for us to climb out.

"Are their parents here?" asked the officer.

"Yes," nodded TB. "They are to be in library."

"Will you young men be OK?" Officer Ivie asked us.

"We're fine," Jeff and I both said. TB was a little weird, but it was just a short walk to the house, so I didn't really think anything of it. We watched and waved as the helicopter took off again, blowing leaves around and causing the nearby trees to sway back and forth—or rather, forth and back.

"In the library?" I asked TB as the helicopter turned and flew back toward the city.

"Yes," nodded TB again. "I show you."

"We know where it is," I said.

"Yes," said TB, but he continued to act like he was planning to take us there. Whatever.

I looked around the excavation site and started to realize how much things had changed because of the mudslide. Where everything in the old mission courtyard had been well organized and neatly dug out when we had first seen it, now it was a mess. There was still a large enough flat area for the helicopter to land without a problem, but the back wall of the mission was now mostly buried again. Only the door to the priest's room, where we had been, was

189

visible anymore. I guess they had simply worked to free us, but nothing else. There were now several huge mounds of dirt near the doorway that had surely been left by all the digging to get us out.

It seemed to take longer than usual to get back to the house from the excavation site where we were dropped off. Maybe it was just because I was tired. Or maybe TB was starting to act a little creepy. Anyway, after we reached the patio doors I found myself almost hurrying to the library to see Mom and Dad. Jeff was right with me, and TB was not far behind.

"We're home," Jeff called out as we entered the library.

Stunned that he would call this place "home," I quickly turned to him as we stood just inside the library doors and said, "What?"

"What what?" asked Jeff.

"This is *not* home," I said. "We're back, maybe, but we're not *home*."

Click. I was surprised to hear the doors close behind us. I turned to look at them. As I reached for them I was even more surprised to hear the locks turn and click.

"Nobody's in here," said Jeff.

I pulled on the door handles, but nothing happened.

"We're locked in!" I said, rattling the door handles. "TB locked us in here!"

Jeff grabbed one of the door handles with one hand and started pounding on the door with the other. The doors hardly moved. This was the first time that I noticed how big and heavy they were. They were not like the hollow, flimsy doors at our house. I think I could have easily broken through those if I had to. But not these; they felt like solid wood.

"Hey!" we both started yelling. "Let us out of here!"

Jeff continued to pound his fist on the door and yell, but I gave up after a few seconds. I started wondering who it was that we were hoping would hear us and let us out. Surely the rest of our family was already locked up someplace else. We hadn't seen Mr. Omni

190

anywhere, so there was no telling whose side he was on. He could be locked up with our family, or—the idea that I considered to be the most likely—he could be the one giving the orders. After all, didn't TB work for him?

"Help me!" said Jeff either in disgust or desperation—I'm not sure which.

CHAPTER 15

Seek Ye out of the Best Books

"Help you what?" I asked.

"I'm trying to get somebody's attention," Jeff said.

"Whose?" I asked. "TB's? Do you think he's close to having a change of heart?" I paused for dramatic emphasis. "Did you see anyone else? I'm sure everybody else is locked up somewhere just like we are."

"We don't know that," Jeff said. "Maybe they aren't yet. Maybe they can still hear us."

"I think they would be here by now if they could," I said. "I'm sure TB is probably just waiting for us to shut up." I took off my jacket and plopped myself down in one of the big, cushy chairs. "Besides, my sugar high is gone and I'm tired. Maybe if I had had an apple and a bottle of 100 percent juice—like you did—then I would have the energy to keep hurting my fist on the door."

I didn't look at him because I didn't want to see his smirk. He didn't move for a minute, but then came and slumped into a chair next to mine. He sat there for a minute before taking off his jacket and settling in again.

"You're right," Jeff said.

We both sat staring at the locked doors for a moment.

"Don't you think it's strange," Jeff asked, "that those doors lock from the outside? I mean, wouldn't it make more sense to have doors and locks that kept people away from expensive things like a whole library of books?"

"Maybe we can pull the pins from the hinges," I suggested, looking toward the door. "Wait. Where are the hinges?"

Jeff looked at the edges of the doors and said, "They open into the hallway, remember? So the hinges are on the other side."

"That's weird," I said. Then I asked, "Is everyone wacko who builds huge houses like this?"

"I don't know," said Jeff. "Maybe."

"Why?" I asked. "Why are they all wacko?"

"I don't know," admitted Jeff. "Maybe they're worried about getting robbed or something."

I thought about this for a minute. "You're right," I said. "And that's why they build secret passages in their houses, too. I'll bet this house has secret passages!" Then, with confidence I added, "We can get out of here."

I hopped to my feet and started toward the bookshelves.

"What?" asked Jeff. "What are you talking about?"

"Don't you remember that show we saw?" I asked. "The one about all the old mansions in the western United States that were built like around a hundred years ago? Practically every one of them had secret rooms or secret passages or secret attics or something."

Jeff just stared at me.

I could feel him staring at my back as I began to inspect the bookcases in the library.

"Look," I said. "The bookcases are built right into the walls."

"Well," grunted Jeff, "they would have to be, wouldn't they? You couldn't have that ladder rolling around the room if the bookcases were freestanding and could fall over."

"Exactly," I said. "Which would make it really easy for a secret passage to be hidden behind one of them. One of these sections of the bookcase is probably a huge door. It's probably on a hinge where you have to push a knot in the wood or pull out a particular book or something to make it swing open."

"You can't be serious," said Jeff.

"Aren't I acting serious?" I asked. "What else are you going to do—pound on the door and ask TB to change his mind?"

Jeff didn't respond.

"Maybe that apple and juice didn't give you so much energy after all, huh?"

I knew it wasn't a nice thing to say, but it slipped out. He took it well, though.

"Funny," he said. He even had half a smile. Then he asked, "Do you think someone is watching us?"

"Huh?" I asked. I looked over at him and saw him looking up at a high corner of the room. I looked where he was looking and saw a video camera. It was pointing in our direction.

"Oh, great," I said.

"Let's find out," Jeff suggested. Then he slowly got up, walked to the other side of the room and acted like he was reading the titles of the books. I watched the camera rotate, seeming to follow his movements.

"Someone's watching alright," I said. Then I added, "But if we stay on different sides of the room, it can only watch one of us at a time."

"What are you thinking?" asked Jeff.

"Well," I said, "we don't want them to know what we're doing and certainly we don't want them to see the secret passage open when we find it."

"R-right," said Jeff. He sounded like he thought I was nuts.

"So," I continued, "why don't we sit in chairs on opposite sides of the room and only check out the bookcases when the camera is not pointing at us. The one who's not searching can warn the other one to sit down really fast if the camera starts to move."

"Does that mean I get to sit down?" asked Jeff. "It's still pointed at me, right?"

"Right," I said. Jeff slouched into a chair near where he had been looking at the bookcases. The camera didn't move for a minute, but then started back in my direction. I quickly jumped onto a chair and acted like I might be taking a nap.

"It's pointed right at you," whispered Jeff.

"I don't think there's any sound," I said. "You don't have to whisper."

"You don't know for sure—and someone *could* be outside the door," said Jeff a little louder now, but not much. Then he said, "It's coming back my direction."

After the camera was pointed at Jeff, whoever was moving it must have been satisfied, because it stayed there. I took advantage of the opportunity to begin examining the bookcases and pushing on knots in the wood. Each of the bookcases was separated by a piece of dark wood that was about a foot wide with lots of knots and heavy grain in it. It took a while to examine and push on every place that looked like a possible button for opening a secret book-case doorway.

I didn't find anything on the frames of the bookcases that appeared to be out of the camera's view, so I started pulling out each of the books in groups to see if anything happened. I was careful not to pull them out all the way, so that I could easily push them back into place again.

"This is crazy," Jeff said after a while. "We're not going to find anything."

"We're not going to find anything if we don't look," I said. "Maybe . . ."

Jeff interrupted me by hissing, "The camera's moving!"

I quickly pushed the books in my hand back into place and jumped onto the chair. After a few seconds Jeff said, "It looks like it's staying with you now." He paused before reluctantly adding, "I guess that means it's my turn to search now, right?"

"Yeah," I said.

I was proud of him. I knew he was *not* convinced—even though I was—that there was anything here worth looking for. But he was diligent. Maybe he was doing it just to keep me off his case. I didn't care, though, as long as he was searching.

After a few minutes I said slowly as I looked over the bookcases, "Maybe I should use the ladder and start on the next level when the camera moves again." I was happy to see that the ladder was on my side of the room. I was trying to look over the situation without someone watching the video monitor getting suspicious about what I might be thinking.

"You're crazy," said Jeff. "Do you really think they would have a secret passage up there? What if the ladder wasn't close by when the secret door opened? You'd fall out on your head!"

"Exactly," I said. "Seems like a pretty good place to hide a secret passage, doesn't it?" I pretended to yawn and stretch as I looked over the bookcases again. Then I said, "I'm going to try."

"But you'll have to move the ladder," Jeff said as he continued to work. "They might notice it." He paused. "And you'll have to jump down really fast when the camera moves in your direction again."

"What do you suggest?" I said.

"I don't know," said Jeff.

"I have an idea," I said.

I was pretty sure Jeff was tired of my ideas, but I thought this was a good one. I got off the chair, stretched like I was really tired and climbed under the grand piano and laid down on the thick rug, leaving just my feet sticking out from under it.

"I want the camera to just see my shoes and nothing else," I said. "How did I do?"

Jeff went and stood underneath the video camera. "I think it can probably see a little way up from your ankles," he said.

I pulled my legs further underneath and asked, "How's that?"

"Looks good," he said.

"Great," I said. "But now I can't see if the camera moves anymore, so you better go sit down again in case the camera looks for you."

Jeff certainly didn't argue with that. I think he was happy for any excuse to stop his halfhearted search. He sat down immediately, but it was almost ten minutes before he said that the camera was moving. He said he was watching it out of the corner of his eye and it was apparently still pointed at him. It was time to make my move.

I proceeded to take off my shoes, moving as little as possible so they would hopefully be in the same place. I set them up the best I could to look like I still had them on and was lying in the same position under the piano. Then I rolled up my jacket and tried to make it look like my legs coming out of the top of my shoes, just in case the camera could see more than we thought.

"There," I said, standing up and examining my work. "Now they'll think I'm asleep under the piano and I can use the ladder to check out the upper level."

"You'll still need to jump down and move the ladder back when the camera moves," Jeff said.

"I know," I agreed. "Be sure to tell me as soon as you see it start to move even a fraction."

"I will," Jeff said, but he didn't sound like he thought I would be able to move fast enough for my scheme to work. I wasn't worried. I went over to the ladder and began climbing up.

I was able to search for quite a while before the camera moved back in my direction again. I asked Jeff a couple of times if he was still watching for it and he assured me that he was. Using the ladder and working on the upper level was definitely more of a pain because I could check only a small area of the framing before I had to climb back down and move the ladder over again. And because I was only wearing socks on my feet, they were starting to hurt a little bit.

"It's moving," hissed Jeff after about the third time I had moved the ladder.

Luckily, I was just on my way back up, so I didn't have quite as far to go. I jumped to the floor, pushed the ladder back to where I thought it had started and ran underneath where the camera was mounted so I wouldn't be seen. The camera stopped when it apparently had a view of my shoes sticking out from underneath the piano. It stayed there for only a few seconds before it moved back to where Jeff was.

"I guess it's not my destiny to help you search," said Jeff. He seemed pleased by the idea.

"You can't look like you're talking on the camera when I'm supposed to be asleep!" I hissed.

Jeff didn't respond.

After I was sure the camera was staying put on Jeff I went back to the ladder and pushed it into position again. I was about two thirds of the way across the back wall when it happened. I had just moved the ladder to a new area when I pushed on the first knot I found. The whole board seemed to move a little bit. I pushed it again harder and found that the entire one-foot-wide framing board moved inward on one side because it was apparently hinged on the other side. I had been looking for a button that would activate a hidden door, but I had not expected one of these panels to actually *be* a door itself. The opening was really narrow, but it was about eight feet high and definitely big enough for me to fit through.

"Jeff!" I called. "I found it!"

"No way!" called Jeff in a weird voice, apparently attempting to not *look* like he was talking.

"Way!" I said. "*Totally* way!"

"A secret passage?" asked Jeff.

"Yep!" I said.

I held the hinged board completely open and peered inside. The light from the room shone a few feet into the opening. It was very narrow for about a foot—just until it got behind the bookcases—but then it immediately opened up wide. I couldn't really see what was in there or where it led, though.

"What do you see?" Jeff hissed. He sounded excited.

"I see you apologizing to me," I said, without turning around. He didn't respond within a couple of seconds, so I let the door quietly close as I spun on the ladder to look at him. "I see you telling me that I was right all along and you should have trusted me."

Jeff heaved a big sigh, still obviously trying not to look like he was communicating with anyone. "You're right," he said. "I'm sorry I didn't trust you."

"That's OK," I smiled as I started to climb down the ladder.

"You were right all along," Jeff said. He didn't sound as sincere as I probably would have preferred, but he said the words, so I decided it was good enough.

"Thank you," I smiled.

"I'm sorry that I said you were crazy," Jeff said.

"It's OK," I said again, trying to end the conversation.

"I'm sorry that I thought the idea was *totally* stupid," Jeff said.

"I said it's OK." I was starting to get a little annoyed.

"I'm sorry that . . . ," Jeff began, but I interrupted him.

"Enough!" I said. "I get the point."

Jeff was still trying to hold perfectly still and act like he was asleep, but he had a distinct smile on his face.

"If TB is watching you on camera right now," I said, "then that smile of yours is going to make it pretty obvious that you're awake."

Jeff rolled his head to one side so his face wouldn't be in full view of the camera. "Nah," he said. "He'll just think I'm having a really pleasant dream about getting even with somebody."

"Right," I said. Then remembering what was going on, I added, "I need a flashlight."

"Good luck with that," said Jeff.

"I want to see what's in there," I said. "I want to know where it goes."

"I still don't have a flashlight," Jeff said, helpful as ever.

"Hey," I said. "Maybe I can use the piano lamp."

There was a lamp on the piano for the music. I quickly looked up at the video camera to see if I thought the lamp would be visible or not. I didn't think so.

"You're going to need a pretty long extension cord," Jeff said.

"Maybe it already has one," I suggested. "It's in the middle of the room." Then I asked, "Do you think I can get the lamp without being seen?"

"I can't really tell from here," Jeff said. "But I don't think. . . ."

I didn't bother to wait for him to say what he didn't think. I just snatched the lamp as quickly as I could and said, "Got it!"

"I sure hope no one was watching," Jeff mumbled.

"Hey!" I said. "There's no cord on this thing."

"Maybe it's fake," Jeff suggested.

"Maybe," I said, looking it over. Then I found a switch on the back and flipped it to one side.

The light came on. "Yesss!" I said, and then added, "Can you say 'battery operated?'"

"No way," said Jeff.

"Way again," I responded.

Checking the video camera to make sure it was still pointed in Jeff's direction and not mine, I climbed the ladder up to the panel where I had found the entrance to the secret passage. I pushed the panel open and climbed inside.

"Where are you going?" Jeff hissed just before the panel closed behind me. I could hear the panic in his voice.

Now I panicked, wondering if he was giving something away to the video camera. I quickly found a wooden handle, pulled the panel open again, and stuck my head out just far enough to see what Jeff was doing. He was still sitting in the chair and looked like he was still trying to fake for the camera, but his eyes were bulging hard to the side so he could see where I was.

"I'm going to check this out!" I hissed.

"What about the ladder?" asked Jeff. "If the camera moves, he'll see it's in a different place."

"I don't think he's looking at the ladder," I said. "He just wants to see what we're doing. He won't even notice the ladder."

"You don't know that," Jeff said deliberately.

"I'm willing to take that chance," I said.

"Of course you are," said Jeff. "Because you'll be gone. *I'm* the one who will be stuck here if TB comes looking for us."

"So *you* move the ladder back where it was," I said. "The camera hasn't moved for a while. He's probably not even looking."

Jeff thought for a minute, but then slowly got up out of the chair. He stretched and yawned and then moved under the camera. It didn't move. As soon as Jeff saw that he was out of view and that the camera wasn't moving, he scampered over to the ladder and moved it back to its original position.

"Great," I said. "I'll be right back."

"Wait!" hissed Jeff. "You can't just stick your head out again. What if he's looking? We need some sort of signal."

"OK," I said, thinking. "How about if I knock twice when I get back. I won't open the door unless you knock back, OK?"

Jeff thought for a moment and then said, "OK. I guess that will work. But if I don't knock back then wait for at least a couple of minutes before knocking again."

"I will," I agreed. Then I asked, "How many times will you knock?"

"Uh," said Jeff. "How about three times?"

"OK," I nodded.

With that, I let the secret panel slowly close and then turned around to see what I could find. Behind the bookshelves was a passageway that extended in both directions. It was still narrow, but certainly wider than the space between the bookshelves. Here I could walk without turning sideways.

I might have expected the walls to be unfinished studs without any coverings, but they were flat and smooth. There were spider webs in the corners by the ceiling and floor. The floor was wooden and very dusty.

As I made my way along the passage I began to wonder how long it had been since anyone had been in here. Turning to shine the piano light back where I had come from, my footprints were obvious in the dust on the floor and there were no signs of anyone else's footprints. *Safe,* I thought. Then I turned one of my feet over to look at the bottom. The sock that used to be white was now a very dark brown. I wondered what Mom would say about it.

I continued a few feet farther and then found a little notch in the wall that looked like the one that led to the opening between the bookcases in the library. There was a wooden handle similar to the one at the library, so I pulled it toward me. It opened, but I had no idea where I was. There appeared to be several various fabrics hanging in front of the opening.

Carefully, not sure what I would find or what would be waiting for me, I reached out to the fabric and quickly realized that this was all clothing hanging on a rod. I was in the back of a closet! Looking more closely, I realized that the clothing looked like my mom's and dad's. I figured I must be in their bedroom. As I thought about the layout of the house, I realized that the upper level of the library was probably right next to their bedroom on the second floor.

I wanted to see if anyone was there, but I was afraid of running into the wrong people, so I quickly switched off the piano lamp. Everything was pitch-black for a moment, as I waited for my eyes to adjust to the total lack of light. Slowly, I moved out of the opening and completely into the closet, allowing the hinged, narrow doorway to close gently behind me. Before I went any further, I wanted to make sure I knew how to get back out the way I had come, so I felt along the back wall in the corner of the closet until I was confident in the panel that pushed inward just like the opening between the bookcases in the library. Assured of my exit, I then slowly pushed one of the closet doors open from the inside.

Everything was still dark. Almost not daring to risk it, I switched on the lamp in my hand, making sure I was ready to dive back into the closet and through the secret opening if I needed to. But the room was empty. Everything seemed to be in perfect order. The dresser drawers were closed, Mom's and Dad's scriptures and other things left on the nightstands were arranged neatly. The bed looked like it had been made very carefully—didn't my parents understand what it meant to be on vacation?

Thinking again about the layout of the house, I wondered if the secret passage would also lead to the closet in the bedroom shared by me, Jeff, and Danny. I made my way back through the closet and into the passageway. I continued in the same direction as before until I came to an opening that looked just like the one that led to Mom's and Dad's bedroom, complete with a handle. Pulling the handle toward me, I was not surprised to find myself in the back corner of our closet. I didn't bother to switch off the lamp this time. One of the closet doors was open and I could see out into the room, but I had quite a bit more trouble making my way through because of all the disorganized junk on the floor. There were shoes, clothes, and toys strewn about. I was sort of amazed by the mess we had created in just a couple of days.

I glanced around just to be sure no one was there and that nothing seemed out of place, then I quickly grabbed a different pair of shoes and slipped them on. I was suddenly glad that Dad had insisted that bringing only a single pair was not a great idea. Scrounging through the closet in the dim light, I quickly found

Jeff's second pair of shoes, as well as a pair of jeans, and an extra shirt. I thought for a moment before grabbing a blanket from one of the unmade beds and hurried back into the secret passageway.

Within just a few seconds I found myself back at the opening that led into the library. I suddenly felt shaky again as I hesitantly knocked two times on the secret door and put my ear next to it to listen. Very deliberately I heard two knocks coming from somewhere in the room. Where was the third? Didn't Jeff say he would respond with three knocks? I kept waiting. Maybe I had just missed one of them. Maybe I should knock again. Just as I was about to, I decided that was a pretty bad idea. Maybe TB was in there; maybe he was the one who had responded with two knocks, matching mine. Maybe Jeff was trapped or in trouble. I wondered if I would be able to hear the ladder rolling on the bar when Jeff moved it into position for me. Jeff had said that if he didn't respond then I should wait a couple of minutes before knocking again. But—he had responded, hadn't he? Just not the way I expected. And doesn't the scripture talk about "two or three witnesses?" I was expecting three, but I only got two—shouldn't I just be happy with that? It wasn't easy, but I decided to wait. I put the lamp down on the floor and switched it off.

As I stood there with the bundle I had brought from our room, I tried to be patient. The thought suddenly came to me that if Chelsea were here she would probably think of an Article of Faith that fit the situation. Was there something about being patient in the thirteenth? I began to recite it in my head: *We believe in being honest, true, chaste, benevolent, virtuous, and in doing good to all men; indeed, we may say that we follow the admonition of Paul.* Nothing about patience. I continued: *We believe all things, we hope all things, we have endured many things, and hope to be able to endure all things.* Wait—maybe there was. Doesn't *enduring* mean to keep doing the right things and to be patient until it is over? I thought Chelsea would be pleased. How did it end? *If there is anything virtuous, lovely, or of good report or praiseworthy, we seek after these things.* I figured the most praiseworthy thing to be seeking after at this point was a way to escape—there was that word again. I decided "escape" must be the word of the week.

I didn't know if two minutes had passed, but I was tired of "enduring." I had just raised my hand to knock on the door again when I heard a knock coming from inside the library. I quickly put my ear against the back of the door and listened. Two more knocks—that made three. Slowly, I pulled the door open and peered down into the room.

"The camera started moving in the middle of my knocking," Jeff said as he moved toward the ladder. "I had to wait until it stopped."

Looking at the camera, I saw that it was now pointed at the chair where Jeff had been.

"It's a good thing you waited for the third knock," said Jeff.

"It's a good thing we have the thirteenth Article of Faith," I said.

"Huh?" said Jeff. The ladder was almost where I could reach it now. I didn't bother to explain my comment.

"What's all that for?" asked Jeff. "Where did you get it? Where does that passageway go?"

"There are openings in the backs of the bedroom closets," I explained as I climbed down the ladder, holding on with one hand. "I brought this stuff so we could make it look like you decided to lie down under the piano, too."

"Oh!" said Jeff, a little astonished. "Cool. So where else does it lead? Can we get out through the bedrooms? Or are they locked, too?"

"I don't know," I said. "I just grabbed this stuff and got back as quick as I could."

Jeff switched shoes while I stuffed the blanket inside the extra jeans and shirt I had brought. We put everything partway under the piano, hoping it looked convincing through the video camera. We decided to adjust my shoes as well, so it would look like I was moving around once in a while. Then we climbed up the ladder and into the secret passage. I went in first, picked up the lamp and switched it on.

"What about the ladder?" Jeff asked, still holding the door open.

"I'm not planning to come back," I said. "How about we just push it back in the direction it came from and hope it gets close."

Jeff hesitated, but then agreed. He gave it a shove and I heard it rolling along the bar for a few seconds.

"It didn't go far enough," said Jeff.

"It'll have to do," I said.

Inside the passageway, Jeff said, "This is so cool."

"Yeah," I said. "Let's get out of here."

We made our way back into our own bedroom through the back of the closet. Switching off the lamp again, we carefully tried the door. It was unlocked. The hallway seemed empty, so we crept out of the room and pulled the door closed behind us. Suddenly, I froze.

"Wait," I hissed. "What about the video camera in the hall?"

I backed slowly right against the door. I expected Jeff to do the same, but he was staring intently out the window across the hall. Normally we could see the mountain behind Omni's house through this window, but it was dark outside now.

"There's a helicopter," Jeff whispered.

Sure enough, I saw the lights of a helicopter dropping slowly down in the area of the Old Mission.

"Is it the police one again?" I asked quietly.

"It looks smaller," said Jeff.

"Hey," I said. "Who's that?"

Through the window we could see someone moving quickly along the walkway leading from the back patio to the old mission.

"It looks like TB," said Jeff. We continued to stare out the window for a moment before Jeff suggested, "We better get out of the hall before someone sees us."

We crept back into the bedroom, closed the door quietly behind us, and switched on the piano lamp again.

"We've got to go see who is in the helicopter and what they're all doing," I said.

"What about everyone else?" Jeff asked. "Don't you think we should try to find them first?"

"I want to know what's going on," I said.

"How do you propose that we get out there?" Jeff asked. "At least in the house we can stay hidden in the secret passageways."

"I don't know," I said. I paused, my eyes darting forth and back as I tried to figure out the best thing to do. "I just want to know what they're up to."

CHAPTER 16

What's Mined Is Mine

"Right now," said Jeff sternly, "it's more important to find Mom and Dad and everybody else than to find out what that helicopter is doing here and what TB is up to."

"But TB is outside now," I said, "so he won't be watching the video monitors."

"We don't know who else he's working with," said Jeff. "If we try to go outside and someone sees us—or if someone else is watching the monitors—we'll get locked up again and then we're not going to be able to figure out anything. And this time you can bet that TB won't just leave us in a room; he'll probably tie us up or something."

I knew he was right, of course, but I just couldn't bring myself to admit it.

"Let's go back in the secret passage," suggested Jeff, "and see what other rooms it leads to. Maybe we'll find everybody else and then we'll have a much better chance."

"OK," I reluctantly agreed, but I found myself imagining all the havoc it would create if six other people that TB thought were secure somewhere, were suddenly free just like we were. I decided we would just have to burn that bridge when we got to it.

"Do you want to have another prayer?" I suggested. "This time we got out of a mess without even asking for help—but we still should probably say 'thanks.'"

"We're not totally out of trouble yet, either," Jeff pointed out.

"Right," I agreed.

It was my turn to say the prayer. When I prayed, I not only thanked Heavenly Father for the help we had just received and asked for guidance as to what to do next, but I also asked that we could agree on the best way to get out of this whole situation. I especially asked for protection for the rest of the family, since we had no idea where they were. I suddenly felt a lot of peace when I prayed for them. I didn't worry anymore.

After the prayer, we made our way back through the closet and into the secret passage. Just a few feet down from the entrance into our bedroom closet was an entrance on the opposite wall.

"Did you know there were entrances on both sides of this passageway?" asked Jeff.

"I didn't," I confessed. "I don't know why."

"Where do think this one leads?" asked Jeff.

"Uh," was all I managed to get out. We both stared at the small entrance for a moment without saying anything.

"I just figured something out!" said Jeff.

"What?" I asked.

"This is the reason that this house is laid out so weird," said Jeff. "I mean with the halls at the front and the back of the house."

"What do you mean?" I asked.

"All the rooms off of the front hall look like they back onto all of the rooms off of the back hall," Jeff explained, "but they really don't. This secret passage goes in between!"

"You're right!" I said.

"So this one," Jeff continued, pointing at the entrance, "must lead into a room that you get to from the front hall."

Thinking about the layout of the upper level, I realized that I had never been in the front hall, so I had no idea what rooms were over there. I didn't think Jeff had been in that hall either, since we were pretty much side by side all the time.

"Any idea what this room is?" I asked.

"Nope," Jeff admitted.

"Turn off the light and let's find out," I suggested.

Jeff switched off the light and slowly pulled the doorway open. It looked like another closet—only this one was empty. It didn't take long to find out that it was indeed another bedroom closet, just like the others. We didn't stay there long.

Continuing in the same direction down the passageway we found an entrance into the back corner of the closet in the girls' bedroom. No one was in there, so we returned through the back of the closet. The passageway continued on a little further, but the girls' room was the last one on that side. We did find another empty bedroom on the opposite side. We turned around and headed back toward the library where we had first come into the passageway; it was time to search in the other direction.

"I sure hope this doesn't just go between the bedrooms and the library," said Jeff. "Otherwise, the only one who would benefit from it would be Meg, because she could secretly get new books to read without anyone else knowing it."

He was trying to be funny, but I didn't feel like laughing. "Yeah," I agreed. But secretly I was thinking that if the passage didn't go anywhere else, then I could probably talk Jeff into going out into the hallway and taking a chance with the video cameras. And the sooner we decided to do that, the better, because we knew that TB was outside right now. Who knew how long he would *stay* out there?

"Unless, of course," Jeff continued, "the ladder was out of position, but she tried to reach something anyway and so we all heard the huge thud when she ended up flat on the floor below."

I imagined Meg hanging onto the bookshelf with her feet dangling below as she still tried to reach the book she wanted. She definitely would place getting a book above her own safety.

We continued past the opening into the library. I was sorely tempted to poke my head in there and see if the video camera had moved, just to make sure everything still felt safe. But Jeff was in the lead now with the lamp and so I needed to keep up with him. I figured it was probably best not to take the chance.

At the other end of the passage, on the other side of the library, we found entrances into the back of five more bedroom closets, two on the same side as the library and three on the other. We had no idea that all these bedrooms existed. Again, there was no sign of our family or anyone else. The rooms each looked perfectly straight and clean, ready for any overnight guest who just might happen to show up. Not far past the last unused bedroom, the passageway became a stairway leading steeply downward.

"Looks like we may be able to get to the ground level," whispered Jeff. So much for my hope of getting out before TB returned.

We crept down the stairway and found ourselves in a long, narrow passage that looked pretty much identical to the one upstairs. This passage also had openings all along both sides.

"We need to be really careful with these," Jeff said.

"Why?" I asked, not sure what he was getting at. "Do you think TB might be in one of these rooms?"

"No," Jeff explained. "We were safe upstairs, because none of those rooms had video cameras—they were bedrooms."

"Oh," I said.

"But as far as I can remember," Jeff continued, "every other room in this place has a camera in it."

"You're right," I said slowly, thinking of each room. "I think you're right."

"We need to turn the lamp off and open each door really slow," Jeff said.

"And only open it a crack," I added.

"Right," Jeff agreed.

We tried to be as careful as we could. We found entrances into other rooms that we knew about, including the game rooms and

Anthony's "translating room" or whatever Omni had called it. These rooms didn't have closets, but the walls were covered with solid wood panels. Most of the panels were pretty wide, but they were separated by narrow ones, similar to those that separated the bookcases in the library. The secret entrances were behind one of the narrow wood planks in the back corner of each of those rooms.

We were thinking we might find another entrance into the library on the main floor, but we didn't.

"I guess the ladder is the only way to get out," I said after we had gone forth and back a couple of times between the rooms that we knew were on either side of it.

"Yeah," agreed Jeff.

We also found a couple of rooms that we had never been into before, but we didn't dare go inside. These were very dark, so we just called softly into the room to see if maybe this was where TB had locked up everyone else. There were a couple of rooms that we couldn't get into at all, though. There were stacks of boxes or other things in the way that didn't show any signs of budging when we tried to move them. Still, we tried calling softly to see if anyone might respond. No one did.

"Now what?" I asked after we had explored every entrance there was.

"I guess we only have access to half of the house," Jeff said.

"Yeah," I agreed. "The kitchen and dining room and everything else are on the other side."

"Yeah," Jeff said.

"So we have to go out in the hallway to get over there," I said.

"Do you think there's a secret passage between those rooms, too?" asked Jeff.

"I don't know," I admitted. "Maybe." Then I asked, "Do you think TB is back in the house by now?"

"He's had plenty of time to get out to where the helicopter was and back," Jeff said.

"Yup," I agreed. I wanted to point out that that would not have been the case if we had gone out when I first suggested it, but I didn't say anything.

We stood in silence for a few moments, trying to decide what to do next.

"Hey, Bran," Jeff said. Why he used my name, I don't know—I was standing right next to him and it's not like there was anyone else around.

"What?"

"Where are the monitors for the video cameras?" Jeff asked.

The question surprised me as I realized that I had no clue.

"I don't know," I confessed. "I never thought about it. Any ideas?"

"Not really," Jeff said. "But if we can get to them, then it might be a fast way to find out where everyone else is."

"You're right," I said, thinking of the possibilities. "We could also see where TB is or anyone else that is helping him."

It sounded like a great idea, but since we had no idea what to do with it, it didn't really help us much at the moment.

"It's time to go out and see what's going on," I said flatly.

Jeff thought for a moment and then said, "OK." He looked resigned to the idea. I was relieved that he had finally agreed.

"So which room do you want to go through?" I asked.

"The one that's closest to the back patio," Jeff suggested, "so we are in the hall for the shortest amount of time possible."

"Good idea," I said. I don't think I ever would have thought of anything like that. Jeff was a thinker, that's for sure.

"That means Anthony's translation room," Jeff said.

"Let's go," I immediately agreed, and started moving down the passage toward the room.

Before Jeff moved, he said, "We need to be really careful, Brandon."

"I know," I said.

"There's a video camera in that room," Jeff reminded me, "and the lights come on automatically because of the motion detector, remember."

That comment made me stop and think. "Oh, yeah," I said. "But wait—didn't Omni say that Anthony turned off the motion detector lights when he was working in there?"

"Did he?" asked Jeff, hopeful at the thought. "I forgot that. But it seems like the light came on automatically that one time that Omni took us in there."

"Maybe Irene leaves the motion detector on when she cleans it," I suggested. "So we might be in luck if Anthony was the last one in there. Let's go see."

"OK," Jeff agreed.

We made our way down to the secret entrance into the translating room. Jeff switched off the lamp, set it on the floor of the passageway, and slowly pulled the door open. It was still dark inside, with just a sliver of light coming from underneath the double doors.

"Can you see the video camera?" I whispered.

"Not really," Jeff answered. "I'm going inside."

Slowly, Jeff stepped into the room and began to make his way along the side wall toward the double doors.

"The motion detector must be off," said Jeff, sounding a little relieved.

I had decided the same thing and was stepping into the room as he spoke. Just as I let the door close behind me, the room was suddenly ablaze with light. If someone was watching the video monitors, I was sure that we were suddenly the center of attention. Jeff stood frozen to the wall, but I quickly decided that this was a time for action. I immediately ran for the light switch and hit the button. Darkness filled the room once more. Jeff and I remained motionless as we thought about what had just happened.

Finally, I asked, "Do you think anyone was watching the monitor?"

"I don't know," Jeff whispered, "but the camera didn't move."

"Were you watching it?" I asked.

"The whole time you were running across the room," Jeff said.

"Maybe we're OK, then," I said quietly.

Neither of us said anything else for a moment, listening for any signs that we had been detected.

"Do you think the cameras have infrared," asked Jeff, "so they can see in the dark?"

I had never considered this before.

"That would stink, wouldn't it?" I said.

"Well," said Jeff, "I guess it sort of depends on whether you're the one sneaking around or the one watching."

"Good point," I agreed.

Slowly, in the dark, Jeff made his way along the walls until he was next to me. It was time to see what was in the hallway. I was happy to be in the lead now—Jeff was just a little too cautious for my taste. I opened the door just a crack and looked into the well-lit hall. I could detect no motion and no sound, so I began to open it even further. It turned out that this was a great place to be; I could not only see the hall just outside the translating room door, but I could also see the back patio through the windows and also the intersection with the hallway that led to the front of the cottage. I realized for the first time that this was really the center of all movement to and from any place. The dining room and kitchen were the first off of the back hall on the other side of the house. I continued to watch and listen for another few moments before speaking. I looked down both ends of the hall.

"I don't see anyone," I whispered.

"Should we try 9–1–1?" asked Jeff.

The thought had never occurred to me, and I wondered what made Jeff think of it now. Pulling my head back inside the room, I looked over to where Jeff was standing. Mounted on the wall near the double doors was a cordless phone! I didn't say anything, but immediately began to nod vigorously. Jeff was already picking up the phone before waiting for a response from me. He had to turn it so the light from the partially open door would shine on the buttons. He pushed several and then held it up to his ear. Even in the dark I could see the anticipation leave his face. He pulled the phone down where he could see the buttons again and pushed a couple more, then put it back up to his ear.

"It's dead," Jeff said with discouragement after a moment and returned it to the wall.

"Figures," I said. I stuck my head out again and made sure no one was around. Then I said, "Let's go!"

Without waiting for Jeff to say anything about being careful or going slowly—as I was sure he would—I took my first step into the hall, looking up at the video camera and hoping that I wasn't being watched. Jeff didn't say anything; I was surprised—maybe he was still thinking about the phone. I crept across the hall to get a better look at the back patio through the windows. I still could see no one. Soon Jeff was right next to me. We both turned and looked down the hall that led to the front of the house. Again, no one was there. It looked like all the halls were lit up. Just then we heard the sounds of a helicopter again. We both turned and saw the same small helicopter landing near the old mission. The cottage was far enough away from the excavation site that the sounds of the helicopter were not very loud. We continued to watch as it slowly dropped toward the ground. Suddenly Jeff and I both jumped as we heard the sound of a door closing somewhere toward the front of the house. We scrambled back toward the translating room as we heard footsteps coming from the same direction. It sounded like TB.

"Quick," said Jeff, "let's get back in the room."

"No," I hissed. "I want to see who it is first."

I stood at the corner where the two halls met, waiting to see who was coming from the front of the house. The loud footsteps definitely sounded like TB. It was easy to tell when he was walking on the hardwood floors and when he was on the long rugs, because the sound was much more muted. It was TB alright. He came around the corner from the hall at the front of the house. I probably should have followed Jeff to the translating room at this point, but I continued to watch him coming closer to my position. About halfway from the front hall to the back hall where I was, TB suddenly stopped, leaned down, and began working on something on the floor. It took me just a moment to figure out that he was straightening the tassels on the end of the rug. Irene was telling the truth!

As TB stood again and continued toward me I finally turned and tiptoed over to the doorway where Jeff was standing. We both went inside and pulled the door mostly closed. But I left it far enough open that I could see the intersection of the halls and glass doors that led to the back patio. TB walked past without even glancing in our direction and went out the back doors.

"Brandon," Jeff hissed, "what if he comes down this way to check on us in the library?"

"He already went outside," I said. "And he didn't even look in this direction."

"Well, then you're lucky," said Jeff, "since you had the door open."

"Yeah, I guess," I said. "But if he's watching us on the video monitor and thinks we're asleep on the floor, then he would have no reason to check on us, would he?"

Jeff just sighed. Then he said, "I wonder if that's what he was just doing: checking the video monitors. Do you think they're in one of the rooms at the front of the house?"

"I don't know," I said, "but I want to see what's going on with that helicopter."

Without another word I left the room and scampered toward the back doors that TB had just gone through. I was convinced that he was the only one around and we were perfectly safe as long as we knew where he was.

"Brandon!" hissed Jeff. He was soon right behind me at the back doors. "Now is the perfect time to search the house!"

"Now is the perfect time to see what's going on back there," I countered. "If people are locked in a room somewhere, then they will still be there when we get back. But if that helicopter is here to pick up TB, then we may never see him again. It would probably be a good idea if we saw who is flying that thing and who else is out there."

Again, I didn't wait for a response, but who could argue with such great logic? I should have been on the high school debate team. Anyway, I could see that TB was already on the walkway that led from the patio to the mission. I opened the door, glanced back at Jeff, and then took off after TB. I was hoping Jeff was smart enough to close the door, whether he chose to follow me or not.

Luckily, there was grass along either side of the walkway. There were lights on short poles stuck in the ground every few feet along the side. They were pointed toward the walk, lighting it quite well, but the grass behind the lights was almost completely black. I stayed behind the lights just in case TB decided to turn around.

As we moved toward the mission I noticed that I could no longer see or hear the helicopter that had been landing a couple of minutes earlier. About halfway to the mission I began to notice a very faint whirring sound. I figured it was the helicopter blades still spinning, but not very fast. Because I was thinking about the sound and watching TB, I didn't notice someone coming toward him from the other direction until I heard him yell, "Hey! What are you doing?!"

It made me jump. I was suddenly very glad that I had stayed out of the light. TB stopped in his tracks and just waited for the other person to approach him. It was Anthony. I guess the police let him go—for now at least. If at all possible, I wanted to hear what was going on. So I moved behind some tall bushes along the edge of the grass and inched closer and closer to where TB was stopped. I was only a few feet away when Anthony reached him.

"You are supposed to have some more bags ready for us to load up!" yelled Anthony.

"Bags are being ready," said TB defiantly.

"Where are they?" asked Anthony, surprised.

"At bottom of ladder," said TB, as if he resented being questioned.

"I *told* you," said Anthony, "not to leave the bags alone. I don't want to take the chance of anyone else finding them! You are to bring them from the mine and stay with them until they are loaded onto the helicopter."

"You are being gone 45 minutes each flight," said TB, still annoyed. "It only takes half so long to bring bags. I waiting not with bags for so long. Also must I be checking prisoners!"

"Why?" asked Anthony. "Didn't you lock them up well enough?" Without waiting for a reply, he said, "Then check them first. You can check on them when we first leave. But then get down there and bring the bags for the next trip—just don't leave them alone anymore."

"You being boss," said TB.

"That's right," said Anthony. "I'm the boss. And you're getting well paid for this. You won't ever have to work again when we're done here."

"I being good butler," said TB. "Having joy in work. Having pride in work."

"Yeah, you're the greatest," said Anthony. "Whatever. Let's get back down there and load up the helicopter."

I was so intent on the conversation between Anthony and TB that I didn't notice Jeff right behind me. I jumped big time when I turned slowly, thinking about what I had just heard, and realized he was there.

"Whoa!" I breathed. I took a couple of deep breaths, trying to recover, and then asked, "How much of that did you hear?"

"All of it," whispered Jeff. "I was right behind you the whole time."

"Good," I said. "Makes you glad we weren't searching the house somewhere, doesn't it?"

"I guess," said Jeff. "So let's go search now—since we know what they're up to."

"No way," I said. "I want to see those bags. I want to know what's in them and where they're getting them from."

"What?" said Jeff. "Why?"

"They are robbing Mr. Omni!" I said. "They're thieves!"

"How do you know Omni isn't in on it?" Jeff asked.

"Right!" I said. "What reason could he possibly have for locking us all up and sneaking stuff off of his own property in the middle of the night?"

"Maybe it's not really his property," Jeff said. "Maybe the owners came back early when they heard about the mudslide."

I just stared at him. Sometimes Jeff gets the craziest ideas.

"I'm going," I said.

With that, I spun on my heels, moved back out onto the grass behind the lights, and followed TB and Anthony toward the mission. As they made their way down the steps into the huge pit, I saw that the helicopter was parked down there. The low whirring sound was indeed coming from the slow spinning blades. The sound was quite a bit louder now that we were close.

Anthony motioned for the pilot to join them. A man that I didn't recognize got out of the helicopter and followed TB and Anthony through the door into the priest's room where Jeff and I had gone the night before. The lights were on inside. I quickly made my way down the steps. I glanced back and saw that Jeff was right behind me. I looked closely inside the helicopter to make sure no one else was in there, then I made my way over to the door lead-ing into the priest's room.

I pulled the door partway open just to see what was going on. Anthony was standing just a couple of feet away with his back to the door. He was shining a flashlight down into the open shaft that led to the mine.

"Hurry up," called Anthony. "We have a bunch more trips to make tonight."

Then I saw a large, dirty bag move out of the opening and drop on the floor near Anthony's feet. It looked like it was made of burlap and was very old. I could only see the top of the head of the man who had brought it up out of the hole. His hair was much lighter than TB's. I figured it must be the pilot. He was breathing heavily.

After a moment he said, "We wouldn't need to make so many trips . . ." He paused, gasping for air. "If you didn't ride with me every time." He paused again. "Without your weight in the chop-per, I could carry another two or three bags. It's getting pretty tedious taking only four bags at a time."

"I told you," said Anthony firmly. "I'm not letting any of that silver ore out of my sight. Not that I don't trust you—it's just the way I am."

"Right," said the pilot and he disappeared again.

Anthony continued to stand over the hole and make comments about moving faster. About every thirty seconds or so another bag appeared until four bags had been placed on the floor around him.

"Let's get them loaded up," Anthony said next. "Hurry. We're losing time."

Realizing that they were about to come right out to where we were, I quickly shut the door and looked around for a place to hide. Luckily, the huge mounds of dirt that had been left behind after our rescue seemed perfect. Without even needing to say what to do next, Jeff and I both scrambled around behind one of the mounds, where we had a good view of both the door and the helicopter but seemed to be well out of sight and away from any light.

We watched as TB and the pilot carried one bag at a time from the priest's room to the helicopter and loaded them behind the front seats. Anthony just watched as they did all the work.

"What a wimp," I whispered. Jeff didn't respond.

After the fourth bag was loaded, the pilot climbed inside the cockpit. Anthony yelled at TB, "We'll be back in forty-five minutes! You be ready with the bags! And *don't* leave them alone!"

TB nodded in understanding, but didn't say anything. We all watched as the helicopter rose slowly into the night sky.

CHAPTER 17

Brought into Captivity

The wind died down quickly after the helicopter had risen and was moving away. I had expected there to be more dust flying around, but it actually wasn't nearly as bad as I thought it would be. TB first looked over at the door to the priest's room as if he was trying to decide something, but then turned and headed up the steps toward the house.

"Let's go see where they're getting those bags from," I suggested. "Did you hear him say they were full of silver ore?"

"No way," said Jeff flatly.

"Yeah, he totally said that," I nodded.

"I heard him," said Jeff. "I mean 'no way' about going into the mine. We're going back to the house to find everyone else."

"What, *now?*" I asked, incredulously. "We should do that after TB's come back down here again—not when he's up there!"

Jeff shook his head forth and back. "No way," he said again. "As soon as TB heads down in the mine, then you'll want to follow him to see where he's going, won't you?"

"Probably," I admitted.

"You didn't want to search the house when it was empty," Jeff said, "and now you don't want to search it while he's there. You're just a lot more interested in what's in the mine than in finding out what happened to everyone else."

"Well, what if they're trapped in the mine?" I asked. "Now

would be the perfect time to . . ." I stopped mid-sentence. From the look on Jeff's face I knew there was no point in finishing my thought.

"You wanted to see what was going on down here," said Jeff. "Now we know. And we know that they will be making trips all night long, so there's no hurry. In *fact*, if we can find everyone else, then we'll probably be able to get some help stopping these guys and finding out everything about what they're up to."

"OK, fine," I agreed finally.

"Besides that," Jeff continued to argue, "didn't you hear TB say that he was going to check on the prisoners? This will be our best chance to find out where everyone else is!"

"What if we're the only prisoners?" I asked.

Jeff looked stunned by the thought. "Then where's everyone else?" he finally asked. "And don't say they're in the mine. And— and if we really are the only ones, then this would be the best way to find out, wouldn't it?"

I certainly had to agree with that. Figuring that TB now had a big enough head start, we headed up the stepping stones to the top of the hill. We could see that he was about halfway to the cottage. Staying on the narrow strip of grass behind the walkway lights, we ran quickly after him to see where he was going.

TB went across the patio and through the glass doors. We ran as fast as we could at this point, continuing to watch him as he made his way down the hall toward the front of the house. We watched through the patio doors until we saw which way he turned when he reached the front hall. Then, as quickly as possible, we went inside, pulled the doors closed behind us, and charged down the hall after him. Remembering how much quieter the rugs were than the bare wood, I tried to be extra quiet whenever I had to take a step or two where there was no rug.

We got to the corner where the halls met just in time to see the door at the very end of the front hall being pulled shut. It closed with a loud snap. I took off running and could hear Jeff right behind me. When we got to the door that TB went into we stopped short and listened. All I could hear was Jeff's loud breathing right at my shoulder.

"Stop breathing in my ear," I said as quietly as possible.

Jeff caught his breath and moved back a step. But then all I could hear was my own breathing. I decided to take a chance: I slowly opened the door just wide enough to squeeze my head through the opening. There was a faint glow coming from inside. I stuck my head further in and found a small room with a desk and some file cabinets. The glow was coming from an open door in the room leading to another room. I crept inside and looked between the edge of the open door and the door jamb. I could see a bank of glowing TV screens. We had found the video monitors! This was the surveillance room for the whole security system.

I pulled Jeff over close and pointed through the opening so that he could see what I was seeing. I kneeled down on the floor so that he would be able to see over the top of me.

There were four screens across the bottom row that appeared to be showing various rooms or halls in the cottage. I noticed that each screen seemed to have a different number in the upper right-hand corner. Above the four on the bottom row was one screen that was much larger than the others. TB was standing in front of the monitors with his hand on some buttons next to the large screen. I immediately recognized the library on the large, top monitor. The piano was clearly visible in the middle of the room. I could see the fake legs and feet that we had set up underneath. I was surprised to see that TB not only had the ability to move the camera from side to side, but he also made it zoom in and out. He zoomed in on each of the pairs of shoes we had left in there, apparently trying to get a better look. When he zoomed out I could see where we had left the ladder.

TB seemed satisfied with what he saw in the library and began repeatedly pushing a button that seemed to cause the display on the large monitor to cycle through various cameras. When he stopped pushing the button I saw a room full of people. Jeff had been right all along! What a genius. Everyone was there. Mr. Omni was easy to pick out because of his completely bald head. But I could also see Mom, Dad, Meg, Chels, and Danny. It looked like Irene was there, and Omni's limo driver, too. As far as I could tell, they were all on the floor—either sitting or lying on pillows. But I had absolutely no idea what room they were in. I couldn't see any furniture. I was sure I had never seen that room before.

I was so busy trying to figure out where the room was that I didn't notice when TB was apparently finished and started toward us. Jeff brought me back to reality by grabbing my shoulder and pulling me backward. He almost knocked me over. I immediately realized that we were about to be in serious trouble. I didn't see any way that we could get back out in the hall and out of sight before TB saw us.

But Jeff was way ahead of me. He had left the door into the hall wide open. I was sure that I had only barely opened it and was sort of assuming he would pull it closed behind him. Jeff was through the door and into the hall almost before I realized what was going on. I sprinted after him and quickly pulled the door closed behind me. I was pretty sure that I had it mostly closed well before TB would have reached the inside door.

Jeff stood watching me, but as soon as the door was shut we both instantly took off in a dead run, again trying to make our footsteps as quiet as possible on the bare floor in between the rugs. We didn't slow down after turning the corner but went to the back of the cottage and hid around the corner of the back hall. At least I thought we were both hiding. As I stood peeking around the corner waiting for TB to appear, I realized that I was by myself. Jeff was down the hall opening the door into the translating room.

"Where are you going?" I hissed.

"Let's go through the secret passage!" Jeff whispered, his hand still on the doorknob.

I stopped short and asked, "Were we able to get into that room?"

"I think so," said Jeff. "Let's go."

"Wait," I said, turning back to look down the hall we had just come from. "I want to see where TB is going next."

"We're *not* following him back outside," said Jeff. "I want to get back to those monitors and figure out where that room is. Did you recognize it?"

"No," I whispered, still watching down the hall.

TB turned the corner and continued walking directly toward us. There were no doors in this hall, so I knew he would be coming to the back. I moved over to the doorway where Jeff still held the doorknob.

"Do you think we can figure out where that room is?" I asked.

"I don't know," admitted Jeff. "But maybe if we move the camera around we'll be able to see something we recognize."

"OK," I whispered. "I just want to see where TB is going next."

"*Bran!*" Jeff hissed.

"If he goes out back, then we won't follow, OK?" I said.

"That's right," said Jeff, opening the door.

We moved inside and pulled the door mostly closed. TB's footsteps were getting closer and closer. He didn't go out the glass doors, but instead turned the corner and headed away from us. I pushed the door open far enough that I could see him. He passed the first door leading to the dining room. As far as I could tell, he went in through the second door, which was the kitchen. I really wanted to keep after him, but I had promised Jeff. I stepped back into the translating room and pulled the door closed.

"He went in the kitchen," I said.

Jeff didn't respond, but bolted for the secret opening. I was right behind him. Jeff picked up the lamp and switched it on. We moved quickly through the passage to the last entrance into the front part of the house. Just like that, we were back in the small room with the desk and filing cabinet that led to the room with the TV monitors. Jeff was moving so fast that I was still closing the secret entrance when he reached up to open the door.

"No!" Jeff moaned.

"What?" I whispered.

"It's locked!" Jeff said.

"No way," I said. "What can we do?"

The single door opened inward, so we had no chance of getting at the hinges and opening the door that way. We could see the dim glow coming from under the door.

"Do you think there's a key in here somewhere?" Jeff asked.

We switched on the light and looked around but didn't see anything. The desk drawers and the filing cabinet drawers were all locked.

"I'll bet TB has the key with him," I sighed.

"Great," said Jeff.

I thought for a minute and then said, "He went into the kitchen, though. Maybe he's getting something to eat and he'll put his keys down somewhere."

"How likely do you think *that* is?" asked Jeff.

"Not very," I admitted. "But it's worth a try."

"OK," Jeff agreed after a minute. He didn't sound too hopeful—and I admit I felt the same way. As we were making our way back through the secret passage, Jeff said, "When TB goes back out to the mission, we're not following him. We're going to search the house to see if we can find that room."

"OK," I agreed.

I led the way out of the translating room. Now that we knew where the monitors were and that TB wasn't there, we felt a lot more comfortable moving into the hallway. Still, I looked out the back and down the halls to make sure TB was nowhere in sight. We made our way quickly and quietly toward the door into the kitchen.

"Wait," whispered Jeff. Pointing to the dining room door he said, "Let's go through here."

I nodded in agreement, but didn't say anything. I realized that we were far less likely to be surprised by him if we went through the dining room to get to the kitchen. Now Jeff was in the lead. He opened the dining room door slowly. It was dark at first, but the motion detector light quickly switched on. Jeff immediately turned it off. We made our way to the other side of the room and saw light coming from around the swinging doors that connected the dining room to the kitchen.

Jeff pushed one of the doors ever so slowly inward. When the opening was big enough, he carefully put his head through it. He looked around for a few seconds and then pulled back, letting the door close.

"Guess what he's doing," Jeff whispered.

I had no idea. "Hoarding cantaloupe?" I asked.

Jeff ignored me and said, "He's taking a nap."

At first I was dismayed, because I was hoping for something else. But then I quickly realized that this could be *way* better.

"Are his keys in his hand?" I asked with excitement.

"I don't know," said Jeff warily. "What are you thinking?"

"We can get them!" I whispered loudly.

"No way!" said Jeff. "You want to grab them and make a run for it? Or what?"

"No!" I said, still excited by the possibilities. "We can catch them when they fall from his hand!"

Jeff thought about this for a minute and then said, "He'll still wake up."

"Not if we catch them in something quiet," I said. "It's the sound of them hitting the floor that wakes him, remember?"

"Something quiet like what?" asked Jeff.

"Anything!" I said. "But first we should see if he's holding them. Otherwise this discussion is pointless."

Jeff didn't say anything or even move for a minute, but then he slowly opened the door and stuck his head back inside. He didn't move for a moment, but then went the rest of the way into the kitchen, letting the door swing closed behind him. I opened the door to see what he was up to, but didn't follow him inside. He made his way along the large, stainless steel table down the middle of the room and snuck closer and closer to where TB was napping in his chair. Suddenly Jeff turned around and came quickly back to the dining room.

"Is he holding them?" I asked.

"Yeah," Jeff said as I closed the door. "They're in his hand."

"Yes-s-s," I hissed.

"What are you going to do?" asked Jeff.

"It's time for a 'MacGyver move,'" I smiled, but Jeff couldn't see it in the dark.

"A what?" asked Jeff.

"That's what Katie calls it when you do something really tricky on the spur of the moment," I explained. "A MacGyver move."

"Who's Katie?" asked Jeff.

"That's not the point," I grunted. "We need to move fast. We need something we can catch those keys in that won't make any noise when they fall."

"Like what?" said Jeff.

"We need a basket or something," I said. "I'm turning on the light," I warned him, switching it on almost as soon as I said it.

There was a bowl of fruit on the dining room table. Jeff pointed at it and asked, "Like that?"

"Yeah," I said, "but we need something else in it that will keep the keys from rattling." Then I got an idea.

"What?" asked Jeff.

230

"I'll go get it," I said. "You take most of the fruit out of there and just leave a layer in the bottom. I'll be right back."

"Hurry," said Jeff. "He could drop those keys at any second."

Without answering, I headed out into the hall and took off in a dead run. I ran upstairs and headed for the girls' bedroom and ran into their bathroom. It didn't take long to find what I was looking for. In one of the drawers was a huge plastic bag full of cotton balls.

"I knew it!" I said to myself.

Meg and Chels loved nail polish. It seemed like they changed colors almost every day; so they always had a big supply of cotton balls nearby. Grabbing the bag, I ran back downstairs as quickly as I could, taking the steps two at a time. I made a much louder thump than I meant to when I pushed the dining room door open. Jeff looked up in surprise.

I was happy to see that he had the fruit bowl ready with just a few small tangerines in the bottom. I tore the plastic bag in half and dumped the cotton balls over the top of the fruit. The bowl was almost full.

"That should do it," I said.

"Do you think it will work?" asked Jeff.

"It better," I said, "because we don't have time to test it!"

Grabbing the bowl, I went quickly to the swinging kitchen doors and semi-slowly pushed them open. As soon as I saw that TB was in his chair, I rushed inside and as quickly and quietly as I could, placed the bowl of cotton balls directly under his fist with the keys in it. I got real nervous when I saw how relaxed his hand was, realizing that he could drop the keys at any second. I retreated quickly back toward the dining room, but stayed where I could see his hand.

"What are you doing?" Jeff hissed. "Get in here! What if it doesn't work? He'll see you!"

"If it doesn't work," I said without taking my eyes from TB's fist, "then we're in trouble anyway, because he'll see that bowl and know that someone's up to something." I paused. "But if it *does* work, then we won't know it without looking, will we? I think it's going to work great, so I want to know as soon as we can get the keys."

Jeff grunted slightly at my explanation, but didn't say anything else. I waited and watched for about two minutes before I saw the keys fall from TB's hand. I felt myself jump as they fell, anticipating the rattle—but it never came. TB seemed to jump a little, too, but then he remained motionless in the chair. I could hardly believe it! Then I felt my heart begin to race as I realized that I now needed to retrieve the bowl without getting caught.

More slowly than I had moved in my entire life, I began inching my way toward TB and the fruit bowl. I couldn't believe how loud my heart suddenly sounded in my ears. I actually came to a complete stop two different times in an effort to get myself to relax before continuing. Finally I was close enough to reach the bowl. I somehow had the feeling that as soon as I touched the bowl, TB would suddenly reach out and grab my arm. He was a big guy, and I knew I would be lucky to get away if he was indeed awake. I put my hand closer and closer to the bowl, ready to pull it away and run for my life if I had to. I even jerked it away once in anticipation. Then I finally just reached out and lifted the bowl about an inch off of the floor. Nothing happened. As quickly as I dared, I pulled it toward me and then speed walked back to the door where Jeff stood watching the whole thing.

Once inside the dining room, I reached through the cotton balls and pulled out TB's keys.

"Let's go," I said with a huge smile.

"Let's put all this back first," said Jeff, taking the bowl from me.

He dumped everything out on the carpet and then quickly began stuffing the cotton balls back in the plastic bag. Returning the bowl to the table, we loaded it up with the fruit that he had taken out earlier.

"Now let's go," I said, grabbing the bag of cotton balls.

We switched off the light in the dining room as we left and made our way quickly through the translation room and into the secret passage. I dropped the cotton balls and picked up the lamp, switching it on again. Jeff started to pick up the bag.

"I thought we could leave those here for now," I said.

"Yeah," Jeff agreed.

I handed Jeff the keys. We moved back through the passage and into the small office. TB's key ring had at least a dozen keys on it, so it took a minute or so to find the right one. I was pleased to find that TB had left the top monitor on the room where our family and Mr. Omni were stuck. Jeff immediately began pushing the buttons that TB had used to move the camera around and zoom in and out.

"I still can't tell what room this is," said Jeff. "Can you?"

"No," I said, shaking my head. "But maybe this will work."

I had seen a button with the word "microphone" next to it. I pushed the button and said, "Hello? Can you hear me?"

The response was immediate. Almost everyone on the screen looked up and around. It looked like they were saying something, but we couldn't hear anything.

"Take your finger off the button to listen," said Jeff.

"Oh," I said, releasing the button.

All the sudden we could hear several people speaking at once.

"Who's there?" said Omni.

"Brandon, is that you?" Mom was asking.

"Hello?" Dad was calling. "Hello?"

I pushed the button again and said, "This is Brandon. Jeff's here, too."

Releasing the button I heard Mom say, "Are you two alright?"

I was getting the hang of it now and began to push and release the button at the right times.

"We're fine," I said. "But where are you guys? We want to get you out."

233

"I'm afraid you won't be able to do that on your own," Mr. Omni said.

"Why not?" I asked.

"We're locked in a vault," Dad said.

"No way," Jeff and I both said at the same time. Then I asked, "Where is it?"

"I think it's under the garage," said Omni. I was surprised that he seemed unsure about it. "If you go through the kitchen you will find a pantry," Omni explained. "The door at the end of the pantry opens up to stairs that lead down to a small vault with a combination lock."

I asked, "So can we open it if you tell us the combination?"

"I don't know the combination," said Omni. "I bought the property without even realizing the vault existed. I knew nothing about it until TB brought us down here. I thought the door at the end of the pantry just led to another storage room. I believe I told you that TB came with the cottage. Well, he kept both the vault and its combination a secret from me."

"So how do we get you out?" I asked, a little panicked. "Can you breathe?"

"Oh, yes, of course," said Omni. Mom and Dad also nodded in agreement. "There's a ventilation system in here."

"OK, good," I said, relieved.

"I'll need you to call the security company," said Omni. "I made note of the name on the vault door when TB brought us down here."

"We can't," I said. "The phones are dead."

"They are?" asked Omni. "How strange."

"The police told us that all the power lines and cell phone towers were taken out by the mudslide," I said.

"Well, that explains why my cell phone won't work," Omni said. Then he asked, "Are the police there?"

"No," I said. "TB had us locked in the library, but we managed to get out without him knowing it. He thinks we're still in there."

"Really?" said Omni. "Then how did you get to the security monitors?"

"We—uh—borrowed TB's keys without him knowing it," I said, smiling at the thought.

"OK," said Omni. "There's an alarm button you can push that should bring the police. They should be able to get in touch with the vault company."

"Great," I said. "Where's the button?"

"You should be able to see it on the upper right-hand corner of the display where you're standing," said Omni.

"OK, I see it," I said. "Should I push it now?"

"Please," said Mr. Omni.

I pushed the button.

"OK," I said.

"I don't hear anything," said Omni.

"Are you supposed to?" I asked.

"Of course," said Omni. "The alarm should be ringing throughout the house and then across the property!"

"We don't hear anything either," I said.

Jeff added, "Uh, oh! There's a display here that says 'Alarm Disabled.' That's bad, huh?"

"That is bad," Omni agreed. "TB has taken advantage of me. Do you know what he's up to?"

"Yes," I said. "He and Anthony and some other guy with a helicopter are stealing bags of silver ore from the mine and hauling them away!"

"So *that* is what this is all about," said Omni. "Most unfortunate."

I didn't say anything.

"Well, then," Omni said, "do you think you can get out of the cottage without being seen?"

"Yes," I answered. My finger was starting to get tired from continually pushing and releasing the button.

"Good," said Omni, "Then go down the hill to the nearest home and call 9–1–1, OK? Maybe someone down there has power or a working cell phone. There is a hiking trail right across the road from the front of the cottage."

"OK," I said. I paused before adding, "But are you going to be OK?"

"We'll be fine," said Dad. "TB did leave us some food in here."

"And he let us use the bathroom," Danny called. "So *that's* a good thing. But I'm getting really pretty tired of being in here."

"We were working on the Articles of Faith," said Chelsea, "but he's tired of that, too."

"OK," I said.

"We'll get you out as soon as we can," said Jeff.

"OK," said Mom. "Be safe!"

"Did you guys say a prayer?" asked Danny.

"Yes, we did," I answered.

"Good," said Danny. "That means that Heavenly Father will take care of you."

"You're right," Jeff and I both said.

"It doesn't mean that nothing bad will happen to us, though," said Danny. "It just means that things will be the best that they can be. So don't worry."

"OK," Jeff and I agreed. Jeff added, "We won't worry. We'll get you out soon!"

CHAPTER 18

Seek after Riches

"We ought to be able to go right out the front door," Jeff said as we closed the door to the surveillance room.

"What about TB?" I asked.

"What about him?" said Jeff. "Let's go before he wakes up!"

"What if he doesn't wake up?" I asked.

"Sounds good to me," said Jeff. He had his hand on the door-knob, ready to go out into the front hall.

"Think about what will happen," I said. "The helicopter will come back and Anthony will be mad that TB isn't down there with more bags ready. Then he'll come up here and find him sleeping in the kitchen and they'll both know that the keys are missing."

Jeff's eyes darted around for a moment. "That could be bad," he said.

"That could be bad," I agreed. "They would immediately know that something is wrong and would probably start checking to make sure we're all still locked up. Even if they have another key to get in here to check the monitors, you can bet that they won't fall for our trick in the library any longer."

"And if they don't have another key," said Jeff, "then they would probably immediately start checking the rooms in person—just to see who's missing."

"Right," I agreed.

"So what do we do?" asked Jeff.

"Well," I said, "I don't really want to give up the key to this room, so what if we take it off the ring and put the rest of TB's keys back where he expects to find them. There are so many other keys on there that I'm sure he won't notice."

"Good idea," said Jeff. "He won't know it's missing until he comes to check on us again."

"Right," I said. "And when he does figure it out, I'll bet he won't tell Anthony about it anytime soon. Anthony already told him it wasn't even necessary to check on us at all, right?"

"You're right," said Jeff. He started removing the key from the ring as he said, "So do we want to drop the keys and make him wake up, so he doesn't miss his date with Anthony? Or do we just put them there and let him get into trouble?"

"I don't know," I admitted. "I think we should do whatever will keep them where the police can easily catch them."

"Then we want to slow them down," Jeff said. He tried the key in the lock just to make sure he had taken off the right one. "Let's just put the keys on the floor quietly and leave him sleeping."

"OK," I agreed.

Part of me actually thought it would be safer to throw the keys over where TB was sleeping and let that wake him up, rather than getting close enough again that he could reach out and grab one of us. But we'd likely have trouble getting them to land right where we wanted without getting so close that he would see us. Of course, the time we saw him do this trick, it seems like he did actually yawn and stretch for a moment before eventually opening his eyes. I decided it was scary either way—and if Jeff was willing to even try something like this, I wasn't going to muddy the waters. I was mostly worried about coming up with some way to keep these bums from getting away and ripping off Mr. Omni. Sure, he already had enough money for twenty-seven lifetimes, but still . . .

"Let's go," Jeff said, heading for the secret doorway now, instead of the front hall.

We made our way quickly back to the translating room, crept to the double doors, and slowly opened the one that gave a perfect view of the intersection of the halls. Everything seemed quiet. And there were no signs of anyone coming from the back patio. We scampered down the hall and into the dark dining room. Very slowly, we pushed the doors open that led into the kitchen. TB was still there. I was pretty sure that he was way over his normal fifteen-minute nap by now. We needed to hurry.

Jeff had the keys, and I let him keep them. I watched from the end of the room as he practically crawled along the floor next to the long table until he got to within a few feet of TB. He waited for a few seconds before moving again. Then he crouched over like he was ready to bolt back in my direction and inched closer and closer to TB, all the while reaching out with the keys until his hand was just above the floor, directly underneath TB's hand. I think I could even see him begin to shake as he placed the keys on the floor and lifted his hand away. TB didn't move. I was amazed at how quickly Jeff got back to where I was. His expression was a strange combination of terror and pleasure.

"I did it," he breathed as we let the doors close again.

"Good job!" I whispered.

"Now let's try to find someplace to call 9–1–1," Jeff said between gasps.

I really would have much preferred to get down into the mine and try to find where they were stealing the silver ore from, but we had promised that we would try to call 9–1–1. I knew Jeff wouldn't go for another distraction at this point.

Knowing that TB was still asleep, our only fear was from Anthony coming from the excavation site. We opened the door into the hall carefully and looked through the windows across the patio and over to the walkway. There was still no sign of anyone. We hadn't heard the helicopter since it left either.

We quickly ran down the hall to the front of the cottage and let ourselves out the front door. It was not locked. That was good—in case we wanted to get back in, which was my plan all along. We ran down the front walk and driveway. Everything on Omni's property was well lit. It took only a minute to find the hiking trail across the road because of the extra light spilling over, but the trail was dark and a little scary.

About five minutes later we were on a dark and deserted street off the hill from Omni's cottage. And I mean it was *dark*. The power was obviously not yet back on in this area. There was a little moonlight, but not much. The homes were large and spaced far apart. We went to the closest house, ran up the front walk, and knocked on the door. There were absolutely no signs of life here. No one answered, so we tried again about half a minute later. Still no answer.

"Let's try the next one," I suggested.

It took a minute or so to get to the next door. It, too, showed no sign of life.

"Can Omni really be the only one with a generator around here?" asked Jeff rhetorically.

"I guess," I sighed.

When we tried the third house, someone actually came to the door. Through a window next to the door we could see flickering lamplight getting closer and closer as we waited. The door opened just a couple of inches, revealing a couple of bars like they put on hotel room doors that keep them from opening any further.

"Who is there?" asked an elderly woman. She seemed strong and sure of herself.

"We're from the house up above," I said. "It's being robbed and we need to call 9–1–1."

"Well, you won't be able to do it here," said the woman.

"We don't have to come in," explained Jeff. "But could you please make the call for us?"

"I would if I could," she said. "But my phone service is out. I don't have any power and I don't have a phone. So I can't help you."

"OK," I said.

"But I do have weapons," said the woman firmly. "So don't try anything."

We were stunned by this comment.

"No, ma'am," Jeff said. "Of course not."

"Good night, then," she said. "Maybe you can find someone with a phone that works—a cell phone, perhaps."

"Yes, ma'am," I said. "Thank you."

The door clicked shut and we watched for a moment as the light moved gradually further and further away from the window.

"What kind of weapons do you suppose she has?" I asked.

"Besides her attitude?" asked Jeff. "I'm sure I don't want to know."

We tried another couple of homes, but couldn't find anyone there. We were moving with a lot less energy now. I think the old woman scared us a little bit. California seemed a little different from Utah.

"I think I would rather take my chances in the secret passages than out here," I said soberly.

"I think you're right," said Jeff. I was surprised but pleased.

We found the hiking trail and made our way back up to Omni's road. The trail seemed much longer now; it was probably a combination of failure and the fact that we were now going uphill.

When we got back to the cottage, Jeff suggested that we circle around the side to the back so that we could see the patio and back hall before going inside. I liked the idea. Everything seemed still and quiet. We wondered whether TB was still asleep. Then we heard the helicopter. We looked toward the excavation and saw it rising.

"Would they have come and gone without TB helping them?" asked Jeff.

"I don't think so," I said.

"Then he's probably down there," said Jeff.

"But he'll be coming this way in a minute," I added.

We decided to go into the translating room and watch for TB to return. It took only a couple of minutes before he came into view. He seemed a little annoyed. He came through the glass patio doors and headed straight for the front of the house.

"I think he's going to go to the surveillance room," Jeff whispered.

"Let's go see," I said.

We made our way back through the secret passage, turned off the piano lamp, and opened the secret doorway to watch. We were in place just before TB opened the door. He stood in the doorway with his keys in his hand, fumbling through them. He was obviously looking for the correct key. After a moment he reached over and switched on the light in the room.

"What being wrong here?" TB mumbled to himself.

He looked more and more confused as he looked through the keys. Then he walked over to the surveillance room door and rattled the doorknob. He spent at least three minutes alternately looking through the keys on his ring and rattling the doorknob. I don't think he had a clue what could have possibly happened. It was almost comical to watch him as he became increasingly frustrated and confused.

"Where being key?" TB mumbled again.

Then TB started searching his pockets and looking around on the floor, imagining that the key might have somehow fallen off. He searched for another minute or two before finally returning to the hall. Before he closed the door we could see him again looking around on the floor for the missing key. Finally, the door snapped shut. Jeff and I almost burst out laughing. This was definitely the most fun we had had in days.

We went back to the translating room to see if we could catch up with him. He wasn't in view, so we snuck out and peered around the corner toward the front of the house. Eventually he appeared, walking very slowly, visually scouring every inch of the way in search of his missing key. Jeff and I retreated into the translating room as TB got closer and closer. When he got to the patio doors he stopped and stared outside, thinking. I'm sure he was just trying to imagine what could possibly have happened.

Suddenly, TB turned on his heel and headed toward the kitchen. We followed, sneaking into the dining room and looking through the swinging doors. TB was at the far end of the kitchen on his hands and knees, searching for that key. He must have thought the key was lost when the ring fell from his fist. Again, Jeff and I almost couldn't contain ourselves.

With his back to us, TB stood slowly. He continued to look at the floor for a moment. Then he mumbled something that I couldn't make out. Without warning he pounded his fist on the long, metal table. Jeff and I both jumped.

"First," TB yelled, "I be not waking!" He pounded his fist again. We jumped a little less this time. "This fool Anthony be finding me!" He pounded his fist once more. We were ready for it this time. "He be calling me the fool!" Another pound on the table. "Now!" He drew a deep breath and exhaled loudly. "Now! I be losing key!" He pounded for a final time.

We watched and waited for what would come next. TB was motionless for at least a full minute. His back was still toward us as we peered through the crack between the swinging doors. Then, slowly, he raised his head and looked at the clock on the wall above his napping chair. He just stared at it for a moment before tilting his head slightly to one side. He stepped forward, reached for the card that Irene had shown us earlier and turned it over. It was still the "Back in 15 minutes" sign. Without a word he turned the sign back over and left the room.

From inside the dining room we heard him walk down the hall

H

and go through the patio doors. As soon as we dared, we opened the dining room door and found him walking briskly down the walkway toward the excavation site. He was obviously on his way to get more bags ready for when Anthony returned.

Jeff and I took only a moment to laugh and congratulate ourselves at what we had done. But it was great.

Then Jeff asked, "Do you think we can find the vault?"

"Yeah," I said.

We went through the kitchen, into the pantry (which was full of shelves loaded with various food), and opened the only door we could find. There was a stairway leading down to a huge metal door with a combination lock on it. Jeff pounded on it a couple of times and yelled, "Hello?" Faintly, we could hear someone calling back.

"We better use the microphone," I suggested.

We ran back up the stairs and through the house to the surveillance room. Jeff quickly unlocked the door with the "borrowed" key and pressed the microphone button. The monitor was still on the vault room, but the adults all seemed to be standing just under the video camera.

"It's Brandon and me again," Jeff said. "We were the ones pounding on the vault door. Was that you?"

"We heard you," said Dad.

"That was us," said Mom.

"Did you call the police?" asked Omni.

"No," said Jeff. "We tried half a dozen homes down there, but they're all dark. Nobody has power yet. We found one lady home, but she said her phone wasn't working."

"That is highly unfortunate," said Omni.

"I was going to say the exact same thing," said Jeff. I just looked at him.

We spoke for a few minutes about everything that was going on. We told them about TB working with Dr. Anthony and another man to steal silver ore from the mine. We told them about the secret passageways and that we thought we could stay completely hidden in there. Mom, especially, agreed that she would prefer to have us hidden in the cottage than roaming around through the dark streets looking for help.

"If we can't get some help by morning," Dad said, "then we'll probably need to send you two out again."

"Morning is fine," Mom agreed. "But not before then. We'll be alright until morning."

I looked around and saw Meg, Chelsea, and Danny all lying motionless on the floor.

"Are the kids all asleep?" asked Jeff.

"Yes," Mom answered.

Chelsea immediately popped up and said with a yawn, "I'm not! Did you tell them the scripture?"

"Uh, no," Mom said. "I'm sorry. I forgot. Chelsea has a scripture for you."

"It's not for them," Chelsea said. "It's for TB."

"OK," said Jeff. "What is it?"

"Ether chapter 8, verse 18," Chelsea said. "I didn't already know it, but I found it while we were in here because there's nothing else to do."

"You have a copy of the Book of Mormon with you?" asked Jeff in disbelief.

"Meggy and I have been reading it together," Chelsea explained. "That's what we were doing when TB made us come in here. He told us to leave everything behind, but she didn't."

"I believe that," said Jeff. "Meg never lets go of a book if she doesn't have to."

"Don't forget to tell TB that scripture," Chelsea said, yawning and lying down again.

"OK," said Jeff.

Mom and Dad and Mr. Omni wanted to know more about what was going on and what we had been doing. After Jeff explained how

245

we had gotten the key from TB so that we could talk to them, Mom said, "No more of that! That man has a gun. You stay away from him."

"He has a gun?" asked Jeff.

"That is how he convinced us to get inside this vault," explained Omni.

"Oh," said Jeff. "You never told us that before."

"Well, now you know," said Mom. "So stay away from him."

"OK," Jeff agreed. "We will."

Suddenly, we heard pounding from the vault. Everyone on the monitor seemed surprised.

"That's not us," Jeff said.

Omni looked up into the video camera and put his finger to his lips to tell us to be quiet. Jeff released the microphone button and we just watched as they all moved away from the door.

"It sounds like the door is opening," Dad said.

"Yes, it does," Omni agreed.

A moment later we heard TB's voice say, "You be standing back!"

Omni held his hands out in front of himself and said, "You don't need the gun. You're just scaring the children."

"Children being all asleep," said TB. "This being good. Everybody being OK, yes?"

"We're fine," said Omni. "But when do we get out?"

"Not yet," said TB.

Then we heard the door close.

"What was that all about?" asked Dad.

"I think he probably just wanted to make sure we were still here," said Omni, "since he can't get into the surveillance room anymore."

"Jeff!" I practically yelled. "He's going to check the library next!"

Without another word Jeff and I ran out of the room, slamming the door behind us. We knew TB was far enough away that he would never hear it. As fast as we could, we took off back through the secret passage and up the stairs. In just a few seconds we were at the entrance to the library. The only light we had was from the piano lamp. The ladder was too far away so we just jumped for it. I went first and Jeff was right behind me. The movement caused the lights to come on. I dove under the piano and curled the jacket and shoes I had left behind underneath me. Jeff did the same.

Less than five seconds later we heard the key rattling in the lock. TB opened the door slowly and looked inside. Neither of us moved. I was trying my best not to let TB hear my panting from the frantic run we had just made. After just a few seconds we heard the door snap shut again. We waited quietly for just half a minute or so before checking the door. It was locked again.

"Do you think he's headed back to the mission?" asked Jeff.

"Probably," I said. "Let's go see."

We decided there wasn't any point in rearranging the pants and shoes again. We just moved the ladder into position, grabbed everything, and took it with us. We went through Mom and Dad's room and out into the upstairs hall. We could see TB walking toward the excavation site. He was about halfway there by now. We figured he was on his way to get another load ready for the helicopter. We had some time.

We went back to the surveillance room and told them what had just happened. Mom was worried about us being where TB could get to us, but Dad thought that making him think we were still locked up was probably a good idea.

"Young men," Omni said. "I need you to check something for me."

"OK," we said. Jeff was running the microphone controls.

"The four screens at the bottom of the panel are usually set to automatically cycle through the different cameras. Are they doing that now?"

247

"Yes," said Jeff.

"On one of the screens," Omni said, "please change the switch from 'auto' to 'manual'. Do you see where to do that?"

"Yes," said Jeff. He flipped the switch on the first screen and said, "Done."

"Wonderful," said Omni. "Now will you push the 'monitor' button on that screen until you come to the pantry?"

"OK," said Jeff. He pushed the button a bunch of times until we saw first the dining room, then the kitchen, and finally, the pantry. "Got it," Jeff said.

"Good," said Omni. "Now if I remember correctly, pushing that button one more time shows a black screen. Is that right?"

Jeff pushed the button and said, "Yep. It's black."

"I remember seeing two black screens in a row when I have cycled through them in the past," said Omni. "Obviously, one was inside the vault—and now I'm wondering if the other camera isn't in the stairway leading down here. Its lens may still be covered up in some way. Do you think you have time to check it out?"

"Sure," we both said at once. Mom looked a little nervous at this idea, but Dad seemed to be telling her it would be fine.

"We'll be right back," Jeff said.

"Stay together," said Mom.

Knowing that TB was outside, we made our way to the pantry in just a moment. Mr. Omni was right: there was a camera mounted right at the top of the stairs. It was pointed right at the vault door, but it had a lens cap on it.

"TB must have done that so that Omni would never know about the vault," Jeff said.

"Yeah," I agreed. I was starting to feel bad for him—and for the way I had felt about him before.

We removed the lens cap and headed back to the monitors. We now had a perfect view of the vault door. We explained the situation over the microphone.

"Can you zoom in close enough to read the numbers on the combination lock?" asked Omni.

"No problem," said Jeff. He zoomed in until the dial practically filled the whole screen.

"Fantastic," said Omni. "These cameras record everything they see. So the next time TB opens the lock, if you're not there to watch it, then all you need to do is run the recording back and read the numbers!"

"No problem," Jeff said again.

"Yes, problem," I said.

"What?" asked Jeff.

"When he's doing the combination, he'll be standing right in the way," I said.

"Oh, you're right," Jeff said to me. Then he added, "I have an idea."

Jeff pushed the button and said, "This might work, but we have a problem to take care of first."

"What problem?" asked Omni.

"No time to explain," said Jeff. "TB might be on his way back now, so we need to hurry if we're going to make this work."

They all wanted to know more, and so did I, but Jeff just shut the door and headed for the secret passage.

CHAPTER 19

Secret Combinations

"What are you going to do?" I asked Jeff at least three times.

"I'm still working on that," Jeff finally answered. Then he said, "We need something really sticky."

"Like soda?" I asked.

"No," Jeff said. "Something that TB can't miss—something dark and really gooey."

By this time we were in the pantry and looking around. Jeff pulled a gallon bottle of molasses down from the shelf and said, "Yes! This will be perfect."

Jeff took the molasses down the stairs and poured it on the floor right in front of the vault door, right under the combination lock.

"What are you doing?" I asked.

Jeff got a huge smile and said, "Do you think TB will stand there?"

"No way," I said.

"That's right," explained Jeff. "He'll stand to the side the next time he opens the door and we'll have a perfect shot of the whole thing!"

"But he'll know something is wrong when he sees that mess!" I said.

"Exactly," said Jeff, "so he'll be sure to open it. He'll be sure it was us and come to check, but we won't be there—and it won't matter, because we'll have the combination by then!"

"You're a genius!" I said. "That's another MacGyver move. Katie would be proud!"

"Only if it works," Jeff said.

We closed everything up and returned to the translation room to watch. Jeff was so excited by what he had set up that he wanted to know when TB headed to the vault again.

"It's just too bad that we can't do something to stop them from getting away," I said.

"Yeah," Jeff agreed, but he didn't offer any ideas.

I was getting tired of waiting around, so I switched on Anthony's desk lamp to take a look at the priest's journal on the desk.

"Hey!" hissed Jeff. "What are you doing?"

"I want to look at this stuff," I said. "Tell me when he's coming and I'll turn it off again."

Jeff didn't like the idea, but he agreed. I started looking through the journal and reading some of the notes that Anthony had written on the left-hand pages. We had read most of them before, but then I found a note that caught my eye:

Named as the children of Amulon

I remembered the note with the same words that we had found in Anthony's Book of Mormon in the tunnel. I laughed to myself, remembering how he had misunderstood the scripture. Then I thought about all the other Book of Mormon names he had written on the paper. I wondered what it all meant.

I looked over at the original journal that was covered in plastic. I really wanted to take a closer look at it, so I pulled out a couple of the latex gloves and slipped my hands into them. There was powder inside that felt weird. Carefully, I pulled the journal out from under the plastic and opened it, turning page after page, examining the writing. Of course, I couldn't understand any of it since it was all in Spanish. It was about half full and then there were a bunch of blank pages.

I continued to carefully turn through the blank pages until I got near the end. The last few pages had writing again, but not like the first part of the book. The first page here had "I Nephi" written at the top. I thought that was strange because these were the first two words of the Book of Mormon. There were three columns of writing on the page. Down the left-hand side of each column was what looked like a date on each line. There was a number, followed by a Spanish word, followed by the number 1845. Each date was followed by something like "3 shiblons" or "1 shiblon." Partway down the first column the 1845 changed to 1846, and then partway down the middle column it changed to 1847.

I turned the page and found "II Lehi" at the top of this page. There were similar columns with similar markings of dates and amounts of "shiblons." This was a ledger! The priest was keeping track of amounts of silver on various dates. The next page had "III Laman" at the top, but there were only a couple of entries below it. The next page had "IV Lemuel" at the top, but also had only three or four entries.

Next came pages "V Alma" and "VI Ammon" at the top. These pages had lots of entries like the first two had. I kept turning until I got to "VIII Korihor" before I finally understood what was going on.

"Jeff!" I hissed. "I get it now!"

"What?" said Jeff, still watching at the door for TB.

"I think that every one of those mine tunnels was given a number to start with," I said.

"I know," Jeff said. "The Roman numerals. So what?"

"But then," I continued, "after they figured out whether a tunnel was going to be good or bad, the priest added a name from the Book of Mormon, using a good person or a bad person."

"We didn't see any names on the tunnels," Jeff reminded me. "Just Roman numerals."

"I know," I said with excitement. "But this ledger has both!"

That got his attention. He turned to see what I was looking at. "Ledger?" he asked.

"Look," I said. "These are the names that Anthony had written on the paper in his Book of Mormon! He was trying to figure it all out, but never did. In fact, he was probably at the visitors' center the other day because he was returning a census with these dates on it. Maybe he stole it because he thought he'd find the names of Amulon's children on the census and that would give him a clue as to what everything meant. But, really, the tunnel was named Children of Amulon—it must have been productive."

"This is so cool!" Jeff said. He started to reach for the old journal, but I made him put on latex gloves first. Then he started turning carefully through the pages just as I had. "Go watch for TB," he breathed without looking up.

I hesitated, but stood and moved over to the door, taking a quick glance out the windows. I was much more interested in the journal by this time.

After a few minutes, Jeff asked, "Well, then, which mine shaft was the one the priest chose for himself?"

"I don't know," I admitted. "He said it was one of the good ones, didn't he?"

"Yeah," said Jeff. "But wait. Didn't he also say it was the one that represented the Lord?"

I walked back over to the desk and watched as Jeff continued to turn pages. He stopped when he got to a page with " 'X' Jesus Christ" at the top.

" 'X' marks the spot," whispered Jeff. "Mr. Omni had it right all along, didn't he?"

"It sure looks that way," I agreed. "We should have remembered that 'X' is the symbol for Christ, huh?"

"Wait a minute," Jeff said. "Do you remember how the 'X' was carved on that tunnel?"

"Yeah," I said, thinking of the two hands with the wrists together.

"Do you remember the extra lines coming from the thumbs and fingers?" Jeff asked. I did, but before I could say anything he said absently, "Is that drawing in here?" Jeff turned to the front of the journal as he spoke. "That's it!" he said with excitement. "The hands in this drawing are the same as on the mine tunnel."

"Oh, yeah!" I agreed. "Except the lines here cover the whole page, making a huge 'X' across everything."

"I hadn't thought of it that way," Jeff mused. "'X' really does mark the spot."

"Do you know what this means?" I asked.

"What?" said Jeff.

"It means that we know where TB is getting the burlap bags from," I smiled.

"So?" said Jeff. "We can't stop them."

"Probably not," I agreed, "But do you still have that GPS thing?"

Jeff reached into his pocket and said, "Right here."

"Do you know what we could do with that?" I asked.

"What?"

"We could," I said, pausing to increase the anticipation, "Go down there when TB is here and the helicopter is gone, and put that thing in one of the bags. Then . . ."

Jeff finished the sentence for me. He said, "Then we can use it to find out where they're taking it all!"

"Exactly!" I said.

"Check the door," said Jeff suddenly.

I did, but there was still no sign of TB. The patio doors made enough noise that I was sure we wouldn't miss him even if we weren't watching.

"I have a plan," I said.

"I can hardly wait," said Jeff.

"The next time the helicopter leaves and TB comes back to the house," I said, "we'll go to the mine and plant this GPS device in one of the bags in tunnel 'X.'"

"What if he checks the library and finds out we're missing?" asked Jeff.

"Perfect!" I said. "He's been checking both places, so when he checks the vault, too, then we'll have the combination!"

"What if they don't take any more bags because they know we got out?" asked Jeff.

"Anthony is way too greedy for that," I said. "You know he'll want to grab just one more load."

"You're right," Jeff agreed. "But what if the molasses doesn't work? What if the camera still can't see the dial when TB does the combination? Shouldn't we stay and watch the monitors just to make sure?"

I was ready for that one. I said, "If we can't get the combination from the video, then our best chance of getting it will be to know where these guys go, won't it?"

Jeff thought about this for a minute and then said, "You're probably right."

"Let's do it, then," I said. "And the closer we are to the mine when TB heads up here, then the more time we'll have to get in and out before he returns."

"OK," Jeff agreed.

"Hold on a minute, though," I said, grabbing a small, blank piece of paper from the desk. "Do you remember the scripture that Chelsea wanted us to give to TB?"

"I think it was Ether 8:18," Jeff said.

I wrote the reference on the paper and stuck it in my pocket, then stood up to leave. As Jeff and I came out into the hall we caught a glimpse of the helicopter returning.

"Good," I said. "That means TB should be down there waiting with bags to load up."

Jeff and I went outside and made our way toward the mission, all the while staying on the grass behind the walkway lights. We watched as the three men repeated their ritual, loading four more bags into the helicopter. We hid behind some bushes when TB climbed up the stepping stones and headed for the house. As soon as we dared, we ran down the steps and went into the priest's room. The lights were still on. We picked up a flashlight and made our way down the ladder and into the tunnel.

"Hold on," I said, pulling Anthony's Book of Mormon from the place we had found it the night before.

I opened the plastic bag just enough to put the small paper with Chelsea's scripture reference inside. I was sure to place it such that the reference was clearly visible through the plastic bag.

"OK," I smiled, still holding the book in my hand. "Let's get to tunnel 'X.'"

We made our way quickly to the tunnel, pausing to look at the carving of the hands above the entrance. It was pretty cool. We didn't have to go very far down this tunnel to find what we were looking for. There were probably about twenty burlap bags all lined up on one side of the tunnel. Jeff opened up the very first bag and shined the flashlight inside.

At first I thought it looked mostly like dirt and rocks, but then we ran our fingers through it and found lots of shining bits of metal, silver in color, mixed in with the dirt clods and embedded in the rocks.

"I guess it still needs to be refined," said Jeff.

"Yeah," I agreed.

Jeff pulled the GPS pager from his pocket and put it into the burlap bag. I stuffed the book inside the same bag and we tied it closed again.

"Let's get out of here," said Jeff.

I agreed. We raced back to the ladder and up into the priest's room. We opened the door carefully to be sure no one was there, then we quickly climbed back up the hill out of the excavation pit. Just as we got to the top of the hill we saw TB practically running toward us. He kept looking back toward the house over his shoulder. He hadn't seen us, so we jumped behind some bushes and waited for him to pass. TB went down near the door for the priest's room and began pacing back and forth, looking at his watch about every fifteen seconds.

"I think he knows we're out," Jeff said.

"Yeah," I agreed.

"Should we go check the video?" asked Jeff.

"Let's see if he goes to get any bags first," I suggested.

We didn't have to wait long. TB finally took a good, long look at his watch and apparently decided that he had time to go into the mine. It was painful to wait for the fifteen or so minutes it took for him to return, but I wanted to be sure. Eventually, he emerged with one bag and then another. Then he started pacing again, regularly checking his watch, and looking into the sky.

"Do you think he got the right one?" whispered Jeff.

"He better have," I said.

"Do you think he only got two this time?" asked Jeff.

"It looks like it," I said. "Maybe that's all he could bring himself to do, being as nervous as he is."

"Yeah," said Jeff. "Or maybe that's all the helicopter can carry if he's going with them this time. He might have decided this better be the last load since he doesn't know where we are."

"I'll bet you're right," I nodded.

The night was starting to feel cool—or maybe I was just getting nervous about whether or not our plan was going to work. Either way, I felt myself beginning to shake a little.

Within a few minutes the helicopter returned. TB practically ran to it with one of the bags and quickly explained something to Anthony, who immediately began to look around nervously. TB went back for the second bag, loaded it into the helicopter, and then climbed in after it. The helicopter then lifted off from the old mission for what I assumed would be the last time. They didn't act like they were coming back. As we watched the helicopter disappear, I realized that the first hint of morning light was starting to show over the top of the mountain.

"Let's go see if we got that secret combination," said Jeff.

We ran all the way back to the cottage, down the front hall, and into the small office. Jeff pulled the key from his pocket and unlocked the door. Everyone looked pretty much the same on the monitor. Pushing the microphone button, Jeff said, "I think they left for good. Did TB open the door again?"

"He did indeed," said Omni with a yawn. "Do you know how to check the video recording?"

"No," said Jeff.

Mr. Omni explained which buttons to push, and we quickly rewound to the point where TB had opened the vault. It was funny to watch TB's reaction when he first found the molasses on the floor. He actually went up and down the stairs several times (or is it down and up?). He tried to clean up the mess first, but eventually just gave up. He stood way off to the side as he turned the dial.

"It looks like the numbers are 7–21–90," Jeff said. "Let's go try it! We'll be right there!"

"Ninety?" I questioned. "Are you sure?"

"I'm sure," said Jeff, already on his way to the vault.

It was a huge dial with a lot more numbers than a normal combination lock. I had never seen a combination with numbers that went so high. When we got to the vault, we were able to open it the very first try. I think Danny was the most excited to see us. As soon as he was sure that TB wasn't the one opening the door, he took off past us yelling, "I need to go to the bathroom!"

"Remember that internal hydro-alarm we discovered on the last fathers and sons camp out?" asked Dad. "I think Danny still has it."

We all went back up the stairs and took turns eating and telling each other what had been going on all night. Jeff and I were especially excited to tell them what we had done with the GPS device.

"Well, let's check it out then," said Omni.

"I believe the road is still impassible," said Omni's driver.

"The last I knew," said Omni, "they were planning to work through the night and hoped to have it open by this morning."

"Very well, sir," said the driver.

We all climbed into Mr. Omni's limo.

"Is the beacon sending a signal?" Omni asked the driver.

"Yes, sir," said the driver. "Shall I follow it?"

"Of course!" said Omni.

We headed down the street. The road had indeed been opened during the night. Omni tried his cell phone, but it still didn't work. After we had been driving for about fifteen minutes, though, he got a signal and immediately called the police, giving them the current location of the GPS device. It apparently was no longer moving.

A few minutes later we found ourselves on a lonely road near the top of a hill. We came around a corner and saw both the helicopter and a large cargo truck. As we drove up and stopped near the helicopter, we saw Dr. Anthony, TB, and the pilot with their backs to us, huddled in a semi-circle staring at something. There was an open burlap bag lying at their feet. When we got out I noticed the whirring of the helicopter—maybe that was why they hadn't heard the limo pull up.

Just then two police cars arrived. They made much more noise and dust as they came sliding to a stop. The three men all turned to see what was going on. I almost laughed when I saw Anthony holding the Book of Mormon we had put in the burlap bag. It was open. I wondered if he was reading Chelsea's scripture reference that we had left for TB.

At first Anthony was clearly shocked to see everyone there. He stammered, "This is impossible! H-how did you find us?" But then he quickly recovered and tried to hide his surprise. "What's going on, Officer?" he asked in that sickly sweet voice of his.

"We received a report of items being stolen from Mr. Omni's property," said the officer. Turning to us, he asked, "Is one of you Mr. Omni?"

"That would be me," smiled Omni.

"Stolen?" said Anthony. He looked around as if trying to imagine what the officer could possibly be talking about. Then he held up the Book of Mormon and said, "This is mine. We were just reading . . . um . . . a passage . . . together."

"That's his book alright," I agreed.

"See!" Anthony said, anxious for support. Pointing to the bag on the ground, he added, "This bag was dropped, and the book fell out. I'm not sure how it got in there, but it's proof that the bag also belongs to me."

"What about all these other bags in the truck?" asked the officer. Looking at Omni he asked, "Are they yours?"

Anthony didn't give Mr. Omni any time to respond, quickly saying, "He has never even seen those before in his life!"

"That's true," agreed Mr. Omni.

"See!" Anthony said again.

"But we have," said Jeff. "Brandon and I put that book in the bag."

"And the GPS as well?" the officer asked.

"That's right," I said.

The officer went to the bag and quickly found the GPS device and handed it to Mr. Omni, asking, "Is this yours?"

"Yes, Officer, it is," answered Omni.

Anthony went completely red in the face. His eyes darted around between the police, the rest of us, and the burlap bags in the truck.

"Well," Anthony said, "it's obvious that it simply got mixed up with my belongings. I apologize, but I can assure you that it wasn't stolen. It was simply an inadvertent mistake."

"What's in all of these bags?" asked the officer, pointing to the stacks in the back of the cargo truck.

"Well," smiled Anthony, "I admit that I had been working on a different project, totally unrelated to my employment with Mr. Omni. I suppose that I am guilty of not giving my full attention to my employment with him."

"Those bags are his!" I practically yelled. "You stole them!"

"What an outrageous thing to claim," Anthony said calmly. "Mr. Omni has admitted that he has never even seen those bags before. I'm sure he'll also admit that he didn't even know of their existence before this moment. And where they came from is absolutely none of your business."

"Too bad we actually *saw* you taking them from his property," Jeff said.

"Impossible," Anthony said, still trying to look calm.

"And where do you think the bag was when we put the GPS in it?" I asked.

Anthony opened and closed his mouth several times as if he were about to say something, but he never managed to get anything out.

"I think we can take it from here," smiled one of the police officers. "It's time to read these men their rights." Turning to Anthony, TB, and the pilot, he added, "You three are under arrest."

"By the way," smiled Omni to Anthony, "is that my helicopter? Were you stealing it or just borrowing it?"

A while later we were gathered around the dining room table at Mr. Omni's cottage. Irene is amazing. She hadn't gone with us on the GPS hunt. Instead she had stayed at the cottage and made breakfast for everyone! We had a great time telling our stories about everything that had happened. So far, Jeff and I were the only ones there that had actually been inside the mine or the secret passages.

261

We wanted to show everyone, but they were too tired. We agreed to do it later.

"Hey, Dad," Jeff said. "I've been thinking. Do you remember last year when you said we had a theme for our vacation?"

"Vaguely," Dad said.

"Well, I've been thinking about what the theme is for this vacation," Jeff said.

"I can hardly wait," Dad smiled. "What is it?"

"Symbols of Christ," said Jeff.

I don't think that was anything like what anyone was expecting.

"You certainly have seen the letter 'X' or the Greek letter *chi* a lot this week," said Omni.

"Right," agreed Jeff.

"On your license plate," said Danny.

"And on the picture in the priest's journal," said Meg.

"And on the tenth tunnel in the mine," I added.

Chelsea said, "I remember talking before about the Book of Mormon being a symbol of Christ. Jeff and Brandon found Mr. Anthony's Book of Mormon."

"That's right," Mom said.

"And Brandon also got one on the airplane," Meg said.

"Oh, yeah!" said Chelsea.

"What about all of you being in that vault overnight," said Jeff, "and coming out in the morning? That's just like what happened to Jesus."

"That's a good one," Dad agreed.

"How about this whole week?" I asked. "Do you think there's any chance of resurrecting this vacation?"

Everyone laughed.

"For now," said Dad, "I think the best chance we have at that is trying to catch up on some sleep."

Everyone agreed.

"Hey, Chelsea," I said. "Are you going to tell us what is in that scripture reference that you found for TB?"

"I have it right here," said Meg. "It's Ether 8:18, right?"

Chelsea nodded. Meg read the verse aloud and everyone laughed. It was perfect.

About the Author

Carl Blaine Andersen holds a bachelor of science degree and a master's degree in mechanical engineering from Brigham Young University and is a software engineer at Novell. A former member of the Mormon Youth Symphony, Carl enjoys music and teaches cello. He has served in The Church of Jesus Christ of Latter-day Saints in various ward and stake callings and as a full-time missionary in the Switzerland Zurich Mission. He is married to Shari Lynn Tillery Andersen. They are the parents of six children and reside in Orem, Utah. Brother Andersen maintains an Internet Web site dedicated to these books and welcomes your comments and questions: www.cbandersen.net